Satan's Touch

By Forrest Carlyle

Satan's Touch is a Cold War spy thriller, based on the author's real life experiences working for CIA. The novel is a tale of malice and greed, the fast-paced action of Ludlum spiced with the sinister logic of Le Carré. *Satan's Touch* is the story of a man trained by the KGB and still having its power behind him. Driven by twisted obsessions, he's determined to find something he was forced to abandon years ago. What's he looking for? It will be difficult to answer that question. Satan's Touch destroys all clues to his search with fires so hot they melt concrete into glass. (His arsons are based on a series of unsolved burns, done by professional arsonists who've eluded Interpol and our FBI.) The arsonist made certain his only opponent is a broken ex-CIA operative, Alec Ryder, now working for Interpol. Following the arsonist's trail, Alec discovers the closer he gets to the truth, the more Ryder himself becomes a hunted animal.

The novel is told in alternating chapters from the viewpoints of the villain and his pursuer. You hunt with Satan's Touch in the past and Alec Ryder in the present – until the men collide in a stunning twist.

Based in Silicon Valley, these authors write comic fiction, thrillers, mysteries and adventures. Un-Tied Artists donate proceeds from sales of their books to Doctors Without Borders.

In 1999, the Nobel Peace Prize was awarded to Doctors Without Borders for their work in relieving the suffering of underprivileged countries. Why a peace prize for doctors? Because terrorists find eager recruits among the despairing millions of this world, living in unthinkable conditions.

See more about Un-Tied Artists and their books at
www.SiliconValleyNovel.com

Other books by Un-Tied Artists

Why is Paris burning? For money, a lot of it, more than you can possibly imagine. A serial arsonist killer is loose and American Interpol agent Nicki Foster fights to stop him. To stay alive, Nicki and Fire Captain Paul Denis race to solve a puzzle leading to an immense fortune. Lose the race and a flashover fire will burn them alive, leaving only an x-ray of them behind.

Everest is Hollow is an adventure novel, featuring a teenage Indiana Jones-style archaeologist. His nickname is "Trouble." Together with his friends Nuru and Tattoo, Trouble climbs Mount Everest's difficult West Ridge. Trouble enters a cave and realizes Everest is hollow. He discovers an abandoned city, the key to a lost civilization built on treasures of the past.

The theme of *Wire* is Watergate meets *The Fugitive*. A spunky investigative reporter uncovers a conspiracy involving a Presidential candidate. She finds herself stalked by a pro hit man. She lives on the run, chased by an assassin code-named Elijah. His connections reach everywhere she goes for help, including the FBI.

Stir outrageous characters in a thick sauce of greed and you have the recipe for *Silicon Valley Game*. This is a humorous, naughty book that really dishes. Everyone searching Google is curious to peek inside lives caught in the Silicon Valley Game. What will they find? Answer - backstabbing, gossip and juicy scheming.

Satan's Touch

By Forrest Carlyle

This book's story and characters are fictitious. The story is set in Budapest, Hungary and Los Angeles, CA USA. Some well known public agencies, locations and establishments are discussed. But the characters in this novel are entirely imaginary.

ISBN-13: 978-0-9817702-9-1
ISBN-10: 0-9817702-9-0

Published in the United States of America by Un-Tied Artists

1

1990
The Berlin Wall has been torn down.
Germany will be reunited.
The Cold War is over, yet its legacy remains in Budapest, Hungary.

Last night pleasured him, but it was only a taste. There was such eroticism in killing. A lifetime of planning had gone perfectly as that warehouse melted away, killing the firefighters. His KGB backer was pleased, and this was merely the beginning.

He sipped tea in a room at the Grand Hotel on Margaret Island and gazed at the twinkling lights of Budapest, pondering his next move. He liked to pace, but this room was too small. He couldn't get the suite he really wanted, because it would've drawn attention, started rumors. But this one would do. It had a magnificent view, very inspiring to his thought processes.

He remembered the night his life was given real meaning, here in this hotel, decades ago. Hungary's beaten Army was arriving home on ambulance trains. He'd never forget the smell at the railway depot of ointments and rotting human flesh.

Budapest's mood was so somber that it came as a shock when he was asked to wait tables at a gala party. There were few young men available for catering an important occasion, you see. They made him feel inferior just by mentioning how few were left, so they had to take even *him*. Yet the pay was good and food could be stolen from the kitchen. A tuxedo would be supplied, as well as shined shoes. He was required to practice the night before, but he'd be paid for that as well. He must be prepared for his role.

They hadn't prepared him for the splendor that would arrive at the Grand Hotel on Margaret Island, elegant men in top hats and women in furs with sparkling jewels in their hair, on their ears, around their necks and wrists. He'd never known such wealth existed in the world, much less under his nose. They were very gay. Obviously they'd been partying in small groups already, as a prelude to this gala. Their laughter sickened him.

He couldn't help staring when one girl caught her dress getting out of a polished Daimler limousine and was forced to reveal a flash of thigh where hose met garter belt. She caught him gawking at her exposure, but wasn't angry. She actually looked smug that he was touching her open thigh with his eyes. In a moment, she vanished like the rest of them into the swirl of another world, one where he was only a servant.

He caught snatches of her that night when he placed fine china or poured another glass of wine, but never did she return his intense look. It was as though he didn't exist. He'd been there for one moment when she wanted affirmation of her power. He hated her. She was spoiled and had been given everything in life. Even the war hadn't touched her.

The orchestra played a waltz and he carried a sterling silver tray with yet more champagne for the inebriated guests. He approached a little knot of bystanders that weren't dancing. They parted to accept glasses for a toast and he found himself staring at her cleavage. He dragged his eyes slowly up her throat onto her lips. She examined him mockingly and he blushed. He was humiliated, furious with himself. He forgot to balance the tray. It tilted and glasses fell. She giggled and stabbed him with a condescending look. He picked up the mess and she dropped her glass on his tray. She gave him a disdainful glance, chose a partner and danced away.

The maître d' scolded him. He would pay for the crystal from his wages. He knew the crystal was worth more than he'd earned, so all his work was for nothing. He wanted to cry, but he wouldn't give them even more satisfaction.

Hours later, as dawn turned the Danube red, he watched the party break up. They no longer looked glittering, just dull, haggard. Where was she, this arrogant rich nymph? He waited for her to leave. He wanted her to feel his hatred.

He stopped looking and gave up. He must have missed her. In the kitchen, he changed clothes and hid as much meat as possible inside his folded jacket, carrying the garment under his arm rather than wearing it, even though there'd be a bitterly cold walk across the Danube. He didn't bother waiting for payment. There'd be none. That was her fault.

For reasons he didn't understand to this day, he wandered from the kitchen into a curious passageway leading him to the hotel's opulent lobby. He began surveying the ornate coffered ceiling.

"Do you have permission for those sausages? They'll fire you if you don't, you know," she teased. Her speech was slurred from champagne. The nymph sat alone, legs crossed, examining him with distant curiosity, as if trying to decide something.

He didn't answer, just stared back, surprised at himself for not being more angry with her.

She broke away from his gaze and giggled at him. "Haven't you ever seen a girl before? Why do you stare at me so?"

"I haven't seen you before. Where do you live?" This wasn't what he thought he was going to say. His words tumbled out.

"I live here, in the hotel, at least for a while. My father arranged it. He's out of the country. When he sends for me, I'll leave."

He didn't comment, just stroked her hair visually. His eyes came to a magnificent earring, a brilliant green stone circled by diamonds. "Is that a real emerald? I've never seen one before, only pictures."

"Oh, yes. The gems are real. Each earring holds a carat of diamonds, in platinum setting, with an emerald of unmatched beauty – or so the jeweler assured me. You really have the best jewelers in the world here."

He was supposed to be impressed, so he looked bored and yawned.

"I'll show you something else you've never seen before – if it isn't past your bedtime." She got up and looked bemused. The nymph walked past, turned around and hesitated to emphasize her offer. Then she continued across an empty lobby toward an elegant stairway. He followed, catching her on the second red-carpeted stair.

They stopped outside her suite and she posed a wicked look, slipping polished nails across a breast, sliding them beneath thin silk. She teased a room key from her breasts.

He whispered, showing his apprehension. "Where are your guardians?"

"Asleep." She tossed a hand carelessly across the hall in their direction. She mocked him again. "Don't come inside if it frightens you." Then she unlocked the door to a suite he'd wanted to book many years later. He took another sip of strong black tea.

Now he was following up on that night and all it led him to do for the rest of his life. He sank into a comfortable chair and savored thoughts of his next move. Success at the warehouse came from elaborate planning and careful execution. But killing the Budapest Fire Department's arson investigator in the blaze was an unexpected bonus. Afterwards, he arranged for the investigation to be shifted to a washed out ex-CIA agent, Alec Ryder, working as a Hungarian Interpol Liaison. Ryder was another enjoyable piece of good luck. The KGB knew all about Ryder. He was a nobody going nowhere. He wouldn't be a problem.

2

Fire

Alec Ryder stood on smooth discolored glass that had once been the concrete floor of a warehouse. Heat from the slab seeped through the thick leather soles of his shoes and made his feet sweat even a day after the fire stopped. The floor had been melted into a block-long scorched glass table top. Acrid stench burned his lungs. All he wanted to do was leave as fast as possible. He had to ask some questions for appearance sake. "Why do you think this is where they died?" Ryder shifted restlessly.

"The colors. Yellow for the helmet and boots, black for the coat. Here's some reflective striping material, I think. But this is the conclusive proof." The newly promoted Fire Captain poked at a large green disc stuck in the floor. He chipped away with his crowbar until he could pry the disc loose. Using a gloved hand, he turned it over to inspect the rounded bottom. A stamped manufacturer's name and serial number were legible. "It's the bottom of an oxygen tank. I found a lump that was probably the regulator a hundred yards away, blown there when the tank exploded."

Ryder stared at twin graves, then looked away at short melted candles, all that was left of steel I-beams. A waxy, reddish-brown hedge only a few feet high had once been a twelve-foot brick wall. He mused aloud. "What burns like that?"

"Nothing burns that hot, Inspector, not even magnesium." The firefighter kept alongside as they walked.

Alec stopped when he reached a blackened hulk at one end of the building. He examined a fire truck's twisted remains. "You know this other Fire Captain. Was this a dumb mistake?"

"He trained me, Alec. He was a real pro. I want whoever did this. Find that bastard for me."

"This was probably burn for the buck, an owner cashing in his insurance policy." Ryder turned away from the young man's intense stare and watched his own breath condense in the icy morning air.

The replacement Fire Captain looked down and scuffed at the concrete turned glass with his crowbar for a long minute. Finally, he jerked his head up and caught Ryder's eyes. There was fear in his voice when he spoke. It was clear the man wasn't used to being frightened. "I'm not just looking for revenge, Alec. This bastard will do more burns. How will we know we aren't walking into a trap every time we get an alarm?"

"What makes you think this was a trap?" Alec stared into the man's eyes. There was something about all this that made the skin crawl on Ryder's neck.

"A night watchman called in the alarm. Said he saw suspicious activity that looked like arson. Thought he saw fire inside the building."

"So?"

"There are no night watchmen in this neighborhood, Alec. The call came from a pay phone – and the timing was perfect. I think he was watching with glee the whole time. He'll want a repeat performance."

"You're just tired and upset. I'll find who owned this place and that'll end it." Alec patted the young man on the back reassuringly and swung into the patrol car. A knot in his guts told Alec Ryder that he was lying to the firefighter and to himself.

* * *

His fingers ran along the tarnished brass frame, then jumped to her photo. You're lucky to be out of all this, Ryder told his late wife. He eyed his gun. Shitty luck to be Catholic, he thought. If he used the gun on himself, he wouldn't join her. But he was kidding himself. He didn't have the guts to pull the trigger.

Alec dragged out the bottom desk drawer and studied a nearly empty scotch bottle. Was now the time to finish it? He tried to ration himself to one a week. Decent scotch cost too much even on the black market.

The phone let him avoid finishing the scotch five days early. The handset kept ringing at him until he snapped up the receiver. "Yeah, Ryder here. I can't be late if you never told me to come. Yeah, I'll be there right away."

Alec Ryder put the phone down and swung his wooden chair around. He scowled out a dirty window at the modern office complex built on the former State Police Headquarters site. Why'd they always call him? He was just the Interpol liaison, not their chief of detectives. He should have liked being wanted. But the real truth was he didn't want them. He wanted to be back in the CIA. Yet it was easier here than being in prison for the rest of his life . . .

The radiator vibrated against his knees. Central heating was again resurrected from its grave. The clanking and whistling broke his reverie. Alec skirted the edge of his battered wooden desk in the narrow clearance of his private cubicle and opened the office door, careful not to pull off a fragile knob that passed for a lock. In two steps he crossed the office space allotted to the detective "squad" and stood over the Budapest Police Department's sole full time detective. The man was lost in a lurid expose on the Budapest Fire Department, a headline screaming how incompetence at a simple warehouse fire killed four firefighters and a Fire Captain.

Ryder growled. "We're wanted. Get your coat."

"What's it about?" Detective Sergeant Usulak smoothed the newspaper, folding it to the front page picture of a burned out fire truck.

"That!" Alec snapped, rapping his knuckles on the newspaper. "It wasn't your Chief of Police who called. It was his highness, the new Commissioner of City Services."

Usulak rose and pulled short coat sleeves down in a vain attempt to make his sportscoat fit. "Be sure to kneel and kiss his ring."

"Kiss his ass, you mean," Alec snorted. Afraid of the building's temperamental elevator, Ryder skipped down three flights of stairs and jaywalked across protesting traffic. He trotted into a lobby of elegant glass and chrome, flashing his badge at the security guard.

Ryder caught a departing elevator and jammed its door open. "Police emergency. Top floor." Alec caught a sideways snapshot of Usulak gaping in astonishment. Ryder ignored the stare, riding in awkward silence until stepping out on the plush carpet of the thirteenth floor.

As they approached the receptionist's station, a leggy brunette got up and scowled at them. "He's been waiting for you. This way."

When they entered, the Commissioner of City Services was staring out his window and didn't even bother to turn around. He ordered them to sit down.

Alec fought back anger at being yanked across the street only to wait for the Fire Chief to arrive.

The Commissioner abruptly turned around as if reading Ryder's thoughts. "No, we're not waiting for the Fire Chief. I dismissed him this morning without pension." After a calculated interval, the plump face resumed talking. "This warehouse arson is most troubling to me. As you know, Alec, I was appointed to make certain the old, incompetent party apparatus became modern and efficient, that it didn't interfere with our blossoming trade relations. Hungary depends on trade for its future, Alec." The Commissioner waited placidly for an acknowledgment, hands folded on a tooled leather blotter.

"Then why are we here instead of the Fire Chief, Commissioner?" Ryder asked. "Arson investigation is the Fire Department's job."

The clasped hands slowly unfolded and a little, unpleasant smile crept onto the inflated face. "The dead Fire Captain was their arson investigator. So I'm giving you the job." He rose to dismiss them. "I'm certain a man with your abilities and resources will make easy work of this case."

"Resources, Commissioner? You mean my billion dollar forensics lab and my thousand man staff?"

The soft, inflated face turned icy and spoke with chilling calm. "If you don't like it here in Hungary, Mr. Ryder, you can always return home. I understand they have an unfinished investigation in Virginia that your return would facilitate . . . a murder, I believe."

The Commissioner's charm returned as abruptly as it had fled. "Besides, you just said that an old Fire Captain alone was sufficient resource. He would have had no laboratory, no staff. Yet you are known for your skill, Alec. I'm certain you can eliminate this nuisance before he does any real damage. Unless . . ." He rose and sat on the edge of his desk, feigning the inviting body language of a Father Confessor, but his mouth twisted sarcastically. "There are ugly rumors, Alec. Rumors that not all your paycheck comes through Interpol. So far, I've chosen to ignore these whispers. If you fail to solve this case, it may be that you are motivated by sources other than Interpol. Report to me daily in writing, Alec. I'll phone if I need any clarification." He went behind the imposing desk and concerned himself with his appointment calendar, ignoring the detectives.

They flipped around and exited the luxurious office. This time they walked to the corner and waited for the light to change before crossing. Ryder was pissed. "What's the Commissioner up to, Usulak? This whole thing is crazy. The Fire Department screws up and we get thrown in the oven and cooked. What the hell's he doing?"

"Cleaning house, so he can have his own *apparatchiks*, loyal to him. In the old days, my friend, I had something on everyone, something I could squeeze back with, if I had to. But this one, he came from nowhere only a month ago and is moving very fast. Too fast, perhaps. Even if we pin this arson on some businessman trying to collect an insurance policy, he'll find another excuse to get rid of us."

"So what are you going to do?"

"Me? I'm going to make finding some dirt on this bastard my full time assignment." Usulak flagged down a patrol car and got in the back seat. "What are you going to do?"

"Hope the whole thing goes away," was Ryder's weary reply. Alec slammed the car door, wondering just how much dirt had been dug up on him. How much did this new Commissioner know about what had happened in McLean – or the favors he'd done since he'd gotten here?

Budapest was recovering its pre-World War II status as the Paris of Eastern Europe and the price of everything was rocketing. Did this city really expect him to live on his paycheck alone?

Ryder went back inside. He took the building elevator and hoped it got stuck. For once it didn't. He collapsed the wire cage and headed for the bottom drawer of his desk. There was no hesitation this time. The scotch bottle was emptied into a dirty glass. Alec picked it up, saluting the chrome and glass edifice staring at him through a grimy window. "Fuck you, fat man. You want action? OK, this is the action you get." He slugged down the drink. Recovering a bit of self-preservation instinct, Alec dialed the phone. It rang only once. "Hello, Otto."

There was a tight, precise voice on the other end, forcing itself out of a gnome-like body. "Hello, Alec. Finally called for a game of chess?"

"No, I'm not in your league and I'm enough of a man to know it."

"A favor, then."

Alec dodged the blunt reply. "Why are you working so late? Are they finally getting their money's worth from your salary?"

Otto ignored the sarcasm. "We're converting to a computer system for the City's property records. A beautiful file server. You really should stop by for a demo, Alec. Plus, it came with an American software consultant and I have to stay late to work with her."

Ryder played with the empty glass and tried to conjure more scotch in it. "You know everything there is to learn about computers, Otto. What does she have to offer?"

"She's cute. Plus, I learn a lot from letting her help me."

The Inspector saw a picture of the hunchbacked gnome's girlfriend – brunette, short because Otto was very short. Opposites attract, so probably on the chubby side since he was incurably underweight. Alec had a vision of them reading aloud to each other from long technical articles, exchanging shy glances. "How long have you been dating this consultant?"

"Oh, we haven't been dating exactly. She plays a decent game of chess and I've been helping Jeanette to improve."

With chess as a common bond, Alec added facial acne to his image of her. "Jeanette? How did you arrange to get both a state-of-the-art computer and a girlfriend?"

"Oh, I didn't," Otto replied. "The new Commissioner of City Services arranged everything. Clearing up title to property is very important in making a transition to Western-style economics. For once we have priority, instead of being a dump for obsolete paperwork."

"So this computer system would know who owns what piece of real estate now?" Alec probed.

"Better. When we're done, it'll know everyone who ever owned a building."

Ryder talked casually. "You know, Otto, I think I'll take you up on that offer of a demo. By the way, how long has our Commissioner known this Jeanette?"

"Don't know. Why don't you ask her? When you come by, I'll introduce her."

"Yeah, that's a good idea. When?" Ryder shoved the empty bottle in his trash basket.

"Tomorrow's good. Come by just before closing."

"Yeah, thanks. Bye." Ryder hung up. He walked into the other room and put a clean sheet of paper in the department's sole typewriter, a pre-*glasnost* Soviet copy of a Remington manual. Alec typed a one line report to the Commissioner, put it in an inter-departmental envelope and dropped it in an out basket. He flipped off the fat man and then flipped off the light. How much was scotch tonight on the black market, Ryder wondered?

3

Sources

The rhino cage at the Budapest Zoo was a major tourist attraction. He wasn't there to admire its ornate art nouveau façade. He stood in front of the rhino cage because his KGB mentor arranged a drop here. The encoded message was taped to the bottom of an empty Coca Cola can, left at the curb only minutes ago.

The rhinos lounged inside their elaborately decorated "house," ignoring workers cleaning walkways around the cage. Blue uniformed janitors continued for another ten minutes, then hopped in an electric cart and drove off.

The workers' cart disappeared behind the rhinoceros house and its doors opened. A pair of leathery beasts disdainfully sauntered out. He got up for a better look at the rhinos, and crossed the pavement. He stubbed a foot on the Coca Cola can and muttered a soft curse, picked the can up and dropped it in a nearby trash receptacle. The message was now in the palm of his left hand. He gave the rhinos a lengthy inspection, scanning for anyone who might be observing him.

At last, he returned to the park bench, decoding the message in his head. His KGB "handler" told him to proceed with the next stage of the plan. It didn't matter. The mentor wasn't "handling" him anymore. It was he who was running this show, he who was telling them what to do. It was the mentor who needed him. For him, the KGB was only a convenient source of information and materials.

The KGB message was placed atop an inch-thick stack of computer printout. What really mattered was the information he held in his lap, and that *he'd* arranged and financed. The file server system he'd put into that archives department was essential. Without it, he couldn't track where the contents of suite 115 of the Grand Hotel on Margaret Island might have gone.

What the data told him today wasn't good. His next target was occupied, unlike that warehouse. Should he try to enter each apartment in turn, slipping in when the occupants were away? No, that would increase his chances of being caught. He'd have to return so many times. It would also risk leaving clues behind . . . and if someone else was looking, they might beat him to his treasure. No, the thing to do was enter the building only once, in the middle of the night, when they were home. That way, if they'd traded, sold or moved what he wanted, he would extract the trail from them, before he terminated them. Afterwards, he'd destroy all clues. His next arson would give him another chance to teach the Fire Department a lesson.

He ran his fingers lovingly over the printout. That computer system he bought the archives department had indeed been a stroke of genius.

4

Origins

Alec shook rain from his umbrella and leaned it into an irregular corner of the stone lobby. He descended two flights to the sub-basement. A workman in blue coveralls was carefully razoring lettering off a frosted glass door. A single edge razor blade patiently extinguished "Archives Department."

"What will they be called?" Alec asked.

Without stopping, the painter muttered an answer. "Department of Property Titles and Vital Statistics."

"Oh, yeah, far more capitalistic." Ryder waited for a response, but his sarcasm was lost on the blue coveralls. "Excuse me."

The razor blade followed the door and kept chopping as Ryder eased past.

Inside, Alec stood on an elevated platform. Piles of ledgers were heaped on battered tables. It was a place that paperwork came to die, like old people went to hospitals. A question murmured its way to him. It came from another room, part of the catacombs-like maze of old storage areas that wove along under the riverbank. The Danube flowed against the farthest wall, rotting irreplaceable records rushed here when Allied bombs turned Budapest to smoking rubble. Alec made his way to an ancient, heavy door and pulled it open. Ryder stood in the doorway, shocked at what had once been a musty cellar. Warm indirect lighting flowed up stone walls from copper sconces to an acoustical ceiling and back down to burgundy carpets. The mildewed cellar was now an elegant conference room with a rosewood table and black leather chairs. Ryder counted ten chairs, occupied by Hassidic rabbis. The men were spaced along the table, softly plying ledgers with arthritic fingers.

A rabbi spoke in Russian and was answered in Russian, then one spoke in German, was answered by the same feminine voice, but in German. Then another question, but in English. "Do you have any of the Nazi registers left here by the Resettlement Commission after the war?"

The same feminine voice answered the question. "I don't know, Rabbi. I'll ask Otto when he returns." She was bent over the table with her back to the doorway.

Ryder's eyes traveled down the buttocks of her tailored skirt to admire very athletic tanned legs. Alec startled her by announcing, "Nazi registers are kept in another room. Perhaps you'd like to see where they're stored?"

He'd wanted her to turn around, to see more of her, but hadn't been prepared for her looks – green eyes, full lips, soft brunette hair, beautiful. No, that was too simplistic. He felt stupidly aware of his soiled raincoat and the plainness of his face.

"Yes, I'd very much appreciate your showing them to me. Thank you . . ."

"Inspector Alec Ryder." He broke off his awkward stare and went down the hallway. He pulled a dusty volume off a shelf and handed it to her.

"Thank you. This'll be a great help to them. I was worried they'd made their journey in vain."

"Their journey?" He didn't give a damn about them. He simply didn't want her to leave right away. Ryder assumed she was their tour guide.

"The rabbis are sponsored by the Holocaust Foundation. Their findings will go into a central repository in Israel. From here, the group will be going to Austria, France and Germany."

His heart sank. As their guide, she'd go with them. "How long will their tour stay in Budapest?"

"A week, I'd guess. No sightseeing for them, just work."

"Have you seen Budapest, though?" This was stupid. What would she want with him? At least he hadn't blundered into asking her out.

"There's been no time for that."

He heard Otto's uneven footsteps on the stairs leading down. "Listen," he tried to speak his words before the Hunchback took him away. "Why don't I show you a little bit of the city?" The door opened. Alec blurted out an invitation. "How about dinner tonight?"

"That sounds very special." Her eyes traveled to the landing behind him.

Alec turned around. He saw jealous hatred in the form of Otto. Ryder's guts twisted. Many times the Gnome saved him by finding long forgotten links. He needed Otto now more than ever.

She covered his blunder smoothly. "Otto, we should celebrate your success with the computer system. Why don't the three of us dine out tonight? My treat. After all, I'm the one getting paid a nice consulting fee."

Otto softened. "Sure, Jeanette." He looked down at Alec. Ryder saw the hardness return to Otto's eyes.

* * *

Rain streaked French doors overlooked a charming garden and framed Jeanette's face. Alec tore his eyes off her. He forced himself to ask another question about Otto's domain. "How will you get all those records into the computer, Otto?" Ryder vainly sought eye contact to emphasize the sincerity of his respect.

Otto used his fork to impale a Gundel pancake as if it were Ryder's ego. "Everything is scanned as a bit map. We make write-once compact discs when the hard drive is full and cross-index on a relational database manager. It isn't hard, Alec – if you're smart."

Ryder caught himself looking at Jeanette and groped for another place in the room to stare. The maître d' rushed over and oozed concern, responding to Alec's accidental focus on a waiter as if it had been a sign of disappointment in the service. "No, no," Alec assured him. "Everything is very much up to standard."

Attention paid Ryder just made Otto all the angrier. "Excuse me," the Gnome blurted out and left without waiting for a reply.

Jeanette broke the silence. "He's used to having me all to himself. He'll adjust, Alec."

Yes, her behavior made sense. She knew Otto had a terrific crush on her. Of course, she did. A woman like this had to deal with that problem all the time. She was using Alec to break the spell. He was a convenient tool, a pry bar close at hand to dislodge a mistake before it really got ugly and interfered with her career. Ryder relaxed. This made sense. Thank God he'd gotten it straight before he followed in the Gnome's footsteps and made an ass of himself.

"Otto has an incredible mind," she continued. "He knows all those documents in the repository like they're some kind of magic carpet woven together in his mind. It's as if nature put into his brain all the passion it left out of his poor body. I admire him as a genius, Alec, not as a man."

The green eyes locked on his and said "man" all over again. Jeanette's fingers slid around the wine glass. "This isn't the table they were going to give me, was it? When the maître d' saw you were in the party, he suddenly found a much better one for us. Do you come here often, Alec?"

"No, I just did him a favor once."

"In your role as head of police?"

"I just sort of help their detectives." What the hell possessed him to be so honest, he wondered?

"He seems very grateful to you, though, just the same."

"The maître d's son was homosexual and the boy's lover committed suicide. The suicide note was very explicit. Somehow an unfortunate lapse in police procedure occurred and the suicide note was lost." He decided he was going insane. Nothing he did or said made sense around her.

"You're a very kind and sensitive man, Inspector. I knew that the moment I saw you."

As she smiled, Alec saw the suicide note in his files. The bribe had been paid in U.S. dollars. It was his scotch fund. Some of the bills were still in an envelope taped to the back of his refrigerator.

His peripheral vision saw Otto returning. Ryder instinctively stood up as a welcoming gesture. The room spun a bit. Must be the wine he decided. At least he hoped it was the wine, not her.

* * *

Today there was no rain so Alec carried the folded umbrella with him downstairs, walking toward a newly christened "Department of Property Titles and Vital Statistics." The ten Hassidic rabbis had returned and were seated at chairs on one side of the room – nine professors and one Doberman. The Doberman's obsessed eyes bore into Alec for a split second, then reluctantly darted to a high shelf. Like a hawk striking a field mouse, the Doberman stabbed a volume above his head, left hand pinning the binding in a neck-snapping claw. The Rabbi's sleeve fell back. On the forearm, Ryder saw the man's fixation explained in a tattooed number that whispered tales of hell – the death camps . . . Auschwitz, Buchenwald, Bergen-Belsen.

The heavy Nazi register was slid carefully off and placed softly on a wooden table. Pages flowed open in loving caresses and Alec deflected his course away toward the far door. Ryder didn't need to look to know the ledger's contents. With characteristic Teutonic efficiency, the Germans had recorded each number's origins, name, family, belongings – and the number's fate.

Inside the well lit, pristine hallway, Inspector Ryder found his path blocked by a new metal door with a keyboard cipher lock. He veered left. The linoleum floor turned to cobalt blue carpet with a tinge of red on its fiber tips, very plush. Alec blinked twice before accepting the vision ahead of him – an office whose back wall was glass rising a story and a half, with a miniature garden behind the glass. Light filtered down from street level onto manicured plants. The office had a feeling of déjà vu. It was a scaled down, subterranean version of one he'd been in just two days before – the Commissioner of City Services' office. But the door to this office was labeled "Otto Tolnai, Director."

Otto sat behind a power desk intent on a computer screen tiled with data. The Gnome was fixated on a scrolling table of numbers that rolled past faster than Ryder could believe it was possible to digest anything. At last the waterfall of data flashed to conclusion and the Gnome turned.

"Hello, Alec. I was just 'flying' over the database. Thank you for waiting. Come in. I have some very comfortable new chairs. Try one out, won't you?" The Hunchback pointed to a small table with four matching leather chairs. He got up and joined the Inspector in an unusual display of calculated manners, as though he'd been to some finishing school for power managers. "What can I do for you?"

Ignoring smugly folded hands that mimicked the City Commissioner, Ryder said, "Just thought I'd stop by and admire your new quarters. Quite an improvement."

"For once, I'm in the right place at the right time . . . plus a bit of talent. Coffee?"

A silver plate service and china cups emerged from a credenza near the table, complete with sugar cubes and cream. While the coffee was poured, Ryder let his eyes roam the office. Rosewood wall modules kept clutter hidden behind closed doors.

Otto sipped his coffee in silence. An alarm chimed softly from the computer. "I'm sorry, Alec, I'd love to sit and chat with you but that's a notice that my staff meeting is starting."

"Yes, of course, Otto. So many detectives, so little time. Before you go to your meeting, just one quick fact."

"Anything to cooperate with Interpol. What did you need?"

The Inspector shoved a scrap of paper toward the Gnome with the address of the ruined warehouse. "Who owns this building?"

"Oh, that's easy. Jeanette looked it up before. I'll just open the history log and find it . . . There. It's printing now."

As a green light blinked on a laser printer, Alec assumed his most casual poker face. "That was certainly impressive. By the way, who got that data from Jeanette?"

"The Commissioner of City Services, about a week ago." The Hunchback stretched long fingers into the paper tray and plucked out the sheet, handing it to Ryder.

"A week ago? Before the fire?"

"Oh, was this the building in which those unfortunate firefighters died? I didn't know that. I'm sorry, Alec. I see now why you wanted the data. My staff meeting can certainly wait a bit. Is there anything else I can help you with?"

"Does Jeanette attend your staff meeting?"

"No."

"Where can I find her?"

"She doesn't have an office. She usually works in the conference room. My staff meets in here."

Alec filed past eager young faces and strode toward the conference room. Around a bend that took him out of Otto's sight, he stopped in front of a dusty full length mirror had been taken down and propped against a bookcase. His image stared back at him from the warped glass and he didn't like what he saw – a foolish man in his best suit with a silk handkerchief carefully folded into the pocket and matching his only unstained tie. He considered going home and changing back into himself, but that thought only made him feel more the fool. What the hell had he been thinking that morning? Jeanette, the answer came back.

He stopped involuntarily when he saw her at the conference table. She had her hair tied back with a rubber band and was wearing mauve-framed half-glasses, her fingers tracing through an open printout and softly muttering to herself. The look made her more human, more approachable. It also reminded him that he knew absolutely nothing about her.

Jeanette looked up and saw him. She smiled.

He smiled back in a very un-detective like manner. "May I sit down?"

"Yes! What a pleasure to see you again after last night's disaster. Why don't you shut the door so we can talk more freely?"

He closed the door and tried to gracefully sit down, but struck his foot on a table leg.

Before he could recover, Jeanette spoke again. "I'm sorry it didn't work out better last night."

He shrugged. "It doesn't matter all that much. As you said, Otto will come around." He brought the warehouse address from inside his breast pocket and opened the paper in front of her. "Does this look familiar?"

"No. It's a response to a database query."

She looked genuinely puzzled, either a great actress or innocent, he thought. "Didn't you look up the owners of this warehouse a week ago as a demonstration for the Commissioner of City Services?"

"No, Alec. He came over for a demo, but the module that prints this wasn't integrated into the system then." She pivoted her chair and typed at a console. "Come here. I'll show you the history log of all inquiries made. It's one of the security features of the system."

He moved around the table, closer to her and leaned over. His lips were inches from her neck and ear. Her blouse was open. She wasn't wearing a bra. The view gave him an erection. He jerked away and sat down again, putting the table over his trousers. He was grateful when she kept typing, glued to the screen. It bought him time to think of other questions to ask, stall long enough that he could leave without embarrassment.

"This is very strange, Alec, but the history log was truncated somehow. I see that Otto looked this data up for you, but I'm afraid I can't prove anything else. There must be a bug in the system. I'm sorry . . ." She looked at him apologetically. "Is it important?"

"Well . . ." he stalled.

"By the way, who told you I looked up this data before? Was it Otto?"

"Yes."

"That makes sense. He's the only other person with the system operator privileges required to wipe the history log. I'm sorry, Alec. He's a petulant little boy and is playing games. I'll speak to him. It isn't right and he must stop." She said it as though she would spank him.

Alec didn't doubt that a verbal spank from her, even just a snub, would hurt. That would shape up Otto– if it was Otto who was lying. Was that glimpse of her naked breast an accident, or did it give her just enough time to "wipe the history log?"

He politely excused himself and went out, wondering what the hell he should put in tonight's progress report to the Commissioner. The daily report was a way of turning up the heat. Was it also a way to find out how close he was getting to the truth? He physically climbed stairs up, but it felt to Ryder that he was instead spiraling downward. He had no idea what was really going on here.

Alec went home and poured himself a tall glass of scotch and a short glass of water, realized he'd done it backwards, then concluded he'd done it appropriately after all. He sat down in the one chair of his one room apartment, sipped the drink and stared at the warehouse address. A German bought the warehouse only a month ago. Well, good. Now it was easier. Find a way to pin it on the German and Alec was off the hook. He didn't have to make an airtight case, because the German probably couldn't be extradited to Hungary, even for homicides caused by an arson job he bought.

Ryder got up, opened the scotch bottle and carefully poured back its precious contents. The case would be over tomorrow and he would ask Jeanette to dinner. Alone. Fuck you, Otto.

He got into bed and turned out the light, then turned it on again and wrote on a little pad next to the bed – call Interpol Headquarters about the German. Something in Herr Mueller's past would suffice as a motive for the arson, of that he was certain. He clicked off the light and tried for sleep.

But all he could see was her tan line and her creamy breast. He could smell the naked skin of her neck only inches from his tongue.

Shit, it was going to be a long damn night.

5

Again

Icy wind off the Danube razored through thin cotton gloves and bit his neck. He bent down and opened a military style green case and with great respect lifted out a magnificent Questar telescope. The small but powerful instrument's legs fit indents on an observing table, molded for this particular telescope.

Instead of focusing on Saturn ascending above the ancient town site of Pest, he used the telescope to view a building more than one mile away. He focused incomparable optics on a street in front of an elderly seven story apartment building, a place where he'd worked all night, until only thirty minutes ago. Dawn was an hour away.

He had a telephone call to make. He rubbed his arms, frozen through a thick leather jacket by damp cold, then picked up another case and approached a telephone pole hugging the building's wall. He unwound a twisted pair with alligator clips on its ends and attached twin leads inside a telephone junction box. He plugged in headphones and practiced his lines a few times, then dialed. A minute later, he disconnected and packed his phone equipment, rolling it across the rooftop to a spot marked in white chalk on the black tar surface.

There was a long silence and then the reaction to his phone call began. A wail of distant sirens grew louder, approaching him. A long firetruck flew past his nest, its orange and red lights screaming alarm even more than its vocal wail. From three directions fire engines came and braked to a halt exactly where his telescope was pointed.

Little needles of excitement thrilled his groin with stimulation.

Lights blinked at the building's top story and he carefully opened the red cover of an arming switch, then flicked it. That top floor shuddered the tiniest bit and he waited for screams to reach him across the intervening space. Their fear seemed unsatisfying to him by the time the voices traveled a mile, distorted by reflections and interference. Disappointment made him angry and the anger built to fury. He shook uncontrollably and it took all his discipline to subdue himself, to wait until the proper moment to use the second arming switch.

He looked again. Flames boiled from one side of the building, eating away dry lumber leading to the rooftop. The fire escape was now useless to those trapped inside. Fools who opened their apartment doors to the hallway paid for that mistake. Flames spread into their quarters, showing at their windows. A burning man and woman held hands and jumped.

Their lives stopped at the street below, but the flames continued. A firefighter rushed over and smothered their pyre with a canvas tarp.

His plan was working. Energized, he danced gleefully. He squinted into the Questar's optics.

The Fire Captain anguished, then moved his long truck forward. Its crew worked feverishly to unlock a huge extension ladder and position stabilizers. Firefighters were on the mechanical extension ladder and ascending to those trapped even as the ladder pivoted and rose. Curved lines of water fingered apartment windows where red flames poured upward.

He flicked the second arming switch, rocking back and forth in his chair to stroke a vivid erection. He'd never felt such ecstasy. He stopped and peered into the telescope. The powerful ladder was fully extended, tapping the building's wall. Yet the ladder quit several feet short of the top story. A child was lowered as far as possible, then dropped. Next a woman jumped and was urged down the ladder. She moved fearfully downward until the ladder bounced as another person jumped on the rungs. She froze in terror, blocking the way for all others.

The Fire Captain shifted aim and tried to stop the fire's progress, pouring water into windows, hoping to buy time. Hundreds of gallons streamed into the hallway and cascaded down the stairs.

In the lobby, water came first as a trickle, then a torrent. The liquid soaked and flooded and sought to go lower still. Water found the basement stairs and poured down those too.

He couldn't see that waterfall, but he knew it was there. He smiled wickedly. It was coming, just as he was coming, ejaculating.

A vicious glow seeped from the basement, reddening grimy windows. The entire building sagged when its foundations melted. For a precious second, brick facade and wood framing leaned into the extension ladder. Then an explosion lifted the entire building. Brick, wood, metal and people fell, burying fire crews and their equipment under tons of burning debris.

Dresden, he thought. He'd learned this tactic from the Allied fire bombing of Dresden, Germany. Time your attacks so a second wave of bombs kills the fire brigades. Let a fire storm sweep air from the lungs of those not burned to death, sweep babies from pregnant mother's wombs. The blitz was nothing compared to the fire bombing of Dresden. The Allies did it right. He learned from them how to do it right.

In five minutes, he stowed all his equipment and dragged the gear to a portable crane system on the rooftop. In another two minutes, the stuff was safely in the alley behind the warehouse.

He brought the pallet up and climbed into it himself, descending smoothly. He dragged thick foam from the back of his truck. He yanked on heavy ropes and the portable crane fell, cushioned by the foam. In a moment, all was wheeled into the back of his van.

He drove away carefully. He'd failed to achieve the goal destiny had assigned him fifty plus years before at the Grand Hotel. Yet he was smiling. He was reveling in sexual ecstasy from tonight's killings. He didn't mind that he'd soiled his trouser front.

6

Tap

Sleep left him like an ugly hangover. Ryder sat upright and rubbed his face.

"Alec!" Fists thumped his door again. "Alec, wake up!"

Dully, Ryder plodded to the door. Alec realized he was naked. He grabbed a towel from the bathroom and slipped the lock, staring at Szige Usulak in bewilderment. "Usulak, I know I forgot the damn Commissioner's report last night. That bastard thinks he's God now, getting you to harass me because I didn't feed him his daily crap. Come on in. Let me have some coffee and a roll, OK?" Ryder headed for his shower, leaving the door open behind him for the Detective Sergeant.

"No shower, no breakfast, Alec. The problem isn't that stupid report."

"What is it then?" Ryder picked up a little traveler's clock he kept by the bed. 6:16 A.M. blinked at him. He'd fallen asleep about four, enough time to get into deep sleep when the pounding started.

"I'll show you. I drove past the scene on the way here." Usulak bent down on the floor and put Ryder's telephone receiver back on its base. "They tried to call you and when they couldn't get through, they called me."

"Who in hell is *they*?" the Inspector demanded, pulling on a faded pair of dress trousers.

"The fire department."

Ryder stopped pulling on his trousers. "Again?"

"Worse than last time, Alec. A lot worse."

* * *

Alec Ryder's patrol car drove into the middle of the disaster. Ambulances waited at every exit, engines running, miniature lighthouses atop the vans spinning urgency into the chaos, as if it needed any. There were rescue workers and small cranes crawling over the debris. Sheets covered corpses on stretchers.

Ryder looked at an apartment building left standing across the street. Every window was smashed in. Between the second and third stories, a section of the fire ladder was impaled through a wall. Ryder stepped out of the patrol car.

On a pile of rubble sat a much older version of the Fire Captain who'd shown Alec the warehouse. Blood dried on the man's face from a jagged cut tearing his cheek open to the jawbone. His coat lay draped over tired shoulders and around an emergency cast on the right arm. The eyes were dull from a pain killer. He looked like a young man turned old by sending men to their death and knowing his own death, too, was inevitable.

"He was here, Alec, like I told you he would be. He tricked me. He killed my men and I let him do it. I had no choice. I couldn't let those people jump or burn. He knew that and he used it. Find him. Let me kill him. Slowly. Painfully. Let me burn him alive, a little at a time."

"What makes you think it was *him* again, Captain?" Stupid, Ryder. Who the hell else could it be? But Alec didn't know what to say.

"Buildings don't collapse because their top stories catch fire, even when it's arson – and they don't fall over at just the right instant to kill the fire crews, without warning, either. He was watching, Alec. I felt him." He looked into Ryder as though he were driving a knife into the Inspector's skull. When the fireman saw Alec recoil, the rage drained away and with it went the life force. Only pain showed in the man's eyes. The Fire Captain tried to get up twice before he managed to stand. He waved off assistance and staggered to a waiting ambulance, collapsing on a stretcher inside. Paramedics slammed the doors and a wailing began. The ambulance grew smaller. The wailing died away.

Usulak spoke. "They were trying to get him to leave when I stopped here, on the way to get you, Alec. He wouldn't go until he talked to you, no matter what they tried. He said you had to know. He just kept saying it was up to you, now, Alec."

* * *

A little after seven A.M., the elevator doors opened and a startled Commissioner of City Services stared into Ryder's angry eyes.

"I need to ask some questions, Commissioner."

"Then get on the calendar when my secretary arrives. I think I have an opening at four this afternoon." He suavely moved around Ryder and headed for his office.

"I need to know the answers now."

The Commissioner stopped and turned around. He glanced at his watch. "Ten minutes, max. Then get your butts out of here." He flipped a switch and the ceiling fluorescents blinked to life.

They went into the office. Usulak and Ryder stood. The Commissioner sat. He looked up expectantly.

"Do you know who owns the warehouse that burned?"

"Yes, a prominent German merchant, Hans Mueller from Stuttgart. I'm told he plans to invest heavily in Budapest, and we need foreign capital badly, Inspector. That's why you're supposed to solve this case quickly."

"When did you find out he owned the warehouse?" Ryder stopped looking at the man and toyed with a heavy glass paperweight instead.

"About a week ago. I attended a demonstration of a new computer system I recommended the City purchase. It was a major investment, but we must get property titles straightened out or we'll never get outsiders . . ."

"Yes, I know. Hungary needs foreign capital badly." Ryder looked unblinkingly at the Commissioner. "Who ran the demo for you?"

"Otto Tolnai, the director of that department."

"He alone?"

"Well, his staff was around, and a consultant. But I wanted him to prove the technology was being transferred to us and we wouldn't need an expensive consultant to run the thing. What does this have to do with your solving this case?"

"Lots."

"Like what in particular, Ryder?"

"My ten minutes are up. I know how demanding your schedule is. I wouldn't want to keep you, Commissioner. I'll put everything in my report."

Ryder and Usulak spun around and left, avoiding any further conversation with the Commissioner. The elevator was busy. They took the stairs. On the first landing, Usulak halted. "You really endeared us to him, Alec. You got two jobs lined up for a pair of fired detectives, huh? So we won't starve. You shortened our careers back there, guy."

"No. Our careers were short to begin with, Sergeant. Unless you dug up something on this turd." Ryder cut to the lobby of the next floor and hit "down" on the elevator panel.

"Yeah. He's Austrian. Got a Ph.D. from University of Göttingen in Applied Statistics. Chosen as the top candidate in a worldwide search for city managers that included the U.S. He was the dark horse entry, though, came out of nowhere."

The elevator doors opened. It was empty. "Why'd they pick him?" Alec asked.

The elevator doors shut and they started down. "All I got is rumor."

"So give me the rumor."

"He could bring in big time capital with his connections."

"What kind of capital?"

"German."

"Great. First Hitler invades, then you get his grandkids with their Deutschmarks." Ryder stepped into a crowd of workers waiting to go up from the lobby. Alec whispered as they exited to the street. "No dirt?"

"Dirt? The guy's a saint. Supports the orphanage he grew up in. It brings tears to my eyes, Alec, just thinking about it."

Ryder laughed for the first time in three days. Jeanette had been telling the truth about the history log. He could ask her out to dinner and enjoy her company. All he had on his mind these days was a lunatic torching buildings so he could kill the Budapest Fire Department and a Commissioner who wanted his scalp. But at least it had been Otto who'd lied, not Jeanette. Then an inner voice warned him – "Maybe Jeanette called the Commissioner and asked him to cover for her. They burned Otto because they didn't need him anymore."

Instead of going back to his office, Alec veered into a pharmacy and bought antacids for the first time in a decade.

* * *

The young girl plucked a cassette from the console in front of her. "We have that tape right here, Inspector. I thought someone from the police would want to hear the emergency call."

"You always tape fire calls, or just this one?" Alec asked.

"We just started, since that warehouse burned. We didn't tape the warehouse call, unfortunately." She handed the cassette to Alec.

He turned it over in his hand, thinking. "Can you play it for me?" He added, "It would save time."

"Of course." She snapped the cassette into a deck. "Here, use these earphones. You can hear it better. This button is play and this rewind. It's easy to use. Even your generation shouldn't be intimidated." She talked as if he were ninety.

He scowled. "How do I know which call it is?"

"Don't worry. I queued the tape. You start listening at a time mark before the call. You'll hear a really old lady talking a few seconds after the time code beep." She pressed the play button for him.

Ryder heard the call, rewound it, heard it again, then listened to the voice a third time. Was the Fire Captain just paranoid? The voice sounded like a panicked old lady, not a demonic killer. Ryder thought for a while. "Where'd the call originate?"

"From a phone inside the apartment building that burned."

"What floor, what apartment exactly?"

"Third floor, number 313."

"Not the top floor where the fire was first seen from the outside?"

"No." She looked annoyed at his questioning the obvious.

"What about that mechanical, tinny sound to the voice? Not quite an old lady, is it?"

"Well, I asked our technicians about that. They said the apartment's local junction box was hot already in the basement. Sort of a piezoelectric effect that distorts the voice. The fire started there."

"Let me listen to it one more time . . . you sure this call was made from inside the building?"

"Yeah. We got the phone number and traced it through records department to its owner." Angered by his attitude, she jabbed the play button hard enough to pop the cover off the tape deck.

Ryder ignored her glare. He focused on the frightened old lady's plea for help yet one more time. How could the Fire Captain be right when the call was made from inside? "Suppose," he said, "you had some gadgets and insider knowledge. Could you fake the call?"

"I don't think so, Inspector." She folded her arms to emphasize her conviction.

"Then get someone who doesn't just *think* so. Get someone who knows for sure," Alec snapped. When she left, he slid the tape into his coat pocket.

* * *

Half an hour later, Ryder scanned a telephone pole hugging the backside of a two story warehouse. "So this is where you'd tap in?" he asked the telephone lineman beside him.

"Yeah. Our stuff is primitive still. It's getting upgraded, but we didn't start with this neighborhood. Fact is, it'll be the last area to get anything new. Not the important side of town, Inspector, you know what I mean?"

"Yeah. Where'd you have to make the tap to fake that call?" Alec screened the sun with his hand and squinted up the pole.

The phone man pointed to a large shining box fed with thick black cables from all directions. "Junction box, just above the roof. If I plug in there, you can't tell me from the real thing. It's where all the twisted pairs come from surrounding buildings."

"How do you find the right spot, though? It must be very complicated."

"No, once you open the box, everything's labeled."

"You show me, OK?" Alec started into the building.

On the roof, Ryder stopped before getting to the pole and knelt at a chalk circle with a large number in its center. There were other cryptic markings nearby. At the third set of chalk marks, Alec saw scrapes on the wall and peered into the alley behind the warehouse.

"Find anything, sir?"

"Yes. Choreography of sorts, I think. The dance of death, perhaps."

Ignoring the puzzled looks of the telephone repairman, Ryder walked to the street side of the building and gazed off, lost in thought. A movement in the distance awakened him from reverie. A crane was turning. It was hovering over a wrecked building. He had a clear line of sight to the tragedy. Ryder leaned over the parapet and gaped. "He was here. Right here. Damn. That's how he knew when to pull the trigger."

"Inspector?" The phone man walked over to Ryder.

"He stood right here and killed them all. The son of a bitch is for real." Did the same German own that apartment building, the guy who owned the arsoned warehouse? He'd see Otto later and find out. That would make it easy. God, how he wanted this case to be easy. Alec felt stomach bile churn into his mouth and he reached for the antacids. Eight a day maximum adult dose was printed on the box. He'd chewed eight already and it was only noon.

* * *

Alec Ryder stared at the back of Otto's head as if he were tearing off the skin. Before Ryder could bark out the man's name, Otto turned and looked at the Inspector. "I've been expecting you, Alec." The Gnome plucked a sheet of paper from his laser printer and shoved it across his desk. "Here's the owner of that apartment house. The fire was horrible. I heard about it at lunch. Was it arson, Alec?"

Ryder ignored Otto's question and read the paper he'd been given. "Not owned by Herr Mueller, too. Just a lonely ward of the State of Hungary waiting to be sold to some foreigner. Why would anyone buy it, though? It was old and run down. A poor investment."

"Perhaps, but someone put a down payment on it. Maybe they wanted the land. Maybe they were going to raze the building and put in light industrial space, you know, tilt up concrete."

Alec stared at him. "Who was in the process of buying the warehouse when it burned, Otto?"

"A limited partnership with a Hungarian as its head. But German backers really. My guess is they put up an Hungarian front to prevent a local backlash against Germans buying apartments and kicking Hungarians into the street."

"Which Hungarian? Which Germans?" Alec demanded.

"Was it arson, Alec?" Otto looked impish.

Ryder hadn't seem him look like this before. Was it a childhood mannerism – tell me what I want first or you won't get what you want?

Alec debated. Finally he caved. "Yeah, it was arson. Which Hungarian, Otto? Which Germans?"

The Gnome continued in his smug way. "Do you think the arsonist wanted to kill so many people, Alec – or was that a mistake? Who could have done such a tragic thing deliberately?"

"A nut, Otto. Now, cut out the fencing. Who was buying this old tenement house when it burned?"

"Ah, you think they wanted to save the cost of demolition and things went awry, so to speak. That's what I wondered, Alec. But it can't be so."

"Why the hell not?"

"Because they wanted good will, not bad. Or the Germans wouldn't have cared about their image and fronted a Hungarian on the deal."

Otto no longer looked impish. He was smug and defiant.

Ryder wondered what would happen if he smashed that cocky face through its beloved computer screen and ground broken glass into the jugular vein. He imagined blood spurting over the keyboard and Otto's body spasming in death throes. Then Alec turned and left. There was no point in asking again who was buying the building. That would only give the son of a bitch more satisfaction.

One call first. If it didn't work out, he'd be back.

7

Voyeur

The eroticism of killing awakened an unquenchable demon in him, an evil he'd thought long exorcised. He found himself slipping down the spiral of his past until he stood again outside that very special room of the Grand Hotel, teasing its lock with a thin steel prick until it yielded. He slid inside and eased the door shut behind him with a muted click. His fingers caressed wallpaper through soft cotton gloves until he flicked the lights on. With their glow, a flame rose inside him, like that wave of searing heat that bullied its way to him from the collapsed apartment house, sweeping along the screams of men and the rending of walls until it enveloped him.

The flame brought her back to him across the years. "Don't feel obligated to come inside if it frightens you." She mocked again and once again he was in her room. It was all different and yet the same – different decor yet still very feminine – different furnishings, yet still the suite of choice for a longer stay, if you had the money – different smell, yet still his pulse was loud in his ears. The sitting room still opened on an elegant bath chamber to the right and a bedroom to the left. There was a splay of fresh roses in a leaded crystal vase on the entry table, their number doubled by the mirror behind them. He averted his glance from the mirror when he passed, not wanting to see himself in the present. Curiosity pulled him toward the bath, but he followed her into the bed chamber instead, just as he had before.

A jewelry case lay open on the dressing table just as it had before. But this one was black leather, not magnificent walnut burl inlaid with maple parquetry. The jewels he fondled were a pale imitation of those she'd had. He dropped them into their simple drawers and turned to the closet.

Business suits, a fur, a matched set of Ghurka luggage – and then, seven revealing silk negligees, one for each night of the week. He was angry. She would have had them folded into the drawers by her maid, not hung in the closet. It wasn't right. Someone violated his chapel and must be made to pay for it.

Muffled sounds came from the outside door. A briefcase or parcel hit the floor with a dull thud. Jiggling of keys on a ring. Scraping of a key in the lock. He reflexed inside the closet and slid the door almost closed, his rage diminished by fear. The Impostor was coming and frightening him like she had done – and it aroused him like she had. He hated the Impostor for it and the more he hated, the more his erection gave him pain, straining to move upward but trapped inside his underwear.

Brass keys tittered against the marble top of the entry table and a briefcase clicked on the parquet floor. He heard her come toward the bedroom across blue Persian carpet, then stop. Did she sense he was here? Or had he disturbed something and she saw it? Was she able to see him reflected in the bedroom mirror?

Indistinct movement. Was she going to the phone to summon help? He groped for a knife, found his stiletto and stopped. How would he open the blade without her hearing its distinctive click? He wrapped the handle inside her fur and pressed the release button. Steel flew out and slashed the silk lining. He didn't care. It was what he wanted to do to her.

One shoe dropped on the carpet, then another. Bare feet on bathroom tiles and water rushing in the tub. Could he escape when she got in? He struggled to remember whether the mirror reflected the bathtub and couldn't be certain. It would be best to leave, best for his mission, best not to risk the goals of a lifetime. But he knew he wouldn't leave, not leave this room without making the Impostor pay.

The water stopped. He thought of her lifting one leg over the side and testing the temperature with a reluctant foot. He ran his knife over her, saw the terror, felt the power. His heart was going to explode. He fought to calm down and wait. Wait for the right moment. Wait like he had for the firefighters to commit. Wait for his climax.

Soft, delicate sound wove itself inside the closet. What was it? She wasn't getting in yet. The water was still running. Ah, now it was shut off. She would be getting inside and closing her eyes. Yes, that was the time to violate her, to rip off the illusion of safety and take his revenge.

He jumped and nearly hit the sliding closet door. The damn bedroom telephone jingled and its sister in the entryway echoed the same undeniable intrusion. She would go to the closest phone, the one beside the crystal vase in the entry hall.

But she didn't. She came into the bedroom, draped loosely in a satin bathrobe. Damn, he couldn't kill this one. Damn, damn, damn. Killing her would ruin everything . . . or would it? Perhaps, he thought . . .

She pulled off a pearl earring and lifted the receiver. Her expression changed. She relaxed and crossed her legs. The bathrobe fell open.

He'd never seen her before this way, without clothes, a vulnerable and pleased expression on her face. He wanted to slide the door open, to get a complete view, but the mirror would show his face.

"Yes, I'm free. No intrusion at all, I'd love to. What time? Certainly. Where? Oh, you're spoiling me. It isn't necessary. A sidewalk cafe would be just as lovely and more the real Budapest I crave. Do you have a favorite cafe? That sounds enchanting. Where is it again? No, I'll meet you there. Bye." The phone slid into its cradle. She turned to freshen her makeup in the mirror and the satin crept up her buttocks above a high tan line.

He licked her legs with his eyes until they caught wisps of pubic hairs showing between her taut buttocks. He felt mesmerized, unable to move. That telephone call had stolen his will. No, it was how she looked. He wanted her to look that way for him. He knew it must be for him that she was preening.

She turned and for the briefest moment looked straight toward him, then flew to the other side of the closet. The doors slammed to his side and she pushed clothes into him, fingers sliding across hangers as though she were practicing scales on a piano. Her scents came to him, both the perfume on her neck and the musk between her thighs. He choked back a whimper. She left the closet with arms draped in clothing.

He gently slid the doors back to see her dress. Red silk blouse, red earrings, red shoes, black pants flew on her. No panties, no bra. The moments she stood naked before him were immortal in his memory.

She came right at him now. He trembled, immobilized.

The door slid open, exposing him completely.

Her hand reached out and felt for the fur coat, pulling it off its hanger and sliding the door shut behind. She'd stood within a half yard of him and never looked his way.

Lights clicked off. The room door shut. Her steps faded. He opened the closet. All was blackness. He groped his way to the wall and found the lights. Leaving them on, he went to the entry. On a chair were her panties. He put them in his pocket, took them back out, smelled the essence of her sex and began rubbing them against his cock.

As he stroked himself closer to the edge, the flame rose again inside him. He spun down the helix of time and the room changed around him. There was no Impostor. The real one was back.

"Don't come inside if it frightens you," she dared him.

8

Sin

Red silk blouse, red earrings, red shoes, black pants. On another woman it would have been a simple, casual look. On Jeanette, it was not simple. The look was stunning and the effect on Alec Ryder was anything but casual when he slipped a fur off her shoulders and draped it around her chair.

She graced him with a generous smile, emphasized by lipstick whose red hue was a custom color matched to the earrings. The dazzling green eyes painted warmth on him, then looked puzzled when she fingered a tear in the coat's silk lining.

Alec fumbled for something that wouldn't be entirely imbecilic. "I know a great tailor. He'll make the cut invisible to the magnifying glass, much less the naked eye."

"Oh, it's really nothing, Alec. I was just surprised. I haven't worn the coat since arriving in Budapest, so I don't know how I could have torn it like that."

"Probably happened when you checked your fur at a restaurant. You just didn't find it until now. I'm sure they have many fine restaurants in . . .?"

"Los Angeles. No good restaurants, only expensive, trendy, noisy ones. I spend as little time there as possible." She accepted a menu from a white gloved waiter, who bowed and glided away. She fingered the menu and looked at Alec.

For a second, he forgot he was desperate for information she could obtain. He smiled back and stammered. "I hope this cafe is all right. Did you have trouble finding it?"

"No, your directions were excellent. I got off the subway at East Station and walked right here. The furnishings are beautiful. I've only been to Gerbeaud and it was, well, a disappointment."

"Gerbeaud is for tourists."

"So I found out." She squinted at the menu, then reached in her handbag and donned the same mauve-framed half-glasses he'd seen before. She gave him a shy wink. "Vanity must cede to practicality." Jeanette scanned Hauer's inventory of caloric sins, tracing the edge of an elegant Herend porcelain saucer with an equally elegant fingertip.

Alec formed his image of her beauty framed by 1890's white lacquered furnishings. She interrupted his dream, looking over the glasses and asking, "What do the natives order?"

"Ice coffee, unless they're on an Olympic Team and can run it off. The temptations here are the caloric equal of weapons grade plutonium." Ryder regretted his comment instantly. Would she be insulted? Would she think him cheap? He rushed to add, "But you obviously have no trouble staying fit."

"I wish that were true. Is the Dobos Torte your favorite or is it the Punchos? Perhaps the Sacher Torte?"

He answered limply. "Sacher Torte. Chocolate with an apricot jam filling." Crap, he thought, she sped-read that entire menu in Hungarian and memorized it. A lump of twisting ice formed in his stomach. What the hell was she doing with him? He'd called her and asked her to come, that's what – and she was diplomatic enough to indulge the local constabulary. Yes, he'd be polite and she'd be polite. Then he'd try to get her to find the history of that gutted tenement building for him. That's all the evening would be, if even that much.

"Would you help me rationalize the calories by splitting one? Two forks, one dessert, half the disaster for each of us. But if you're hungry, have one to yourself. I'll just radiate guilt toward you all evening."

She looked so beguiling, so genuine. Damn, was she nothing more than what she seemed?

A starched white collar and black tuxedo loomed next to him. He peeled his eyes off her impish smile and ordered. "A Sacher Torte. Please bring two plates so we can each try it . . . and two glasses of apricot brandy. Thanks."

He looked into her vortex and forced himself to ask a question. "How did you ever get into computers? I mean, you should be modeling or acting, not staring at numbers on a screen."

"In this profession, my looks are a disadvantage, it's true." After an awkward silence that found Alec scurrying for his next question, she put her hand on his. "I own jeans, a T-shirt and tennis shoes, too. Next time I'll wear them."

Her touch and "next time." So much for a simple, polite, isolated evening. Next time. Ryder was an excellent swimmer. He could never before understand why people drowned. With her touch, he saw himself in the middle of an endless, shoreless lake, exhausted, going under, and not giving a damn. But it wasn't suffocating and cold to drown. A warmth was suffusing into his frozen heart that hadn't been there since the doctor found him in the waiting room. That surgeon hadn't spoken, just shaken his head – and with a simple gesture, Alec Ryder's world disappeared into bitterness.

They'd grown up together, married as teens, been best friends and lovers. Then a coked-out truck driver was a little stoned and a lot stupid. No one understood why Ryder didn't care when the man didn't go to prison. A tragedy, an injustice, his friends lamented. The man responsible was out and free and still driving trucks.

Three years of patient waiting for Alec. All was forgotten by everyone but him. Then, one crisp Virginia autumn dawn, Alec stood in an alley watching that man loading his truck. Inexplicably, a forklift rolled down the loading dock and trapped the man against his truck, breaking his back and ending his life. There was a perfunctory investigation of the accident, but it stopped when he accepted exile to Interpol. Hungary was, after all, better than being in jail, where he'd be dead meat for the inmates.

A tough protective scab formed over his heart, aided by scotch and unrelenting hours of case work even when there was no case worth working on. Now, he was being pulled down by a vacuum, drowning, and he didn't care. The cafe's pianist was accompanied by a gypsy violinist. They were playing *The Third Man Theme.* He saw Joseph Cotton and Orson Welles spinning around, riding a Ferris Wheel, 1930's Budapest in a black and white film. Spies, intrigues, no one for real. How appropriate. Her voice came to him through the mental fog.

"There are very few men left in the world, Alec. Even fewer of them have brains, and they don't work with computers. They're heartless bastards who play with business empires, not keyboards. Men like that don't look past my face to see me. They just want me on their arm at a party when the wife is in St. Moritz screwing the ski instructor. I hoped that as a detective, a policeman, you knew people no matter what the surface said about them. Being a woman in the computer game is very isolating." She held his hand tighter and he responded, wrapping his fingers around hers.

Their order came and he ate a few bites, drank the apricot brandy and spilled out his life to her. The detective in him sat back and watched the spectacle, disgusted, frightened, impotent. Finally, the investigator relaxed. The evening was over. She'd leave and go her way. Tomorrow, the fool would be contained and the precious information probed for, carefully, smartly.

Alec pulled out an American hundred dollar bill, taken from his envelope on the back of the refrigerator, and put it on the tray.

They got up and he thanked her, told her he would call her soon, escorted her to the door, made his excuse at having to thank the owner for that special table. He went into the kitchen to reason with the waiter about exchange rates between the American dollar and the Hungarian forint.

Ryder listened patiently to the waiter's indignation, supported by the management and two burly dishwashers. Alec yawned, told them this was all very entertaining, but he had an early day tomorrow and they must return his hundred dollar bill. He explained it to them logically. His logic was his badge and gun. They, in return, sullenly but logically handed over his money.

He went into the closing restaurant and toward the elegant frosted glass front door. Beyond lay the cold night air. He'd go home and try again tomorrow to remain sane around her. He pushed the door open and his sanity vanished into her eyes. She'd waited for him.

"It's selfish of me, I know. You must have a very early and busy day tomorrow, but I enjoyed myself so much in your company. Perhaps, well, you'd like a nightcap? The bars close so early in Budapest. We could just go back to your place and talk."

My place. Talk. This was an LSD trip, of that he was sure. His speech was an involuntary reflex, instantly regretted by every logical faculty of his mind. "My place! My place is a crime scene. Someday I'll have the police lab take photos and show 'em to you. That's as close as you should ever get to my apartment." He laughed and she looked shy, puzzled, vulnerable.

Her voice was almost a whisper when she talked. "I'm staying at the Grand Hotel. Why don't we go there instead? I have a bar in the room." She perked up a little and laughed herself. "Besides, I have maid service daily, so I know you won't have to call the crime lab before entering."

Now it was his turn to look shy, puzzled and vulnerable. Somehow they got on the right streetcar. Somehow he put his arm around her. Somehow, her head leaned on his shoulder. Somehow, how he could not begin to reconstruct, he found himself standing in front of the door to suite 115 of the Grand Hotel on Margaret Island, and she was fumbling in her handbag for the key.

He surveyed the elegant suite as she dropped her handbag in a chair.

She joked. "You see, it isn't a crime scene. Having a maid come twice a day works wonders. They even turn down the bed and leave a chocolate on my pillow."

Alec remained in the open doorway, feeling uneasy. It'd been so long since he'd been alone with a woman. Add to that this woman. Add also that there'd been no women since . . .

"Come in, you shy boy. Close the door and I'll fix you a drink. Brandy all right?" She pulled out two large snifters and a bottle of five-star Remy Martin.

"Sure." Ryder warily closed the door behind him. "Just the two rooms, a bath and the bedroom?" What the hell was bugging him, he wondered?

"Yes. I'm sure there are nicer suites in this hotel, but I try not to soak my clients too badly. Enough to get their respect, but not so much they won't tell the next person how much value they got for the money. It's a tough balance."

She lit a low candle and warmed his snifter over the flame, swirling the magnificent cognac in hypnotic circles. Its scent came to him – masculine, powerful.

He took the warm glass from her and inhaled, sipped, then instinctively moved to where he could see all doorways and closets. He unbuttoned his coat, rubbed his arm against the shoulder holster for reassurance. Alec glanced at her. Jeanette wasn't warming her cognac. She was staring at him in curiosity.

"Why don't you sit down and be comfortable? That chair is my favorite. It's a great antidote to a mean day." She fluffed up the pillows of a chaise lounge, offering him its envelopment.

"Inspectors are always on duty, I'm afraid. I feel more relaxed over here, where I can see everything. It's an old survival instinct." He sipped again and the cognac's aroma jolted him.

"Well, then, I'll turn on some music. Maybe that will take some of the cop out of you." Jeanette moved to him, put an arm around his waist and pulled him over a foot. She knelt down and reached inside the cabinet he'd been blocking. Beethoven's eighth symphony announced itself from bookshelf speakers.

It didn't soothe him. He felt annoyed with himself. This was asinine. A beautiful woman. Great brandy. Beethoven. And something wrong. Her?

The place? Fear of sex with her? Now that was supreme arrogance on his part. First date and she lays you, Alec. Right, stud. Dream on. Stop being so damned self-absorbed. She's asked you about everything from cradle to badge. Ask her something, for Christ's sake. "How did you ever get into computers in the first place?"

"I graduated from UCLA in math and got one job offer, from Software Systems International. SSI had only done work for the Department of Defense, but was trying to expand into state and local governments to cover a slump in defense work. They had contracts with cities in the Los Angeles area, but couldn't make any money. Every aerospace firm had the same idea and all the cities wanted a custom solution for a shrink-wrap price tag. So SSI just abandoned the work. Their existing customers still needed support. I left and consulted with them. I saw all my friends consulting outside the USA, making big bucks in Saudi Arabia and Singapore. I went to Berlitz and found I had an aptitude for languages. I guess FORTRAN and Hungarian have some common root in my brain." She looked embarrassed. "I don't think that makes me a genius, though. I never did that well in school."

Half of what she said he'd missed in the smell of her perfume and the nuances of her lovely face when she'd talked. Somewhere in his brain the estranged detective was taking notes, jotting down alleged facts that could be checked tomorrow for authenticity, but he didn't care right now if anything correlated. "It doesn't bother me that you're smart. I wish I could spend more time around you because of your intelligence."

"You can." She kicked off her shoes and sat on the sofa. Her eyes invited him to also sit. He obeyed. She snuggled against him. He stroked her hair. Just as fear began to tighten his chest, she impulsively kissed him – a little soft, brief caress of her lips on his. Then another, longer, firmer kiss. She loosened his tie, ran a fingertip inside his shirt and stroked his chest hair. He pulled her to him and possessed her lips with his, found her tongue probing inside his mouth, turning his groin to fire. He pulled away and licked his way along her neck until he found an earlobe. She moaned and unbuttoned his shirt, found a nipple and gave it an erection with her touch. He slid his left hand along her waist and up, loosened her blouse and returned the favor. She squirmed in arousal and pressed against his hand.

Her musk came to him, mixed with her perfume and the cognac . . . and something else, familiar but incongruous. Little hairs on the back of his neck bristled.

Her breath teased his ear when she whispered. "I want to change into something else, something I've been dreaming of wearing since I first saw you." She pulled away, reluctantly, got up and started toward the bedroom. A thousand alarm bells rang in his brain. His erection melted. She was two steps away when he leapt up and grabbed her arm.

"NO!" he shouted.

She looked so innocently bewildered, then ashamed. Finally, anger hardened her face. "I didn't mean to force myself on you, Alec."

"You didn't. Now get over to the front door."

"What's going on?!"

"Just move it." He was up and the coat was off. One hand was on the gun, still holstered.

She hesitantly moved to the hallway door, buttoning her blouse and straightening her hair with a quick glance in the mirror.

"I don't get it . . ."

"Open the door and stand in it." He waited until she'd done exactly as he said. The smells came to him, the warning alarm – her skin, cognac and . . . "If anything happens, get out. Get help. Be quick. You got it?"

"Yes, but . . ."

"No. Just get out, get help."

"OK, Alec, but . . ."

He didn't wait past the OK. The American 9-mm automatic was unholstered, cocked, pointed. He pressed himself against the wall leading to the bathroom door. He slid, pivoting in the bathroom doorway, spiraling on toward the bedroom. Alec rolled across the bedroom entrance in a crouch, scanning all he could, making himself as small a target as possible. He glanced back at her, then swept the bedroom. He could see the closet open in the mirror, her bed turned down, a chocolate on the pillow – and he could smell the blood intensely now. That's what had been wrong from the beginning . . . her perfume, her musk, cognac and fresh human blood.

Where the hell was the blood smell coming from? He had to go in to find out. What if someone else was waiting inside, someone who had done the hurting, not someone who'd been hurt? Should he call for backup first? No, he didn't want anyone to know about his date. If they were still inside, they would have made their move when he was on the couch, oblivious to anything but Jeanette. At least he hoped that was their logic.

A quick spin inside, almost firing at his own reflection. Nothing. A feeling of lunacy, idiocy, nausea for making a fool out of himself swept over him. Then he looked along the far side of the bed.

The maid was there, her face and apron soaked in blood. There was blood splattered on the mirrored closet doors. A wet pool of red soaked into the carpet, fed by a stream running down her face. A long, black-handled knife was stuck to its hilt in her left eye socket and her hands were convulsed about the knife handle. A pair of torn panties were snagged between her clenched teeth.

Ryder slapped the closet doors to one side, pushed the clothes away, slammed them back to the other side and finished making damn sure no one was still there. He hesitated a second, then flung the bedspread off and slid backwards to the doorway. Alec went prone and swept under the bed with his eyes, hoping all the other guy had was that knife, not a gun. He took a deep breath, popped up, turned around to see Jeanette sitting on a parlor chair, hands on her knees.

She looked detached. It startled him. Was it just a protective shell she wore in times of extreme shock? Or was it a professional calmly examining the improbable event and what it meant to her plans, finding alternatives, running down the implications?

He stared at her as he dialed the front desk. "Hello? This is Alec Ryder of Interpol. Yes, the Police. Get hotel security up here at once." He looked questioningly at Jeanette. "Room?"

"Suite 115. Alec?"

"Send them to room 115. Then patch me through to Police Headquarters. I'll wait on the line . . . So cut in and kick them off. This has priority. Yes, it's that important."

"Alec?"

"Yes."

"Is she dead?"

"Yes. Very dead."

9

Mistakes

He could only stand there, peeking at her through a barely open door leading to the Hotel's fire stairs. Abruptly she disappeared inside suite 115, but her room door was still open. He started toward her when a man's voice came from suite 115. He backed out of view. He considered forcing his way in, checked his Uzi, released its safety. Then caution won and he "safed" the weapon. There was no point in adding to his mistakes.

In less than a minute, hotel security arrived, two burly thugs who'd once served the local KGB office. Suite 115 swallowed them also. Still, he could take them even if the hotel men were armed. The Uzi would cut them down like a scythe. Did it really matter, other than his ego? His pride and confidence stung from how badly it'd gone.

How many mistakes he'd made! He'd thought the maid to be Her, the Impostor, until it was too late. The poor maid opened that closet door just as he'd expected Her to do, to replace the fur. He'd driven the knife home in her eye, just as he'd planned. But he hadn't expected the woman to scream and claw at him for a full minute before she became a dying vegetable. To stifle her screams he'd been forced to stuff the panties into her mouth, and then she'd clamped down on them at the end and he could only tear away a part of them. She'd pulled a glove off as well. He'd twisted the knife into her brain, cutting away more and more of her mind until she convulsed, a steel-like grip on his stiletto.

He'd panicked at sounds outside the door, mistaking them for a rescue party. He climbed out the window and went down the fire escape, re-entering the Hotel through a kitchen entrance. Once he fled to his room, his faculties returned and he'd realized he needed to go back and clean up. He had blood all over his clothes and had to change, go to the trash incinerator in the basement, burn his outfit. After that, he'd come to the door of suite 115 only to hear music and soft voices through the door. It was too late to clean up – unless he killed them too. Once again he went back to his room, climbed into a ceiling access hatch in the closet and dragged out his Uzi.

But he was too late again and all he could do now was watch and count his mistakes. There had been many errors. They had his skin from under her nails, his semen in the panties, possibly a fingerprint and worst of all, the knife. His precious switchblade, carried for decades, often used as the weapon of last resort to save his life. Damn, of all the things he'd done wrong, leaving that knife behind was the worst. It had been a gift from those who'd first tortured and wronged him, those to whom he was so closely bonded in a paradox of hate and loyalty.

Sirens. Police would soon be everywhere. Well, he consoled himself as he returned to his room, his mission wouldn't be impaired. They'd never connect this isolated incident with his other brilliant successes. Soon he'd be gone from Hungary, leaving them with all their evidence. Perhaps he'd even find a way to get his knife back. That would be daring, but worthwhile. It was his identity.

10

Unfolding

"A full set of prints from the left hand, skin samples for a DNA analysis and the murder weapon – an old switchblade stiletto. Plus his semen. The guy's a real psycho, Alec. By the way, did you ask her about the panties? Are they hers?"

Alec stopped tapping the brandy glass and snorted toward the pimple-faced coroner's second-assistant. "No. Now take your teenage curiosity and get the hell out with the rest of them."

The nineteen year old shrugged insolently, dropped three evidence bags in Alec's lap and fell in behind a body bag strapped to an ambulance dolly. Hotel security held the door open and made certain they left by a service elevator. No upset guests. Murder never happens in fine hotels.

A pair of uniformed policemen remained, looking questioningly at Alec for instructions.

"Wait outside. I'll be with you in a few minutes – and stay alert. If anyone comes around, detain them. I have a few things to go over with her." When they'd closed the door, he looked at Jeanette sitting opposite him, stiffly erect in a parlor chair. She looked to him like she was bracing for the dentist to do a root canal.

"They were my panties."

"It doesn't matter if they were yours. The guy was a nut. It was all some crazy freak thing, part of coming into the real world from being hidden behind the Iron Curtain for decades. Pack some things, Jeanette. You can't sleep here tonight. We'll get you a new hotel and have the rest brought to you."

She got up like a robot and left him with the endlessly repeating Beethoven. He heard luggage dragged out and snapped open. Drawers were slid out and pushed in. Alec sipped cognac, then took a long drag from the snifter and forced himself to swallow the burning liquid. Could this be related to the arsons? It was hard to believe this weird, half-baked murder belonged at the feet of the same cunning professional who set up those burns. Or was it done this way to make it seem like the crimes had no connection? He fondled the bloody knife in its plastic bag. Weird choice of weapons, weird place to stab someone. Not a slasher's style of attack. Slashers jabbed into the chest, over and over. Professionals come from behind, pin the victim, cut off air to prevent screams, cut the jugular vein in one quick, clean shot. Hold on until the brain dies from lack of blood. Where in the hell had he seen a knife like this before? It didn't matter. The last thing he needed was any distraction from the arsons. This nut was ridiculously careless. He'd get himself caught by hotel security and ID'ing him would be trivial.

Yet he turned the crime over again and again in his mind, rolling the knife in its bag, draining the cognac. The maid's blood was so damn fresh. She died only a few minutes before they'd come into the room. What the hell was the motive? If the guy was nuts, there was no telling. If he wasn't, was he trying to kill that particular maid? Did he want something in the room? Had he gotten what he wanted, or would he be back? It was worth setting a trap for him. That was the only good idea he'd had all night.

He watched Jeanette packing toiletries from the bathroom. She looked like a wooden puppet on strings. She was scared to death . . .

Shit. Did the maid die by mistake? Was the lunatic after Jeanette instead? God, he was glad he'd come back to the room with her. It delayed Jeanette and the maid died instead.

He took the knife out of its bag, held the stiletto. They'd dusted the handle for prints, but found none. Alec wiped off the graphite dust. Ebony wood handle with ivory caps over rivets bonding the handle to the blade. Several old, deep nicks in the blade. New edges had been ground on it many times. An old resistance knife, used to cut many a throat in its time, the deep nicks from chipping against collar bones with enormous force when tempered stainless steel sought a jugular vein. Razor sharp. About a thumb wide . . .

Oh God! He'd been in her closet before she left to meet Alec. The cut in her fur coat's lining! Why in the hell hadn't he struck then? Had the killer been put off by Alec's phone call to Jeanette? More likely, it was really the maid he'd been after all along. Some bizarre love triangle.

He poured more Remy Martin in the glass, swallowed it all. The more he thought, the more every possibility remained. Only one thing he saw with clarity. Jeanette was rigid with fear. Shock passed hours ago.

She stood over him, suitcase in one hand, black train bag and briefcase in another. It was her posture, not her voice that announced, "I'm ready."

"Wait here, just a second." He tried to sound calm, like he was in control of all that might happen. He wondered if he'd even come close to the right tone. Yet she was staying put when he moved to the door, withdrew his automatic, and cracked the entry open. He saw the two policemen intact, holstered the gun and gave instructions.

* * *

Alec rolled down the borrowed patrol car's window to get cold air into his head, then glanced at Jeanette. She was staring aimlessly at the empty streets. "What hotel would you like? I can get you into any of them."

She turned and looked at Alec. There was a long pause, then she talked shyly. "I wish you'd take me home with you. I'd feel so much safer, Alec. Just tonight. Then I'll get out of your hair."

He nodded, not wanting to break her mood. After a gentle pause, Alec resumed his professional, emotionless monotone. "Do you think he was after you, not the maid?"

"I don't know what to think. It shocked me. It was so . . . violent."

"Could the killer have been after something in the room? Was anything missing?"

"I don't have anything valuable. Some good costume jewelry, but I don't even bother to hide it. Next season, it'll be out of fashion and I'll shop Melrose for the next trend."

"How about your briefcase?"

"Nothing. I leave everything at work. Such long hours. Why carry it home?"

"How much longer would you have been here, normally?"

"Only a week's work is left. But I would've stayed to see more of you, if you'd wanted that."

"But now you're frightened. Would you like to leave tomorrow? Officially, I can't condone you leaving the country, but you didn't see the crime committed. It was probably random coincidence that a killing occurred in your hotel room instead of any other. We can gather up your things in a few hours, after you nap, then put you on a noon flight to LA." He knew it was a lie. He wouldn't let her go like that. He couldn't. He rationalized the question as a professional trap, cold, objective manipulation to heighten her need for him, get more information out of her. If he was such a pro, why was his heart jump in his throat while he waited for her answer?

"I was hoping to stay. I can't run out on an assignment in the middle. It would wreck my consulting business to abandon a client."

Alec felt his hands release the patrol car's steering wheel. He stopped at a red light that he could've ignored at four in the morning. But stopping let him focus on her. "Will you feel safe at work?"

"I feel safe around you." She melted back to the Jeanette he'd been with earlier. She looked at him in admiration.

The professional went to war inside him against the man and won for the first time that evening. She was playing him just right. Had she realized she'd become a target because the work was ending? Perhaps she couldn't leave because they'd find her anywhere she went and kill her to bury all links to them. If she was a really good pro, she'd be playing him just like this. But if Jeanette was a pro, she had to switch sides or die with a knife in her eye.

"If we went to my place, could you get some sleep?" he asked. The traffic light had long ago turned green, but he let the car idle and looked into her eyes.

"It's only two hours until I get up for work." She evaded his stare and looked at lights strung along Chain Bridge.

"Tomorrow's Saturday."

"I work Saturdays."

"Alone?"

"Alone. There's still a lot of work before the last application can be integrated."

* * *

Alec Ryder sat in his favorite chair and fondled the empty scotch glass. His stomach churned like a cement mixer, trying to rationalize a cognac/scotch mix. He took the last antacids from his coat.

She still wore red earrings. Her face was like a trusting child's, buried in the pillow. He'd covered her with the bedspread after she'd given in and tried for a short nap. That was hours ago. Now there were children running along the inner courtyard balconies of his apartment house, neighbors flushing toilets and taking showers.

The antacids didn't work. He needed food to calm his stomach. She'd be safe here. No one knew where they were. He'd made sure they weren't tailed. Alec picked up his coat and slipped out to get breakfast. He stood in the doorway and took a last look at her. Ryder told himself she was safe and eased the thin, cracked wood shut, wiggling the door handle to make certain it was locked.

11

Corrections

He tapped his fist against the door to suite 115 of the Grand Hotel on Margaret Island and waited. There was no answer. He knocked again. "Room service."

There was dull shuffling on the other side of the door and a husky, masculine voice answered. "We didn't order anything. Who are you?"

"Room service. Inspector Ryder left a breakfast order for you. It's compliments of the house – for how late you worked last night."

The door cracked open until a chain stopped it. No face was apparent behind the gap.

He waited, looking bored and impatient.

A long pause. The door eased closed. Metal dragged against metal and the chain fell. The metal links swung back and forth, ticking against the wood.

"OK, come in." An invisible force pivoted the door on its hinges.

"How about some lights?"

"Just come in. Then we'll turn on the lights."

Cautious bastards, weren't they? He wheeled the cart inside and was blinded as lights flooded the room. A uniformed policeman stood in front of him, gun pointed down but ready. Deft hands pushed up his arms and patted him, looking for concealed weapons.

"What is this?" Just the right amount of indignation.

"He's clean."

The gun in front of him went inside its leather holster and the holster was snapped shut. The policeman behind him moved to the side of the cart and poked at a stainless steel lid over one of the covered dishes.

"Just leave it."

"OK, but, ah, . . ."

"You said it was complimentary."

"Well, yeah, but, uh . . ."

"Your turn to buy. You tip him." The closest one put a fingertip inside the center hole of a cover and picked it up. The plate underneath was blank.

Before their astonishment could turn to action, he reached under the cart and snapped the silenced Uzi submachine gun off its magnetic holder. He took the one closest to him with a burst to the groin and stomach, knocking the man down. The Uzi swung in an arc, catching the other policeman trying to get his pistol out. Several rounds hit the man in his chest, shoving him to the floor.

He bent over each dying man in turn and pressed the Uzi's barrel to their head. The silenced gun kicked like a muffled jackhammer, "phumping" rounds into their skulls. There was no more groaning from the men.

He turned around and locked the suite's door. Moving rapidly, he assured himself there was no one else in the quarters. On the bedroom dresser, he found what he'd come for – evidence bags, left by Alec Ryder for the policemen to carry to headquarters when their shift ended.

Every mistake he'd come to correct was there – the fingerprints on tape, the panties, skin samples from under the maid's fingernails, even his beloved knife.

He smiled in a wicked manner, looking at himself in the dressing mirrors. Older. Different uniform, but still a waiter. Just as it had been before, with her . . .

* * *

Time melted away. She again taunted him. "Don't feel obligated to come inside if it frightens you."

She vanished inside the darkened suite, but left the door ajar as his invitation.

His heart beat loud and fast. He looked around the empty hallway, afraid someone would stop him – and more afraid they would not. He lied to himself that he wasn't scared and pushed open the door. It was dark inside.

"Have you ever played hide and seek in the dark?" she teased him.

"No," was his flat, stupefied answer.

"It's my favorite game."

"I don't want to play your game. Turn the lights on." He hated how his voice cracked a bit when he talked. Damn her.

"I can make you want to play. Listen."

He stood very still, furious with himself that he didn't just leave this bitch and her weird moods. A clock softly ticked. The bathtub faucet dripped every few seconds, like an unwound metronome. Now there were other sounds – soft, strange. He didn't like it. He reached behind for the doorknob.

"That was my dress. I left it for you to find. Come forward. Touch it and I'll take off more."

He let go of the doorknob, groped his way forward, cursing himself for doing her bidding. But he kept seeing her face, her bosom, her legs. Something he'd never felt before burned in his stomach and the burning was pouring downward, into his groin.

He stumbled into a chair, let out a gasp. She giggled. Damn her!

On the chair was her dress, still warm from her body. He ran a fingertip along the zipper, put his hand inside where her bosom had been. His penis stirred.

A snap, then another and another. More soft unfolding. He waited, forgetting to breathe.

She baited him. "My nylons. Bet you can't find them."

He didn't move, determined to frustrate her.

"Turn right . . ."

He pivoted, following where her voice seemed to come from, took a step, then halted, enraged at her.

"Don't stop now . . . I won't stop, I won't."

His will detached from himself and watched in rebellious silence as he slid one foot after another. A table jabbed his swollen groin. The pain made his cock throb in excitement. He patted the table and found her nylons.

He smelled the stockings, inhaling her perfume and another odor – strange, primitive, overpowering. Did this last scent come from her aroused loins?

"Just one more little piece of cloth and I'm naked. Did you think I had so little on when you saw me dancing, pressed against a man?" She tossed the garter belt at his back and he jumped, knocking over the table with his recoil. Something smashed on the floor. Glass?

"I like breaking things, don't you? I especially like breaking the rules."

He jumped where he thought she was and collided with another table. Its legs screeched across the parquet floor. "Damn you, bitch!"

"Take off your clothes and I'll let you touch me when you find me . . . wherever you like . . . and I'll touch you . . . I know where you want to be touched."

"How . . . ?" his throat was too dry to finish.

"How will you find me? You're a *man*, aren't you? Aren't you *man* enough to find me? I can't run into the hall *this* way . . ."

He stood still, feeling confused. He'd never ached like this, or been this upset, beyond any anger he'd ever felt.

"Take off your shoes, now, please . . ." She begged.

He kicked them off, waited. She didn't say anything. He pushed the socks off with his toes, waited some more.

"Is that *all*?"

"What do you mean *all*?" he barked at her. She sounded farther away. In another room?

"I want you like me. Wearing nothing."

"What if I do that? What then?" God, how pitiable he sounded. She knew he'd do whatever she wanted. He hated himself. He hated her far worse.

"Take off all your clothes. Then, we'll have some very special fun . . . I told you . . . touching . . ."

Where was she, damn it? Where was a light switch?

As if she knew what he was thinking, she spoke again. "Don't bother trying to find a light switch. I pulled the fuses. You have to play by my rules, or not play at all."

He couldn't believe he was doing it when he unbuttoned his coat and trousers, tore off his shirt. Cautiously, he lowered his underwear over the protruding cock. Why was it stiff like this? Why did he want to bury it inside her?

"Are you all undressed?"

"Yes." He tried to swallow and choked.

"You're not lying?"

"No."

"Then follow my voice . . ."

He moved in that direction, but was seasoned enough to go slowly and keep his hands low. It was an eternity until he felt the edge of a doorway and stopped.

She moaned. "Please . . . I need you."

He stepped forward and was hit in the face with a brilliant light. From a dark amphitheater behind the searing illumination, he could hear her laughing.

"You look so funny . . . I never thought . . ." Her laughing was non-stop. "So funny . . ."

"You bitch. I'm going to kill you!" he shrieked and plunged at the light, his penis wilting to nothing, flopping as he charged. His right hand smashed the reflector and bulb to the floor. They stayed on, etching sharp contrasts and ink black shadows across furnishings.

He slowly got his bearings.

She was in her canopied bed, tittering at him, her pupils glowing. She had the covers pulled up, squeezed in a little peak that kissed her mouth. Arrogance danced with satanic delight across her eyes, completing his humiliation.

"You may go now . . ." She announced his dismissal in her most patronizing voice.

She would pay. He didn't know how, but she would pay . . .

He wrapped the covers around his fist with furious deliberation. Violently, he tore them from her hands, exposing her. She was fully dressed, legs crossed.

"That's enough! I forbid you to come closer. Leave my room!" Her face was icy.

How many times had she played her little game before? Had they all left now, at her willful, haughty command? Thrown on their clothes and slinked back to their inferior station in life? He knelt on the bed.

A touch of fear showed in her face finally. She inched back from him.

"I . . . I have bodyguards. They will kill you!"

He grabbed an ankle and made certain his grip hurt. She kicked at him and he pinned the other ankle, too. Methodically, he spread the ankles as far apart as her dress allowed, then knelt over her legs, immobilizing them against the mattress.

"No! I want you to leave! This isn't . . ."

He spat at her. "This isn't supposed to be what happens?"

"What do you want?" She was openly frightened now. The bodyguards were a bluff, he thought.

"What do you *want*?" She repeated the words hysterically.

He didn't answer, just sneered at her, reveling in her growing panic.

"I know secrets. Yes, important secrets. There are important secrets in this room . . . Don't you want *them*?"

"No!" he shouted at her.

"All right then, go ahead. Touch me. I don't care what you do. I'm not here." She closed her eyes and went limp.

He stood up, puzzled. She just lay there. The only sign of life was light breathing. He was again of no importance, again just a pawn to be dismissed.

At the foot of her bed was a nightgown, magnificent green satin with a red cord around its waist. He stared at the rope.

The red cord came off easily. He wound it around his wrists. He moved over her throat.

"I'm going to kill you," he stated flatly.

She didn't react. The same vapid limpness fended him off.

He jumped on top of her and pressed the cord down, cutting into her windpipe with demonic strength.

She struck at him, twisted, flung a leg over his head and peeled him back.

He wrapped the cord around her neck so she was pulled atop him when he fell on the floor. A bed post snapped off and the canopy tumbled down, smothering them.

The bitch scratched cat-like at his face, her head turning bright red from exertion. Soon her skin turned purple and her limbs slackened. Her tongue distended from the mouth.

He thought it another game she had made up, some way to trick him. She was just putting on the face to be ugly, get him to go away. He hung on the cord for minutes, forcing the rope taut long after she died.

He let go of the cord. "Wake up, bitch!" He slapped her. She didn't respond. The same damn limpness that tormented him to attack her was again driving him mad. He would take her anyway. The fight engorged his penis again.

He forced himself inside her despite her passive resistance. It hurt, but the pain drove him all the more furiously to succeed. He kept pushing against her until he spasmed in his first climax.

* * *

How long he'd lain atop her he didn't know. He must've passed out. He opened his eyes. It was all dark. He could feel her clammy chill against his chest and stomach and legs. The room was flooded with an odor of burnt carpet, tinted by his own semen. The floodlight must have scorched the rug before it flamed out.

He tried to get up and found himself pressing on her. He got on one knee and rubbed his eyes. It all seemed a fantastic nightmare, yet there she was, glazed eyes staring at him, the cord fastened to her throat. Revolted, he staggered to his feet. Faint illumination came through a bedroom window and he could see the wall switch.

There was a scuffling noise behind him and he started to get up. A flashlight beam cut across his face. He put up a hand to shield his eyes.

A cruel blow staggered him, then another. He fell hard against the floor, unable to soften the crash. His skull cracked against hardwood, dazing his mind. He fought a losing battle to remain conscious. Blackness wrapped his mind in a painful night. His last thoughts were of dying.

* * *

He faded in and out of consciousness, listening to disembodied voices.

"He's killed her. Looks like he raped her, too."

"She brought it on. I told you she was crazy. This isn't the first time she lured a waiter or a bellboy into a trap."

"What are we going to do? Her father expects us to deliver her in Switzerland!"

"Accidents happen. The Nazis win. We tried."

"Hmmm. Maybe. But what about him? Kill him. He certainly deserves it, even if she was a nut case."

"A quick death is too easy for him. He should be punished. She was a Habsburg. Sick, it's true. But still royalty. He murdered and raped a princess. He should be tortured first."

"We will stoop to what he is, what the Germans are if we torture him. Just kill him and be done with it."

"No. I have a better idea. Let those whom the devil owns have him. They'll torture him for us."

"But he's been in the room, seen the secrets. Here, on the floor, see for yourself!"

"Where he's going it won't matter. No one will believe him. It won't stop us from our goal."

"How will we get them out of the hotel?"

"Get the others. We'll need their help."

"They're already on their way. I hear footsteps."

He remembered being bound and gagged. Chloroform was used to keep him in a stupor as they forced him through the bedroom window and down the fire escape ladder.

* * *

Tonight his mind was clear, eager with triumph. He climbed through the same hotel window again and used the same fire escape. Bitterly cold air sharpened his awareness. His destiny, shaped many years before in suite 115, still lay before him, waiting for him to claim it. He was certain of victory. Last night's mistakes were corrected – the evidence bags were clamped in his left hand, his beloved knife tucked in his pants. Well, all the errors were fixed but one. The Impostor was still alive.

He would correct that error also.

12

Dark Angel

Alec stopped the white patrol car in front of his apartment building and grabbed fast food from the passenger seat. The McDonald's bag held two coffees and a menu assortment for Jeanette. He'd gone to McDonald's because it felt like home. Right now, he needed a home, a place where he felt safe. American fast food was as close as he could get.

Ryder trotted into a courtyard littered with stunted plants that never saw enough sun, never tasted enough rain to be anything but dusty runts. Sunlight angled over the roof and partially blinded him as he squinted up. The usual assortment of laundry lay draped over railings whose bruised metal hinted at having once been painted red, then gold, finally a horrible state-issued grayish blue. Big Wheels and bicycles poked front tires at him, stuck through bars in the railings. A thermal eddy current of dust spun off his level and wound lazily toward the roof, courtesy of an unseasonably warm day.

The Inspector waited. A kid should run out. A wife should yell. A husband in undershirt ought to be stretching himself.

He spun slowly around. There was only the sound of his leather soles twisting on dirty, loose bricks. Instinctively, Alec slid his right hand over the 9-mm automatic and debated. He brought the hand out empty and started up the five flights of stairs to his home.

He tried to be casual on the first level, take a normal pace. It only made him more edgy. By the second story, Alec was moving at twice what he knew he could sustain to the top. At the third, Alec eased into the communal space and looked again. Still an eerie quiet. Was his door slightly ajar? He took the steps two at a time until his lungs burned out.

Alec waited just off the landing and cursed his stupidity at leaving Jeanette alone. The heavy steel weapon burdened his right hand. The left clung to a McDonald's bag he'd forgotten. Ryder became a shadow gliding along the building's wall, dropping into dark archways, pressing on each door to make sure it was closed. No one stirred. Could the bastard have killed them all before he reached Jeanette? It was ridiculous, yet there had been enough time. He could've been waiting outside, seen Alec leave. A pro would be that thorough, very systematic.

Oh shit! What if the building was about to explode in flames, be torched like that other apartment house? Alec was wasting precious time. Maybe Jeanette was still alive, just bound up so there'd be no escape when the flames touched her.

The debate ended when he reached home base and confirmed his door was not as he'd left it. He eased the door open and peeked inside. Jeanette's luggage was dumped open and everything strewn across the bed in a jumble, bringing his fears to life.

Ryder went through the slapped-open door in a crouch and deliberately tumbled head over heels. He came up in the firing position. A muscle in his stomach ached from the commando-style maneuver that a better-conditioned Alec Ryder once did easily.

On its own momentum, the door swung closed behind him. He stood up, holding the automatic with both hands, pointing the weapon chest high at the bathroom door. The toilet area was the only place left for anyone to hide Jeanette.

The sound of quiet feet slipping behind him brought the drumming of Alec's heart to his ears. He raised his gun vertical and hid behind the door.

Cautiously, a body moved on the other side of the wooden panel. Alec put his thumb on the hammer and waited to synchronize the sound of cocking his gun with a squeaky floorboard. The opportunity came and the hammer went back, giving him a split-second advantage.

The back of a head came into view and Alec reflexed, leveling the barrel at the skull.

"Geaneta?" A pause and then again a best effort at "Jeanette?"

Alec's finger came off the trigger just as the toilet door opened. Jeanette exited the bathroom and saw Alec had a gun pointed at his elderly neighbor's head.

In her best English/Hungarian mix, the matron explained that Alec must be nearby because his car was in front of the building. Jeanette should not worry so much. She was with friends here and should come enjoy the birthday cake they were eating in old Domminy's room. So many candles! The man was 102 today and still kicking!

Jeanette nodded and stared numbly. Alec silently brought his gun down behind his back to hide it from his neighbor.

But the old woman tottered outside, leaving the apartment. She never knew Alec stood behind her, an ounce of pressure away from blowing her mind all over the far wall.

The door lock clicked.

Alec Ryder let out a long breath. Jeanette stood immobilized, looking like she was going to cry.

"I'm sorry," he found himself saying by remote control. "I thought I'd go out and get some breakfast for us." He held up the McDonald's bag like a truant student displaying his forged excuse to the home-room teacher.

Anger clouded her face. She jammed clothes into her luggage, ignoring him, turning away so he couldn't see if she was crying. "I have to go to work. I'll catch a streetcar. I've imposed on you enough." Jeanette turned the bag upright and looked around the room for her briefcase. He could see her breasts heaving under the T-shirt despite all her effort at control.

The cotton top was jammed into a pair of designer jeans, making it obvious how slim and fit she was. There were no earrings, no lipstick, no cosmetics on her face. Her eyes were red. She looked very different to him, but even more vulnerably erotic than when he'd felt her press against him. In her hotel suite, they'd tongue-kissed and his hand teased a willing nipple erect. Last night's memory now felt like something he watched on film years ago.

Ninety-nine percent of him ached to forget all the intervening fiasco, grab her, make her submit to him. The sane one-percent knew it was all wrong, knew she felt far too vulnerable to him. If he wanted sex now, he could have it. She needed him too much to deny him – and then she'd hate him forever.

He dropped the McDonald's bag in the trash and reached behind him, groping for her briefcase and cosmetics bag. They must be there. She'd scoured every other place with her glare. "Come on. I'll take you to work. It's the least I can do for scaring the daylights out of you."

"No. I'll go myself."

"Okay. Answer one question first. How long have you known they were going to kill you when you finished this assignment?"

Jeanette sagged on his bed and buried her face. He could hear her sobbing. He sat down next to her.

She looked up, but not at him. Jeanette stared into space with unfocused eyes. "When I woke up and you weren't here . . . That's when I realized I'd be dead soon as the job was completed. It hit me this morning."

"Not last night?"

"Damn you. I didn't come on to you because I wanted your gun." She got up to leave.

He grabbed her wrist. She didn't yank away. She went limp.

"I meant something else. When did you realize it could have been you dead and not the maid?"

This time she looked directly into his eyes and seemed calmer. "I wondered when I saw her . . . and I guess I sort of knew in the car last night, when I wanted to come here instead of another hotel."

He waited for her to come back from the mental fog, but she just drifted farther away. He let go of her wrist and she sat down at his desk, looking lost and bewildered.

He grabbed the McDonald's bag out of the trash. It was, after all, an average day's wages in Hungary. "Feel at all hungry? Coffee?"

He popped lids off two containers and the smell of coffee filled his room.

In the next few minutes of silence, she picked a little at a danish and sipped some acidic institutional brew.

Ryder sipped and ate also. When she pried off a serious chunk of roll, he spoke. "I know my reasons for thinking someone is after you. But I don't know yours. If I'm to have any chance of stopping them, you have to help me. They won't quit when you leave Hungary, you know."

"My reasons aren't reasons at all. They're just silly ideas and things that don't fit together. Maybe I'm crazy."

"I don't think so. I'm convinced it was meant to be you last night. The blood was fresh, not even coagulated. They only missed by a few minutes. It was just good luck and luck runs out." What a heel he was being. Scaring her to death so he could get what he wanted from her about the arsoned property. The chance that the two crimes had any link was very remote, wasn't it? But he hadn't thought so when he nearly blew away his next-door neighbor.

Jeanette stopped eating and pushed aside the food. She looked sick, like she was going to throw up.

It took all his will to continue the questioning, but he needed her help. "What makes you think they want you dead?"

"Because they paid me so much. More than twice what I'd ever gotten before, without my asking. A large advance payment. I used it to buy new luggage and a fur coat. What a fool I was, thinking I'd arrived, a big time international consultant."

He put down the coffee cup and studied her face. "Who brought you the contract?"

"An agent in Europe. Said he'd been asking around and heard I was the right person for the job. He was very flattering."

"Did you know him, work with him before?"

"No, never."

"What was his name?"

"He was a German, from Stuttgart. Hans Mueller. He sent me a check drawn on a Swiss bank. A hundred thousand dollars."

Ryder struggled to mask his surprise and intense interest. He fought to stay calm and look like it was all a parking ticket he'd fix on Monday when the office opened. "Do you have Hans Mueller's address and phone number?"

"Yes, I think so. In my planner. Do you need it now?"

"No, I'll get it from you in a minute. The only thing different about this assignment was the pay?"

"Well, I told you it was just crazy ideas."

"What are these other crazy ideas?"

"The contract. Weird structure to it – all expenses paid. Not customary and reasonable even – all of them. I just had to submit an estimate in advance and they gave me that check too, on top of the hundred thousand dollars."

"Any more reasons?"

"Yeah. The information we put into the computer. It makes no sense to me why they wanted some things prioritized but not others."

"What things?"

"It's very complex. I don't see the pattern clearly. It's a jigsaw puzzle and I only have a few of the pieces. I'd have to show you."

* * *

Alec Ryder bent his patrol car around the Gothic majesty of Matthias Church and then sharply reversed his steering wheel towards the old Jewish Quarter of Castle Hill, where catacombs begun in the 1300s as refuge from persecution were the safest place to hide Budapest's records from Allied bombs in 1945. He pulled on the parking brake in front of a huge arched coach door, its herringbone oak painted a dark brown, framed in stone and isolated in the center of a blank façade whose only adornment was its street number.

Jeanette used her key to let them through an access door. The small portal sat inside the larger barn door that once opened upon lacquered coaches, groomed mares and liveried attendants. Now, the building was partitioned and they could only spiral downward into a portion of the Jewish catacombs. The subterranean quarters were converted to the Department of Property Titles and Vital Statistics.

At journey's end in Otto Tolnai's office, with all doors locked behind them, Alec broke their silence. "What was it you wanted to show me?"

"It's some data, inside the computer. Strange that the system's turned off. It'll take a few minutes for me to boot up."

He watched her carefully, trying to sense her mood. Jeanette rubbed her arms through a bulky sweater that drooped over her T-shirt and swaddled her thin hips while the file server went through lengthy procedures, chirping and beeping, demanding that she use the keyboard.

Jeanette sat down and became absorbed in an abstruse litany of options and responses. Alec realized it had been many hours since anyone was able to contact him. He'd turned off the scratching of his patrol car's radio to concentrate on Jeanette. He hadn't bothered to take the car's portable radio with him. It wouldn't work through the interference layers of construction and iron-bearing stones above him. Absentmindedly, he dialed headquarters and retrieved his messages from an answering machine in his office. There was nothing of urgency.

He debated calling suite 115. The thought dissipated as he stared gently at Jeanette, now wearing half-glasses and peering into the green phosphorescent screen. "Will it be long?" he asked.

"Damn. He's locked up the part I needed to show you."

"Who's he?"

"Otto. I didn't think he knew how to do that . . ."

"Oh. Can you get around it?"

"No . . . not really. The best thing to do is wait until he gets in Monday and ask him to release that section of the database."

Ryder sat in one of Otto Tolnai's plush guest chairs and tapped an anxious forefinger on the conference table. "Won't he think it suspicious that you want him to unlock things?"

"I don't think so. I have to modify the database schema, its root design, to finish the last step of this job. He can't have any part locked up when I do that final step. He shouldn't have any part secure now. In fact, that security feature has always been disabled in the past, at customer request. Otherwise, a disgruntled employee can destroy the database on their last day at work. That Otto wanted this security feature despite my strong recommendations is one of the strange things that frightens me. But Otto should unlock it . . ." Jeanette turned away from the workstation and faced the Inspector. She put her head in her hands and leaned on the desk. Exhaustion and fear showed on her face.

"That means you have to come to work two days from now. It also means we don't have any hints about the killer for another forty-eight hours." Alec rose and moved near her. He sat on the desk and stroked her back with his left hand, dialing with his right. "Hello. This is Ryder. Yes, my codeword's dark angel. Now get on with it. Any messages from the pair in suite 115 at the Grand? . . . No, I didn't know. I had the car radio off . . . Shit . . . No, they don't need me there as well. I'll go over it when we can secure . . . forget that. I'll call back in a few minutes. No, I can't tell you where I am and you forget the phone number where I called from, you got it? No, I'm not bullshitting you. Hit clear on your board now. OK, I'll talk to you in about five minutes. But not from here. Bye." He put the receiver down hard and focused on Jeanette.

"Can you bust the lock now? Without waiting for Otto?"

"There's no reason to do that Alec, and I'm beyond exhausted. Let's wait until Monday, please?"

"You remember the two policemen who escorted us to the patrol car?"

"Yes."

"They're dead. Submachine gun of some kind. They were hit inside your hotel suite. The killer posed as room service. Got the evidence bags I was stupid enough to leave behind." He watched color bleach from Jeanette's face. "Now, can you break in?"

She spun quietly around in Otto's desk chair. "What have I gotten myself into? Oh, God, what have I done?"

"Jeanette?"

"Yes." She was crying.

Too much fear. Too tired. Or he'd pushed her too far. "The only chance we have is breaking into this computer. Otto locked up something. He didn't want us to know important details."

She took off the glasses and wiped her sweater across swollen eyes. "When I built the system, I left a trap door inside, a hole in the security nucleus. The nucleus is very tight, it's got formally verified code. But there's a deliberate hole. I left it in case someone got themselves a disgruntled sysop – system operator."

"So you go in through this trap door?"

"No. In the terms of the trade, you build a Trojan horse and push it through the trap door. Then you trick the system into opening the horse. Zap, you're inside and have every privilege possible. Whatever the computer can possibly be made to do, you can do."

"Where is this Trojan horse you need? Back at the hotel? It's not in the U.S. is it?"

"Worse. It doesn't exist. I never bothered to build a Trojan horse. I figured I could get paid a handsome sum to build one, if someone ever got in trouble."

"How long . . . ?"

"Maybe a day, if I rush. But it may not work, if I rush. In fact, Otto might come here before I finish. He often works weekends."

"Get started. What do you need? I'll have it sent in – and I'll secure this place."

"Food. Coffee. Peace and quiet. Focus. No stress." She laughed a little and he smiled at her, a smile he certainly didn't feel inside.

He slipped away and wandered down the corridor looking for another telephone, then decided against that idea. Alec kept going. When he opened the outside door, the sky was growing dark with another rainstorm and wind bit his unprotected ears. He realized he'd have to leave the outside door unlocked or go all the way back to Jeanette for the key.

Ryder spotted a green cross half a block away and on the other side of street. Maybe from the pharmacy, he could watch the Archives door and make his calls. He hated the clunky radio phones of that era and didn't carry one. CIA had miniature cell phones in their labs, but he wasn't working for CIA anymore. Raindrops glistened on the pavement and he could smell the wet cement. He knew the signs. It was going to pour soon.

Alec trotted across the street to his destination. He bought something to quiet his growing indigestion and stared at the brown arched door across the street, debating risks. The payphone was in the back of the pharmacy.

Ryder scurried around tightly packed display racks and dropped in his coins. Szige Usulak's phone rang and rang and rang. Damn Usulak for being a family man. He would be out with them on a Saturday.

Alec hung up and fished his money out of the return slot. Quickly, he moved back to the front of the store and looked around. No one anywhere loitering on the street. There weren't any cars dotting the curb.

"Miss?"

"Yes?"

He showed her his badge. "Do you see that large carriage door across the street?" He pointed in its direction.

"Uh . . . yes?"

"Watch it. If anyone goes inside, let me know immediately. OK?"

"Sure . . ."

Alec left her astonishment behind and swept quickly to the pay phone. It only rang once before he heard the dispatcher's voice. "This is dark angel again. Write this down. I need a lot of gear – and when I'm through, send someone to get Usulak. No, don't clear this number. You send everyone right here, to this pharmacy. Now, here's what I want . . ."

When he was finished, Alec made his way to the store window where the girl stood.

When she heard him coming, she turned around.

"You see anybody on the street?"

"No. Is it all right for me to go back to work?"

He ignored the urgent curiosity on her face. She wanted to know what was going on and he wasn't going to tell her. "Do your job and be happy you work in a pharmacy, not Interpol."

Alec rocked on the balls of his feet and stared at the brown door. Rain was now pelting the roofs of parked cars and ricocheting off. A woman went by with her scarf pulled close, gripping a rebellious umbrella.

He could leave now. Walk out the door and hail that cab before it goes past. It's not you the arsonist wants. It's her . . . and something else.

Walk out the door and disappear. That message kept repeating itself in his mind, over and over . . .

13

Jew

The Holocaust Memorial danced and waved in the wind. Rain played target practice with thousands of tiny silver leaves drooping in a man-made imitation of a weeping willow tree. He moved inside the Heroes' Temple. It was warm and dry. Water dripped from the brim of his hat onto the lush carpet. He sat in a comfortable chair and pulled out a small, leather-bound notebook with fine linen pages. Writing his memoirs was a major decision, one he'd postponed until certain of achieving his life goal. He looked around to assure himself that he wouldn't be observed. Only then did he drag a Montblanc fountain pen from an inner coat pocket and begin writing –

> *It was the worst moment of my life. Their injections in suite 115 of the Grand Hotel left me in a drug haze. I could barely see the old*

man's face. I couldn't believe he was going to do it. How could he mutilate me like that!? Castrate me! Cut off my penis!

How I screamed and tore against them, but they held me down and he hacked away, tearing into my leg once as I jerked in fury and pain. When he was done, they just threw me a napkin soaked in disinfectant and left me alone to find what I had left of me.

I thought they had made me a eunuch, but they had made me a Jew.

He gazed wistfully through an ivy covered window frame at the growing storm and the Holocaust memorial dancing to nature's fury. How long would it last, this downpour? How long had he waited in that cramped cell to find out what they would do to him next? A month? He put down the fine writing instrument in his left hand and succumbed to the searing memories.

Deliberately they had waited, waited for his wounds to heal and no longer show the bright red flesh that would put the lie to their plot. Food was slopped to him, their food. To live meant to eat it.

One day, instead of food, six men ran into his prison. They pinned him, stripped him, threw clothing at him and slammed his cell closed. "Wear it or freeze. We don't care which you do."

For three days, he held out. Then his lungs burned and he coughed green phlegm. His reason was beaten down. The clothes went on, the Star of David bright yellow over his chest.

Fever burned him and he quaked with chills.

They slapped the peephole open and fingered him with a flashlight beam. His cell door was flung aside and they dragged him out, covered his head with a burlap sack so he couldn't see, pushed him in the back of a frigid truck.

The fever rose and he passed out.

* * *

Rain poured on his face like he was under a gushing faucet. He looked up, struggling to clear his eyes with bound hands. Above him was a round, fat-faced man, water streaming off the brim of his hat. Thin, circular lenses were stuck on his nose with a frame that seemed made of piano wire. He pulled a gloved hand from the pockets of his double-breasted leather coat and pointed downward, laughing to the others.

The man spoke in German. "I must hunt to find them, but this one, they deliver special. Why?" He laughed, his pig face billowing in creases. The others laughed too, just the right amount. "I'll find out why. Get him inside. Dry him off. Give him food. Hot soup. This one is special, that's all I know."

* * *

Days later, he woke up to find the pig face holding a spoon of soup gently over his mouth.

"You must eat to live, *ja*?" The Gestapo man was now dressed in a lively blue pinstripe suit that made him look like a German businessman, not the evil touch of the Fuhrer. His pudgy fingers laid down the soup bowl and took up a cigarette. He lit it, stroking the flint of a heavy silver lighter. Instead of inhaling, pig face offered the smoke. "*Amerikaner* . . . Lucky Strike . . . very good."

Coughing up a light yellow sputum, he waved off the Lucky Strike.

The cigarette was ground out on a steel bar of his jail cell.

"You eat, rest, get well, *ja*? Then, we talk. We talk a lot. How you get here. Why."

A bell-shaped blue pinstripe suit waddled through a quickly opened set of bars. A crisp *"Heil, Hitler!"* was answered by the pig's jaded wave.

* * *

In a week, his lungs were clear of mucous and his energy returned. He sat, waiting with dread for the next encounter with his inquisitor.

But instead, a ramrod straight SS guard appeared, death's head necklace wrapped around a thick neck. A burp gun slung over his shoulder matched the polished bluish steel helmet on his head. The guard tossed him a heavy coat and blanket. The huge Teutonic soldier towered overhead, gesturing urgency and glowering with hard blue eyes. Once wrapped in warmth, he was led outside. Even glare from an overcast day was unbearable to his weak eyesight.

Squinting, he sat next to the pig in an open Daimler touring car, flanked by armored vehicles bearing heavy machine guns. A squad of immaculately uniformed SS soldiers sat on benches in trucks, stiffly erect, like they were on a victory parade through the streets of Berlin. They took off and headed into the countryside, curving down tree-lined rural lanes. Were the air not thick with fear, this could have been a pleasure ride.

The Gestapo man rode the entire day in silence, and for his part, he dared not speak. At lunch, the pig bulled his way past an obsequious village tavern owner and sat isolated at a patio table. All other occupants of the restaurant left at once, escorted outside by sullen SS troopers.

He sat alone in the car and food was brought to him. Once, the pig looked at him and smiled. A moment later, the Gestapo agent threw a tantrum, yelling at the tavern owner. The German smashed a glass of wine on the ground and screamed for a better vintage. The cowering innkeeper scampered away, escorted by SS troopers.

New wine appeared and Herr Gestapo made a prolonged, ornate ceremony of sniffing the cork and swishing the wine in his mouth. With a disdainful look at the wine glass, the German pulled out his Lugar automatic pistol and shot the owner twice in the head.

He tried not to look shocked or intimidated, but he knew he was failing. Vomit filled his mouth and he forced himself to swallow it. He dare not seem weak. An eternal minute crept past before the pig returned to the open car. The German sat next to him as if nothing special happened. For a long time, the Daimler threaded across an open plain that swelled with little hills carpeted in lush green foliage. At a rise, the Daimler slowed and the pig shifted in his seat, trembling with excitement.

Ahead he saw a little valley with a prison compound, wooden barracks sagging beneath the glaring vigilance of watchtowers. Searchlights winked to life, holding back the encroaching night. They drove through the front gate without being stopped or searched. The Daimler turned into a parade ground. Surrounding armored vehicles churned up little plots of meager vegetables, destroying the inmates' food, grinding carrots to juice beneath metal treads.

He would never forget the smells – fresh earth, smashed carrots, diesel exhaust and death. Death in the form of ashes wafted aloft. Death in the form of unburned corpses soiled the earth. Death in the form of skeletons driven out of their last sleep, stood tottering before him. Waving rows of skeletons with sunken eyes flickered hatred and submission as their identity.

The pig waited. The pig waited some more. Finally, the pig waved a gloved hand in dismissal and guards began herding their semi-human flock back into pens.

He and the pig left, not as they had come, but through another gate. On the way out, they passed ovens and an unmistakable stench forced him to vomit. The pig gave him a silk handkerchief to wipe his mouth.

* * *

They dined together very late that night in the pig's suite. It was an elegant hotel and the Gestapo man had the hotel's best rooms, ordered the best dinner possible under wartime conditions, and hadn't spoken the entire time, just looked mirthful.

Finally, the pig dabbed his lips with the bottom edge of a brilliantly white linen napkin. Its top lay pinched beneath the folds of a neck that sagged over a tightly buttoned collar and tie. He pushed away the remains of a newly slaughtered lamb and leaned across the table. "So, my Jew, why were you gift wrapped and dropped at my doorstep, eh? I've shown you today what future is yours if you don't cooperate. But, there is no need, I'm sure, to belabor that point, eh? Cigarette?"

The offered cigarette was taken as well as a light from a solid gold lighter with the red and black Nazi swastika inlaid on its front in semi-precious stones. The pig caught the lingering of his prey's eyes on the opulent accessory. "A gift from *der Fuhrer* himself. I am his hand-picked emissary for purifying the Aryan race. I've been very good at my job and therefore been very rewarded. Frankly, I will miss being a Nazi. It's been the best time of my life. Surprised? Well, you've been sheltered here in Budapest. The war is being lost. Slowly at first, but ever more quickly now. Will it be the Russians or the Americans who capture me? I prefer neither, if I can arrange it. Perhaps with your help, I can arrange a better fate for both of us than what you saw today."

The pig took a long drag on his Lucky Strike and looked away, exhaling. Abruptly, he jerked around and cupped the lit cigarette in his up-turned fingers. He pointed the burning tobacco directly at the target of his words. "Speak the truth or join those you saw today."

* * *

The rain outside paused and he once again resumed his transcription, scratching black ink in jagged, angry streaks across the soft white open spaces before him.

I told the pig everything.

An hour later, I was done. I sat, trembling, wondering what he would do, fascinated by his absolute power. He mesmerized me just by sitting there, lost in thought. I found him disgusting, revolting – and magnetic.

At last, he turned to me. "Undress. I want to see with my own eyes what they did to you."

I shuddered as I removed my shoes and pants. His eyes grew more hooded, more mysterious, more alluring to me as I removed my underwear, exposing my sex to him.

He reached out and grabbed my penis. I was horrified and powerless. I was also shocked at the arousal that came with his touch.

"You will do as I want, my pet, jah*?" he said, "In return, I will spare you – at least, I will spare you as long as I want you." He began caressing me to fullness. My legs quivered.*

"We will see if there is any truth to what you say about that Habsburg slut. I hate that she had your cherry and not me. For that alone, she deserved to die."

14

Smoke

Alec Ryder stood immobilized, watching a police van and two patrol cars pull up in front of the pharmacy. Uniformed officers got out and milled around, unaware of his presence only a few yards away, standing behind a plate glass window.

He felt angry and didn't know why. He saw their confused looks and their youth. Then he knew why he was angry. He couldn't just leave through the back door. These kids would get themselves killed, and so would Jeanette. They needed him and he hated them for it.

With reluctance, Alec opened the pharmacy door. They smiled at him. He was a father figure to them. Shit. He couldn't bear their faces. Soon he'd be on Margaret Island looking at what remained of the faces of two fathers he'd foolishly left behind in that damned hotel suite.

There was a huge plume of smoke rolling skyward from the direction of the river. He watched the black cloud grow, flames tickling outward from an inner core of dark gases.

"Get on the radio," he commanded them. "Call the Fire Brigade. Find out
if it's him."

* * *

Fire Captain Michael Toth tried to grimace when the nurse came into his hospital room, but sutures zipped across his slashed face prevented any show of emotion.

"Time for your medicine," she chimed, with a buoyancy he found obnoxious.

"No more pain killer. I can't think. It fogs my brain." Toth squirmed the words through burned lips.

"The drugs speed your recovery. You must rest and you'll sleep better if you aren't in pain. You needn't feel guilty, Michael."

Toth rolled his eyes in disgust. Right, bitch. The worst day of your life was a dropped thermometer. How many men did I send to their death? Twelve now. Andrew died yesterday of his burns. An even dozen. He looked at her and waved off her pill. He tried to calm his voice. "No, I won't take it. I'm healing fast. I'm young and healthy. But you're right that I think too much about the fire. Please turn on the TV. I'll watch the news and enjoy the rest of the world's troubles."

"The doctor will be in tonight. He'll insist on the morphine, you know."

"Fine. Please just turn on the television."

"After I've changed your IV."

He silently endured her prim, controlling air, subduing his fury. If he yelled at her, she wouldn't turn on the set. Try to reach the controls himself and he would need morphine.

She turned for the door and he gently reminded her of his request.

"Oh, yes. I almost forgot." With an air of casual vehemence, the nurse plucked out a little power button and left, oblivious to any desire on his part for volume control or channel selection.

"Damn her," he muttered. He wanted a news broadcast, some word of progress in hunting down his hated enemy. Instead, a science show blossomed into view, the sound level too low for understanding. There was nothing better to do, so he stared at the screen impaled on a high shelf opposite his bed. Half the image was obscured in glare from the room's window. He could make out a sort of airplane standing on end with a huge red tank strapped to its belly. The red tank had two white rockets bonded to its sides. Michael didn't know English, but he understood the words "Space Shuttle" when the announcer said them.

A dull roaring tumbled beneath the airplane, an enormous spray of water flooding the concrete launch pad. Seconds after the Niagara Falls had begun, blue fury exploded from the Shuttle's main engines, fed by rocket fuel from the belly tank. Flame met water and a concussion shocked the sound track. Nothing happened for the longest, wavering moment and then tons of unbelievably heavy equipment lifted up and lingered, patiently gathering momentum.

The acceleration seemed both nonexistent and phenomenally quick, a paradox that irritated him the way his wife got under his skin on their first meeting.

The damn Americans. Why not send some of their precious technology to him? Oh, hell, what difference did it make? Just shut your eyes and get some rest.

Concrete. Glazed, melted, formed into a glass table top, half a city block long, eroded in the center ten inches from its height at the edges. That was how the warehouse floor looked when he'd examined it with Inspector Ryder. What had that kind of power? What kind of fuel was this maniac using? The fuel was a clue to his identity.

Fire Captain Toth wanted to turn on his left side, to lie the way he always had in bed with his wife. He had his best thoughts before she woke to the alarm and they began herding the children off to school. She went to a job that allowed him to stay in his beloved career. But Michael Toth couldn't turn on his left side. It was burned too badly. Another bit of peace the bastard had stolen. Toth squirmed on his back and forced his mind to again consider a dead-end trail of unanswerable questions.

This time, Toth's imagination seemed to have a separate identity from him. It kept replaying the scene of fire and water he'd just witnessed on television. Why did the Americans shower a building that propped up the Space Shuttle with water? Was the structure made of combustible material? No, it seemed to be a huge block of concrete at bottom and a steel tower above, and the steel tower fell back away from the flame.

What would happen if they didn't pour so much water on the concrete . . . damn, it all made sense now! Why hadn't he thought of this before? Because it was so bizarre, like those pro torch jobs in the U.S. he'd read about. The fires were so hot they destroyed all clues. Then some firefighters were killed and desperate fire departments tried to duplicate the burns. NASA was called and rocket fuel was used. It worked, turning even steel into yet more fuel.

Rocket fuel. That's why the apartment building lifted up like that huge Space Shuttle. Worse, Toth lamented, he'd helped the bastard by pouring water on the fire. The rocket fuel toyed with Michael's water, stripping oxygen from hydrogen, using oxygen to accelerate the blaze. Then the hydrogen blew up, knocking the damn building a yard in the air and demolishing everything in the street – his trucks, his men. Damn.

"Nurse!" He waited and screamed again. "Nurse!" Where the hell was she? Michael tried to get up. His head swam with nausea induced from screaming nerves singing pain to him when he tried to move. He gave up and sank down, panting.

Where was the buzzer that was supposed to summon her? He fumbled behind his pillow with his unbroken arm. He felt the button, jammed it down and kept it clamped until her petulant face appeared in the little window of his room's door.

Toth shouted. "I need my oldest son. He speaks English. He must call America for me. Don't look that way. I'm not crazy. He's always wanted to meet an astronaut. Now he's going to call one."

She looked at him like he was insane, but Toth didn't care. His mind kept whirring with questions. Why did the arsonist use rocket fuel? Rocket fuel was expensive, volatile, difficult to get. Because it incinerated everything, leaving no clues. What was the arsonist covering up? It was possible that demonic mind was just hiding his own trail. Who'd want to follow him – and what would they have learned if the arsonist just used gasoline?

Damn this hospital. He had to get out. He had to find that bastard, somehow. If Toth could just confirm the killer used rocket fuel. That would be a major clue . . .

15

Satan's Touch

He told the taxi driver to stop and rolled down his window for a better view from Margaret Bridge. Burning debris floated on oil-slickened river water. Two fire boats cautiously approached the blaze. The closest one emitted a brief arc of water, but the spray fell short of its goal.

His taxicab driver protested. "I can't sit here. Traffic's already backing up. I'll get a ticket."

"I'll make it up to you." He watched in fascination as fireboats circled the smoking barge, the trio forced downstream by river current. He smiled in twisted amusement. "What happened here?"

"Satan's Touch. He again brought the fires of hell and touched a barge."

"Satan's Touch?"

"Yes," the cabby responded. "That's what the news media are calling him."

"What do they know about him?"

"He's crazy, that's all they know." The cabby shrugged.

Satan's Touch. So that's what they're calling me, he mused.

"I gotta go." The driver turned around. "Sorry." The taxi started forward and he lurched backward in his seat. He cast a last glance at the inferno and rolled up his window against the acrid smoke. It was all going according to his plan. Every fire in Budapest was now his work. No one questioned it. Good. That meant they feared him. Fear was his edge. They'd approach fires with caution now, giving his burns a headstart, more time to incinerate clues.

He jerked forward when the taxi stopped. The cabby jumped out and opened his door. Laying a generous tip in the man's palm, he eased himself out and went inside the hotel to his room.

With his door bolted and a portable metal brace jammed against the room door, he relaxed. He tore loose a Velcro tab concealing a hidden pocket in his coat and withdrew the diary.

At a little desk in front of the balcony window, he drew a line across the end of the previous entry. He wrote his nickname – "Satan's Touch." He felt the thrill he'd known in those last days of Nazi Budapest. Killing was the most erotic thing he'd ever done . . .

It was obvious the end was near. The pig became more desperate. He alternated between experiencing everything he had ever wanted or might possibly want, and ruthlessly seeking a way out.

In me, he found much of both. I was his lover, his pet, his assassin – and his hope that there was an exit from the legacy of his gluttony.

It was dusk when he looked out his hotel window. This was the time of day when they drove into town with the pig's private army of SS guards. Russian planes didn't operate at night, so through the dark hours they prowled. Around them, Budapest licked its horrible wounds and tried for a semblance of normalcy.

As he wrote in his diary, it was all real to him again – flashing and booming of Soviet artillery pieces defined the horizon in strobes of light and sound. He and the pig rumbled along the quay. The Daimler touring car halted before an elegant white apartment building, six stories topped by a penthouse suite with a view of the Danube.

He ran a kid-gloved hand over the crewcut hair he'd dyed blond to please the Gestapo pig. Would *they* be here? A tortured bastard said this would be the place. He'd shot what was left of the man and left the body to rot.

The pig waited in his car and idly smoked a Cuban cigar. He tromped upstairs and dragged everyone into the night, even infants. He didn't bother tearing the place apart for hidden compartments. Instead, he lined them up against the stone wall that kept the Danube at bay and screamed his demand. "Where are the Jews?" He didn't expect an answer. Silence, complete but for the Russian guns inching destruction closer around the battered city.

He grabbed a little girl from her terrified mother. The mother hesitated and then surged forward, trying to smother the child with her own body, protect her from harm. An SS guard drove the butt of his rifle into the woman's head and she crumpled to the ground. The child began crying. Along the thin line of freezing people, children resonated with fear and whimpered almost inaudibly.

Again he screamed. "Where are the Jews?" This time he put the barrel of a Lugar to the child's head. Now he was patient and understanding as he spoke, dragging the cowering child with him, moving along the line. They wouldn't believe he'd kill a little girl like that. One example was always necessary. He cocked the gun. It was a bluff. The gun was unloaded. But his audience didn't know the SS didn't trust him with ammunition.

To his right, toward the end of the line, a man flinched.

The SS guards reacted. They knew it wasn't a man who wanted to talk. It was a man who knew someone would talk, in a matter of seconds. The man tried to claw his way over a stone barrier and into the water, risking death at nature's hands instead of the death that awaited him. He didn't make it. A burst of gunfire sawed across his back and the man quit struggling to escape.

Now they cracked. An old woman tottered forward, shouting at her neighbors. "They're not worth it. I told you this would happen. I told you we'd be punished. And for what? For *them*?" She turned and spat on a frightened couple. The hag began tugging on their clothes to pull them forward, out of alignment with the others. Quickly, the line dissolved into isolated clumps of Jews.

He released his child-anchor and she fell harshly to the cobblestone pavement. He ignored her sobbing when she ran to the dormant mother. Instead, he moved briskly down the parted line, glaring into frightened countenances for what he really wanted. It wasn't there. Not yet.

He gave orders in German to the SS, who were accustomed to this bizarre parade and obeyed him, even though they wouldn't allow him ammunition for his Lugar. "I'll show you what will happen if you don't turn over all the Jews. Where are the rest? So, no cooperation." He signaled the Nazi troopers and they emptied bursts at point-blank range into the huddled mass, then dumped bodies into a river already clogged with the human debris of such atrocities.

The old woman screeched. "Tell them! You know where the Jews are hidden." She waddled to a defiant youth and slapped him. "Tell them. Where have you hidden the four?"

He smiled. Now it would get easier. A few minutes alone with the cocky teenager transformed him into a quivering fool begging for the quick release of death.

* * *

He'd never been so excited in his life. The four men who dragged him from suite 115 were delivered to him, including the *mohel* who took a knife to his penis. For two hours, inspired by his absolute power to inflict pain and death, the pig tortured their prisoners. Now, only the *mohel* remained alive. The *mohel* was insurance the captives revealed the correct hiding place of his obsession. He'd take care of the *mohel* himself, in a manner he'd planned ever since getting circumcised by that bastard.

Excited from his torture session, the pig made love to him, writing his own twisted version of the Kama Sutra, fulfilling every sick fantasy of a lifetime. Afterwards, he lay still, controlling his breathing, stifling the revulsion he felt. Disgust never left him since the first time he submitted to the pig. A seizure of revulsion swept over him, making his rage uncontrollable.

Carefully, he sat up and looked at the naked fat body next to him, focusing on the man's right ankle. White medical tape bound the Gestapo man's last line of defense to a fleshy Achilles tendon. The knife was always there, a warning that even in sex-inspired sleep, the pig was ready to defend himself.

Would the pig cut his throat once the secrets of suite 115 were discovered? The pig had been explicit – "I will spare you as long as I want you."

He crept to the foot of their bed. His hand had a life of its own when it reached out. He felt a thrill stroking the ebony knife handle, exposed between tethers of white tape.

The pig stirred. His breathing became shallow and raspy. Was the pig awakening?

His disembodied hand grabbed the stiletto with crazed fury, tearing off flesh with the tape.

The pig jerked upright, his eyes snapping open.

In one seamless motion, the knife flashed. Its point slashed through the pig's larynx, cutting his windpipe and disemboweling the voice box.

Even in death, the pig clamped iron fingers on the arms sawing a knife across flesh, cartilage and bone.

He rode a bucking rodeo bull for only a moment. The pig threw him off and rolled over. He found himself trapped under 300 pounds of bloodied flab, choking him. Unable to breathe, he stared into the pig's eyes. The Gestapo-trained killer knew he was going to die, knew he couldn't shout to his SS guards for help, knew he could only hang on for revenge. But age and horrible conditioning killed both the pig and his vengeance.

He squirmed from under the bulk pinning him, blood gushing over him. He still held the knife, its thin blade chipped from being forced against bone, used like an axe, not a razor.

The pig couldn't be dead. It was too good to be true. He couldn't convince himself that the inert blob wouldn't rise. Fear of the dead man forced him to strike again and again with the knife, puncturing every body part. He tore at the fleshy neck, sawed at the neck bone, until the pig's distorted face could be held by the blood-soaked hair of a detached head.

He smiled, parading in a goose-step through mirrored rooms, saluting and honoring himself, until he came to the main fireplace. With a sweeping bow, he graced the mantelpiece with the pig's head and went to take a bath.

* * *

Cleansed and dressed, he stooped to retrieve the pig's knife. Lovingly, he wiped blood and flesh from the blade. In the center desk drawer, he found the stones he needed to restore the stiletto to razor-sharpness. He stropped the blade for half an hour, staring in satisfaction at the decapitated body on the floor.

He satisfied himself the knife was ready by slicing a sheet of fine stationary cleanly with the blade. The knife retracted easily and he taped the instrument to his calf, smoothing a trouser leg over the weapon. He checked the look in the room's mirrors, walking to make certain the knife bulge wasn't noticeable. He stopped before the pig's grotesque head, loose flesh sagging on the fireplace mantel like a Halloween pumpkin left too long in the sun. He grabbed a large towel from the bath, swaddled the Gestapo face and pushed his burden down the laundry chute, laughing.

He dragged blankets and bedspread over his lover's corpse and closed the bedroom door. Yanking his leather coat from the closet, he shrugged the thick leather over his shoulders and pulled on calfskin gloves. As an afterthought, he reached in the pig's matching coat and stole all the man's identity papers. He had no plans for the documents, just a hunch they might prove useful. He composed himself before going outside, meeting the SS guard so loyal to the pig. Fear crept into his world, ruining any release he felt. He used the fear to push himself beyond his sanctuary.

In the corridor outside the elaborate suite, SS guards came to crisp attention. As a matter of course, one guard followed him along hallways, winding his way to the street. A sergeant lounged against the front fender of a half-track armored vehicle. He was the same Nazi who brought a coat and blanket to him, before he visited his first concentration camp. The SS Sergeant didn't bother to close the collar of his tunic or put out his cigarette. He stared insolently.

He ignored the man's insolence. "I've been ordered to take the *mohel* with me, to assure success. Bring him to me."

With a dull click of tough fingers, a soldier was dispatched to get the *mohel.*

He talked with a calculated air of indifference. "Bring the car around. We must go immediately."

The SS Sergeant straightened and tossed his smoke on the pavement, grinding out the stub with a dirty boot. He laughed. "You're very funny. Where do you want to go? There are Russian troops in every direction. We're surrounded. Do you think the Russians will cower at the sight of your Gestapo coat? You believe their snipers will hold fire, intimidated by you?"

"I've been ordered to bring back a treasure. The *mohel* knows where it's hidden."

"Where is your . . . patron?" The Sergeant sneered "patron" through a face twisted in amusement.

"Asleep. He wishes to rest until dinner." He felt sweat running down his ribs.

The SS man thought it over. "All right. We'll take one of the half-tracks and three of my best men. You'll ride in the back with them, the *mohel* up front with me. Now, where are we going?"

"I'll give you directions on the way. I don't have an address."

"I thought you made the *mohel* talk." The Sergeant drummed his fingers on the hilt of a sheathed bayonet.

"He only knows part of it. The others . . . the dead ones, knew the rest."

"Perhaps we should confirm your orders."

"He's asleep. He'll be furious if you wake him."

The bayonet came out an inch and went back with a click. Slowly the dangerous weapon lifted again and fell back. The Sergeant's huge palm jutted forward. "The Lugar. You won't need it."

With reluctance, he surrendered the unloaded pistol. There were two stolen clips of ammunition in his coat pocket, now useless. Would they pat him down and find the knife? He fought to remain calm. A tense silence between the men was broken by the clatter of steel treads on cobblestones.

"All right. Get in. But I've changed my mind. You'll ride up front, with me."

* * *

They only got a half mile into the Pest side of Budapest before encountering German infantry, falling back in retreat. The Sergeant turned the half-track and snorted. "Is your patron really asleep, *mein freund*? Asleep enough for you and I to split whatever was worth killing him for?"

"What . . . do you mean . . . I didn't kill him. He sent . . ."

The Sergeant cut him off, slamming the half-track into gear. The transmission clashed, the diesel engine snarled and they jerked past a foot soldier. The ground trooper fired his rifle past the moving half-track, shooting at Russians ahead of them. A heavy machine gun in the half-track pivoted and fired in short bursts. They accelerated. Grenade fragments ricocheted off the vehicle armor plate.

"Your patron wouldn't have let you go alone, not for something he tore Budapest apart to find. I'm no fool. I want a chance to live again when this stupid war is done. Now, where is this treasure?"

"In the basement of the Jewish temple."

"Great. The temple's behind Russian lines. Soviet troops moved forward last night, advancing almost a kilometer."

"It can't be true. I won't be denied."

"You can't kill the entire Russian army just because you fucked too long, idiot." The Sergeant braked to a stop. "Get out. I'll let you take your chances with the Russians."

He sat frozen, shocked.

The Sergeant cocked the burp gun laying across his lap. "Get out. One way or the other, you're leaving"

He'd just cracked the heavy steel door when the world exploded in molten shards. The half-track flipped on its side, throwing him across the Sergeant. Smoke poured into his lungs, choking him. He pushed against the SS Sergeant and found himself pressing on the limpness of a dead man.

Getting out was a long ordeal of only a few seconds. It didn't seem he could force open the armored door now above him, nor crawl out before flames reached him. Machine gun ammunition cooked off, pinging around his metal coffin. With a surge of miraculous strength, he forced his way out and fell hard on the pavement.

His mind came back to what mattered. Where was the *mohel*? He ran to the half-track's shattered back doors. There were three bodies with Nazi uniforms. He found only the *mohel's* bloody shoe, still holding the man's shattered foot.

He followed a trail of gore left by the amputee for only a few yards when brown Russian uniforms sprayed bullets at him. He spotted the *mohel*, huddling behind a pillar, but it was no use. The Russian gunfire was too intense. He could only retreat. He'd gotten so close to the treasures he'd glimpsed in suite 115 of the Grand Hotel, only to be cheated.

* * *

The days that followed were a blur of fear, exhaustion and despair. Swept in a tide of refugees fleeing devastation, he left Budapest on foot. Fear chased him everywhere. He might be found by the German army and shot, revealed by one he'd terrorized and beaten to death by an angry mob. Those fates were terrible, yet preferable to being captured by Russians. The Soviets hated the Gestapo, who'd killed a million innocent Russian civilians on the retreat from Moscow.

A bitter sunset found him staring at deserted watchtowers and concertina wire. This was the concentration camp where the pig brought him. A human flood surged past him, ignoring him. He sat in the icy morning fog and stared at the camp's open gate, ornately wrought in black iron. A phrase woven into the gate dawned on him – *"Arbeit macht frei."* A labor camp. Work means freedom, the lie told slaves of the Third Reich, whose real destiny was death of their body, death of their spirit, death of their race.

Behind the concertina wire were dozens of shrunken, withered faces that stared at him, too dazed to know they were free to leave. They were too far gone to know any identity other than a dying slave.

He got up from the damp earth and walked through waist-high ground fog, parting iron gates with his hands. The fog made it seem he floated rather than walked, entering a gray nightmare without sound. His broken witnesses didn't mark his entry, nor run to escape through the open gates. They stood like painted backdrops in a film set. He alone moved, searching buildings until he found the right place to launder his identity. In this hell, he'd leave the Gestapo behind and become one of their victims instead.

In the abandoned entry hall, he found volumes listing those who vanished in this hole. There, in the chronology of the condemned, he added himself. He found shears and used them, cutting all hair off his head. He moved to the final station and added the last touch. An ID number became an indelible part of his forearm. Shaved, a faceless identity tag tattooed on an arm, wearing pajamas, he fulfilled a fate he'd sacrificed all to avoid.

16

Burn

Injured Fire Captain Michael Toth lay in his hospital bed, exhausted from arguing with his doctor. The doctor thought Toth delusional, perhaps obsessed. A counselor was called, then a lawyer. Finally a release was offered Michael and he signed the paper. They wheeled him to a waiting taxi and dumped him at his panic-stricken wife's doorstep.

His wife insisted Michael return to the hospital. He bargained and they agreed he'd wait until their son arrived from soccer practice. After his son called NASA, it was back to the hospital – if they'd have him. Hours later, Cape Canaveral's Space Shuttle Operations phone number was called, only to find it was too late to get any information.

An obsessed Michael Toth gave up and returned to the hospital on the condition that the next morning his wife and eldest son would be in his hospital room with a phone.

The international call went through at 9:32 A.M. The Fire Captain sat upright, his wounds forgotten in a surge of adrenaline that intimidated everyone with its ferocity. He saw the anxiety in their faces and tried to be patient, but the urgency he felt crept into his voice. "Surely there must be an astronaut available. Look, tell them it's a little boy's dying wish. The Americans have many faults, but they are kind. That excuse should get them moving."

His oldest son translated into his best High School English. After a while, he covered the hospital phone and whispered in an agitated voice. "Dad, I think your idea worked. There are some astronauts-in-training available today." The boy put the receiver to his ear. A moment later, he bubbled with excitement. "They've found one. She'll come to the phone. What do you want to ask her, Father?"

"I need to know why they hose down the launch pad. Would the Shuttle burn up the concrete launch pad if they didn't flood the area with water?" Looking into his son's disappointed eyes caused Toth to add, "Then you can ask her anything. Talk as long as you want." He saw his wife wince. She'd write the check for this call. But it would be worth the money. He was convinced that bastard arsonist must have rocket fuel. Only rocket fuel burned hot enough to cause the glassy warehouse floor and an apartment house lifting up like a Shuttle launching.

Michael tried to sit straighter in his excitement, but just slid into the bed. Damn, why didn't he know English so he could ask the questions directly? This was taking too long.

"Um, yes, I think I understand. Just one moment and I'll see what his next question is. Oh, uh, cancer. Yes, very bad. Just days to go. Thank you so much. Yes, it means the world to him. Oh, . . . , ah, he doesn't speak English so you can't talk to him. That is, I must say it again in Hungarian. Yes, that's right. One second."

"Ask him if there's another fuel that would eat up even the water?"

"Oh, um, yes, that is the boy's father. He's reading the questions for him. Is there a rocket fuel that would burn away even that much water?" Again, the mouthpiece was smothered by a sweaty hand. "She says the solid fuel boosters aren't turned on until the Shuttle clears the pad. Otherwise, the boosters' heat turns the water to explosive gas. The hydrogen and oxygen in a water molecule are torn apart. Separated, they explode. Is there anything else, Father?"

"No, you can ask her your questions now." Michael Toth lay back comfortably against his bed for the first time. He knew the magic. Now, where in the hell did that bastard get rocket fuel? Who would help Toth find the rocket fuel source? Yes, that Interpol guy, Alec Ryder. Where was Ryder now, he wondered?

* * *

"This is Snooper to Dark Angel, you have company. Do you copy?"

Alec Ryder whispered into a radio mike. "Roger, I copy. Who's my visitor?"

"Short, hunched over, Caucasian, older man. Has a key to the place. Drives a white Volvo, license …"

"Got it. Anybody with him?"

"Negative. He's alone."

"Any guns?"

"None in view. No briefcase, no coat. Parked in front. Standing outside, looking around. Acts like he feels us, but can't see us. Do we intercept him, Dark Angel? Over."

Alec Ryder thought through the pros and cons. "This is Dark Angel. Let him go through the net untouched. Stay alert. If he gets any backup, I want to know immediately. You got it?"

"Roger that."

Ryder turned off the volume on the sensitive radio set and altered its mode to relay. He clipped a battery-powered unit on his belt and pushed an earplug in place. Without the more powerful set he'd ordered, normal police radios were useless in the catacombs underneath Castle Hill.

Alec hustled out of his temporary office and rushed to warn Jeanette. He found her face down, napping on a stack of printouts in Otto's office. The desk and table were littered with pizza boxes and coffee cups from a newly opened American fast-food outlet.

"Wake up. Otto's on his way down."

Jeanette stirred and looked skeptical. "Otto? Can't be. He never works Saturdays. Comes in for a little while on Sunday morning, but that's it."

"Well, it's Sunday morning, his usual time."

"What happened to the night?"

"You worked it. Look, I need to know. Is this Tolnai's usual time or is this a special visit?"

She glanced at her wristwatch. "Ten's about right for him."

"You finished coding that horse of some kind?"

"Trojan horse. Yeah, it's done. That is, maybe. The last one didn't work but I fixed the bug. I think. I mean, I won't know until he tries to print something. Then the computer should dump out the guts of what he's protected. That line printer in the security area will document everything."

"Is he accustomed to seeing you here on Sundays?"

"I'm always here on the weekends. It's you, Alec that'll tip him off."

"Right, I thought so. What's the combination to that locked area?"

"Four digits only. The year of the Hungarian revolution, 1956, so we'd all remember."

The sound of Otto Tolnai unlocking the area's outer door came to them. How could he possibly get rid of all the crap in time to hide the fact they'd been there for hours? He should've thought this through ahead of time.

"OK, you stay here. Think up a good story about what you're doing in his office. I'm going to the printer. Good luck." She looked dazed. Can she pull it off? He reached in a coat pocket and put an eavesdropping bug on the table, pulling a pizza box over it. Footsteps shuffled along the carpet. He was trapped. Alec closed the office door and slid behind it. The footsteps stopped in the doorway.

"Hello Otto. I'm sorry your office is so messy. I lost track of time. Here, let me pick up a bit." Jeanette reached for the pizza box hiding Alec's bug, but stopped when she realized Ryder was standing only inches from Otto.

Otto was polite, but his face seemed angry. "It isn't necessary. I'll only be here a few minutes." Alec watched Otto move past Jeanette and head for the computer console. Ryder stepped around the door and slipped down the hallway, followed by Jeanette's stare.

At the main corridor, he ignored a path taking him out of the complex and continued to a cipher-locked fire door blocking further movement. He tried the combination "1956" and heard a muted click. Alec eased the heavy door open and glided inside, closing the door until it latched shut.

Standing in the dark, Ryder fumbled for a light switch he'd spotted a moment earlier, when hallway lights peered into the secured cavern. Alec flipped on a bank of recessed fluorescents. He concerned himself with trying to establish communication with his forces watching the outside of the Archives. He got only static and had to prop open the metal door to receive transmissions. Even then, Ryder couldn't raise Snooper, his primary set of eyes on the roof of the opposite building.

Alec had no choice but to retreat down the hallway until his reception returned. He left the security compartment's door open behind him, fearing that he might have to hide quickly if Otto suddenly left his office. He stood in the relative shadow of a burned-out hallway bulb, past the T-junction to the exit corridor. He turned the radio volume to full, hoping to eavesdrop on the bug he left in Otto Tolnai's office. Jeanette's voice sounded clear, but Otto's was muted.

Jeanette asked Otto to access a new file on the network. There was some by-play between them in computer-ese that he couldn't understand. Jeanette thanked Otto and said she was going to the printer.

She abruptly appeared in front of Ryder, startling them both. In sign language, Jeanette motioned him to follow her.

Once they entered the security compartment, she shut the door.

"I need that door open to talk to my stakeouts."

"The door sets off an alarm if it's left open more than a few minutes. You're lucky the alarm didn't trigger already." She sat at a terminal and flicked on its power switch.

"Is your Trojan horse working?"

"I don't know. We'll see in a minute . . . yes, it looks like I'm inside the security nucleus. I'll start dumping his locked section of the database, but it'll be slow going."

"How long?" Alec fiddled with the antenna draped down the back of his shirt to get better reception. It was futile.

"Ten, maybe fifteen minutes," was her distracted reply. She rose and hit a series of buttons on the line printer. Its cover lifted up. Jeanette glanced at him. "Damn thing's out of paper." She jerked a heavy box from a supply shelf and ripped off its top. She pulled out linked sheets of paper and flipped open a tractor feed, aligning the paper's holes with exposed pins. Jeanette slapped the feed shut and hit buttons to start the lid closing.

After a drawn-out process of mechanical motions and cycling lights, the printer indicated ready. She sat down again at the console and mashed the Enter key hard in exasperation. "There!"

The line printer began a sing-song chant, sucking paper out of the box. Paper wrapped around the top and slid in a folding stack at the back.

Nervous, Alec looked at his watch. "What's he up to, can you tell from your console?"

"Uh, yeah. I probably can."

Ryder debated going into the hallway, but Jeanette's surprise appearance sobered him. It was unlikely he'd avoid Otto when the Gnome left his office.

"Shit." Jeanette looked at Alec. "He's printing the same damn section of the database that I just did."

"In here?"

"Yeah. He'll come in here to check the damn printer. He's probably on his way now."

Alec looked around. There was no obvious place to hide. "You've got to go out there and stall him."

"How am I supposed to do that?"

"I don't know. Talk shop. Tell him you'll get the printout for him."

There were four quick clicks and the door lock snapped. Alec moved to the only place of concealment, behind the opening door, and waited.

"Oh, Otto, I'm sorry. My fix bombed the print manager. Give me a few minutes to back out my patch and then restart your printout, OK?"

"I didn't see any indication my printout was stalled when I checked status." Otto moved further inside. "That printer is going like crazy. What's printing?"

Jeanette shifted to block him. "Just a dump of system memory so I can debug."

"Shut it off. I need to get out of here and I need that printout to study tonight."

"I wish I could, Otto," she nervously apologized.

"How long then?" He inched toward her. If he turned, Otto would see Alec. Ryder held his breath. Any motion would catch Otto's eye.

"Just another five minutes, I promise. In the meantime, I'll restore the system. Don't worry. I'll bring your printout to your office." She smiled coquettishly.

Otto was peevish. "I don't have any other work."

"Oh, good. May I use your workstation, then? It'll be much easier than working over the network."

His reply sounded icy and calculated. "That's a good idea."

To prevent Otto from seeing him, Alec shadowed the door when it closed. His reception blocked by the metallic fire door, Ryder could only fumble for the light switch to restore illumination. The printer whined its irritating sing-song chant behind him, disrupting his sense of time. He looked at his watch and impatiently waited a minute, more than enough time for them to reach the Gnome's office.

Ryder cracked the door and peered out. The hallway was clear. He moved quickly and turned into the exit corridor. He could hear their shop talk in his earphone, a clear indication he could return in safety to the conference room.

Once again in front of the sensitive receiver, he checked his sentinels. There was a new delivery van down the block with only a driver inside. The van seemed to have no connection with Otto Tolnai's arrival. Alec signed off and listened to Jeanette in the Director's office. All he could hear was background noise, no voices.

A growing menace worried at the edges of his consciousness. Who was behind these arsons? A very bright mind, to be sure. Complex, multidimensional chess . . . Otto, the reigning Hungarian grandmaster at chess. Was he behind it all? Was Otto the killer/arsonist?

"Snooper, this is Dark Angel. Has Usulak arrived?"

"Negative, Dark Angel. We haven't been able to track him down."

"Try harder. I need a covert tail on that white Volvo when it leaves. You guys will stand out in the first block. I need Usulak to tail the Volvo. Has anybody been to Usulak's house?"

"Roger, we have a unit outside his house. They talked to neighbors. Looks like the Usulaks went out this morning, but nobody knows where."

"Get someone to his church. Tell the dispatcher to send unmarked cars to his parents and his in-laws. You copy?"

"Roger, Dark Angel. Out."

Ryder should've had Otto tailed from the beginning. What an idiot he'd been, sleep-walking through this thing. He nervously read his watch. Jeanette and Otto had been alone for ten minutes. Why couldn't he hear them talking? Had Otto spotted his bug? How much longer should he wait?

Jeanette's voice came through his earplug. "I'll get the printout for you."

Otto's reply followed immediately. "Not necessary. It's on my way out."

In moments, Ryder heard the Director shuffle pass the conference room door. Alec waited for Snooper to confirm Otto's exit from the Archives. Ryder pulled the mike closer. "Snooper, do you have Usulak?"

"No, Dark Angel. Sorry. Do you want us to tail Otto's Volvo?"

"Negative. Out."

"OK, Angel. By the way, that delivery van just left."

"Did you get the plates?"

"Yes. I'll run an ID for you."

"Great. Out."

Ryder opened the door and headed for Jeanette. He found her in Otto's office, looking upset.

He tried to be gentle but failed. "What happened? I've got to know."

Jeanette couldn't look at him. "He's got both printouts. I tried to mask it as a computer error. But I'm sure he suspects I broke into his protected area. In fact, I know he does. I'll show you."

To Ryder, the data looked like blocks of letters and numbers, all gibberish.

"On the left is hexadecimal, the right is ASCII." She quickly traced a path with her forefinger across the screen. "He erased the files and clobbered part of them with other crap. Most of the data is left, but the relationships are all gone, damn it."

"Isn't there any way to get it back?"

"Not from the database itself, no. I've already tried the usual recovery stuff, but he was smart enough to disable audits before he did his erasing. I'm going to hunt around on the disk, see what I can find. Maybe I can recover his printout."

"How long?" Alec asked in resignation.

"Minutes to hours. I really don't know." She looked disgusted with how it turned out. "All that God damned work on a Trojan horse for nothing."

* * *

Six hours later, Jeanette recovered most of the lost printout. Ryder leaned over her shoulder and stared at numbers. "Can you make sense of the data? Is there some pattern?"

"Well, it's really the result of a lot – and I do mean a lot – of queries, one search after another. He must have been looking for the proverbial needle in a haystack. The problem is, we don't know what the needle looks like and he does. The data that survived all his culling is a large haystack, about a gigabyte worth. I wish I had his criteria used in the searches. That would tell us quite a bit. I could probably guess at some of it though, sort of reverse engineer his questions from the data." She frowned. "How long, right? You always want to know how long. Well, the more time I have, the more right my guesses will be – up to a point."

"You need one day or one week?"

"More like a week than a day." She sat on a table and accidentally pushed over a stack of coffee cups piled there with Alec's nervous energy. A brown residue leaked from the Styrofoam cups and stained a sheaf of papers. She glanced at the mess. Her face said she was too tired to pick it up.

Ryder swept the litter into a garbage can for her. "Can you use that Trojan horse to peek into his private files and find the questions he used in searching the database?"

"I tried. He's on to us – or just super-careful. He's scraped all that off the disk. If it's still around, he's got the data locked away or carries it with him."

"There's no way to shorten all the brain work?"

"No."

There was a knock on the doorframe. Usulak stood there, looking sheepish. He was dressed for church, his one good suit and tie. "You needed me?"

Alec nodded. "Your spare bedroom available?"

"Yeah, especially if the City of Budapest pays for it."

Alec rolled his eyes. "In your dreams. You know how cheap they are." Alec turned up the volume on his police radio. "Snooper. This is Dark Angel. You still awake?"

There was a lag. Then Snooper replied through a full mouth. "Yeah. Just got some lunch finally. Sorry. What's up?"

"Time for operation rescue. You remember what I told you?"

"Yeah, but can't it wait a minute? I just got some food, the first in ten hours."

"All right. There's no emergency. Send the decoy down while you eat, so she and Jeanette can swap clothing. Call back when the cars are in position."

"Roger."

"Oh, and Snooper, did you ID that delivery van?"

"Yeah, Dark Angel, but it took breaking and entering. The automobile registration office has the good sense to be closed on a Sunday and we don't exactly have their files on-line. Fact, I hear we aren't even planning . . ."

"Cut the crap. Who owns the van?"

"Rental van."

"Who rented it?"

"Oh, you want to know that? I never thought of *that* . . ."

"I'll bet. Now, who rented it or I take your damn sandwich away and eat it myself."

"OK, no more threats," came the joking reply. "Hertz says it's on long-term rental to a German staying in Budapest, one Hans Mueller of Stuttgart."

Jeanette looked astonished. "Mueller's the guy who recruited me for this computer job."

Ryder smiled. "Yeah. Look's like we finally got a break."

17

Search the Dead

Once he had Otto's printout, it was easy to narrow the possibilities. Now he was outside the first of them. A quick, brusque knock. Then another. He waited.

There was cautious shuffling on the other side of the door and the peephole darkened, lightened, darkened again. An elderly woman spoke through the closed door in a faltering voice. "Yes, what do you want?"

"Phone man. I need to come in for a second. We're having trouble in the area."

"My phone is fine. I just talked to my daughter on it. Go away and leave me alone."

"Yes, ma'am, but because your phone works doesn't mean the wires aren't crossed with another person's. I only need a few seconds to check it out. Look, here are my credentials. I'm holding them up to your view hole, OK?"

The peephole stayed dark for a full thirty seconds or so, then the disembodied voice spoke again. "I saw your name. I'm calling the phone company. If you're not really a phone man, I'll get the police. You better run if you're lying."

He rolled his eyes and tried to look amused. "OK, lady, but hurry up. I don't have all day." He waited, looking impatient. The slippered feet retreated.

He pivoted out of view and ran at breakneck speed to the junction box in the apartment house basement. He tore the cover open and clamped insulated clips on the outgoing lines, trying each one in turn until he heard the elderly voice. "Well, I want to know if he's for real, dear. Someone there surely knows where your repairmen are, even if you don't. I'm an old lady living alone. I can't be too careful. You never know who's . . ."

He listened to another minute of her drivel and waited to see what the person on the other end would do. Finally, the young girl said she would transfer the call to a supervisor. He tore open a leather pack and dragged out an electronic case. Within seconds, he flicked switches and twisted dials, took a breath, checked the settings and plugged the device in. Satisfied he had a connection, he cut the outgoing line.

With the help of digital electronics, his voice transformed into a facsimile of a young woman. It only took a few careful sentences, with the right mix of frustration and courtesy, to convince the elderly woman she was safe.

There wasn't time to package everything. He left wires dangling and rushed up two flights of stairs to the apartment door. It cracked open, revealing three chains. Age-spotted fingers undid the chains one at a time, taking a maddening amount of time to open the door.

He walked inside and looked around. The living room smelled of medicines and a body odor that only old people give off, a premonition of the decay of the grave. Her curtains were pulled tight. Good. He wouldn't have to close open curtains and risk someone thinking the event was peculiar. It was good, too, that her daughter had just checked in. Most likely, she wouldn't call again until tomorrow.

"The phone's in there." The old woman pointed to a dimly lit hallway. A teapot keened in sharp whistling. "I'll be in the kitchen if you need anything. I take my morning medicine with tea, you see. I don't like water plain. Can't drink it. Never have, even when I was a little girl."

He watched her shuffle two sagging bags of varicose veins that once were legs toward a tiny stove, shouldered between two counters jammed with unwashed dishes.

He went into the hallway and quickly checked the bathroom and bedroom. There was no point in killing her. What he wanted wasn't there. By the time she placed the tea bag in her cup, he vanished from her life forever.

* * *

He drove to Budapest's Central Park – the lush green campus of Varosliget. It seemed fitting that he should resume the chronicle of his tortured life in the company of a monument to an historian. He'd just begun writing when a group of brightly-clad first-graders rushed from the elaborate Transylvanian castle behind him and swarmed over the monument, laughing, giggling, pushing and shoving.

He glowered at them and wondered how they'd feel if they knew he was death come to visit them.

There'd been no laughter, no shouts of joy when the first Russian soldiers had arrived at the concentration camp. He'd patiently waited a week to be liberated, a week of deliberate starvation, of sleeping without a blanket on an icy wooden bunk.

The Russian infantry swarming into the camp were coarse peasants, drafted as twelve-year olds. They filled the slaughtered ranks of adults, men who'd held Leningrad with a death-grip, fighting off a Nazi onslaught. Survivors of that year-long siege hurled themselves at German Panzers to break the Nazi grip on their motherland. Now Leningrad's children were killers at thirteen, ironically filled with the same blood lust that fed German atrocities against the Russians.

These boorish comrades were exuberant with victory and craving more slaughter as their fix. After they went home, they'd wish they'd done more harm and be ashamed of what they'd done. They'd return to find their villages gone, their sisters raped and killed, their families churned into mass graves. Right now, these atrocities were just rumors of what had been done to someone else's village, discounted as merely the blunt, repetitive prodding of their propaganda officer.

They broke down the concentration camp's gates and spilled from trucks, poked and prodded the dead, searching for warm clothing, valuables, boots. Finding none, the comrades-in-arms searched pockets and quickly gave up. Then they ransacked buildings.

It was only when they were about to leave that they paid attention to the living. A Russian officer barked orders to his men. The two dozen inmates left alive were tossed in an empty German truck, without food or blankets.

The officer himself retrieved what few records were left in the camp. The convoy raced out, freed inmates bringing up the rear.

By the time they'd stopped to camp for the night, only he remained alive. The others were dead from shock, disease and malnutrition. There'd been three who were tenacious, but eventually freezing cold claimed them and for that he was grateful. It would be inconvenient for them to point out his late arrival at the concentration camp, arousing suspicions about his true identity.

He lay forgotten in the back of the truck for hours, not daring to move. Finally, it was either freeze or get out. He lingered near a group of soldiers for several minutes before they noticed him. All but one laughed at him and moved away. The solitary child-man-killer gave him a scrap of meat, some hard bread and a cup of water. He returned to the captured German truck and sat in the passenger seat. There was a blanket on the driver's side. He wrapped coarse wool around himself and fell asleep.

In the days that followed, he made himself useful to the Russians in dozens of little ways. They came to accept his presence as normal and supplied him with boots, trousers and a coat. When they fought, he relayed ammunition to them and they gave him a helmet. One day he dared to pick up a dead Russian's gun and supply belt. He stuffed a grenade in a pocket and joined them. He became fluent in the language and dialect of his new captors. He told them he loved to kill Germans. They had killed so many of his people. The Russians never questioned it. He was too good at killing.

The Russians were electrified when they fought to the outskirts of Berlin, racing Americans for possession of the German capital. The outcome was inevitable, but the Nazis didn't crumble. Instead, each room of a house was a place to die, a place to lose your eye, your leg.

The blood lust of his child-killers waned in the sobering fear they'd be the last casualties of this horrible war. Life became precious again. It wasn't certain they'd die as it had been for so many years. They took their time ferreting out the ever-present German sniper. They were in no hurry to move on that next barricade. So he often led assaults, moving in his own crafty, stealthy manner, alone. They waited for him to return, placing bets he wouldn't come back and be found dead in the next house.

But he owned death and dealt it to others as he pleased. He felt immortal, an angel of death come to wreak hell on earth. It wasn't enough to kill the sniper. He caught the man instead, played with the German, tortured him mentally, then physically, and brought back a piece to show the Russians. They may never admit he was as good as them, but he showed them he was more than any of them.

They fought their way inside Berlin hour after tortured hour, berated by their officers for cowardice. Each night the Russians got drunk on poor vodka to forget the Reaper's dice tossed every time they moved from safety to attack. The child killers sobered up each day on the shattered remains of a comrade they'd come to think would never die.

It was in the shadow of Adolf Hitler and Eva Braun's corpses that the Fates laughed at him. They were not even kind enough to kill him outright. He turned the corner of Hitler's bunker and saw *der Fuhrer* lying on a bundle of just-lit firewood. Flames were already devouring Eva.

He stood for a moment, awestruck at being so close to a force of evil that twisted the earth in its grasp. He couldn't let Hitler simply be turned to ash. He wanted that power for himself. He raced forward and never heard the shot, never saw the source. He lost consciousness and when he awoke in a crude Russian hospital, he knew his life had been twisted forever.

18

Kindling

Detective Sergeant Usulak was dozing lightly when he heard the screen door slam. He opened his weary eyes to see Otto Tolnai standing vigilantly on the porch of a small but neat suburban home. Otto's face turned as he swept the street and Usulak brought up yesterday's newspaper to hide his identity. He was surprised to see Otto unlocking the door to a shiny white Volvo. Usulak was as startled by the new, imported sedan as he was by the home. Their salaries should've been comparable and the Detective knew he certainly couldn't afford that house.

Otto got in the Volvo and the car billowed exhaust vapor in the damp cold. Usulak started his car and put it in gear, waiting to leave in pursuit. After a minute, he took the Fiat out of gear and tapped impatient fingers on the plastic steering wheel. Was the bureaucrat letting his car warm up before driving, or was he again surveying the street?

The minutes dragged on. Finally, the Volvo slid down twin concrete strips and dipped into an empty street. He saw Otto wrestle with the steering wheel to turn the large sedan into alignment with the pavement. Usulak winced as he realized the Director was intending to pass directly by the Fiat. Damn, why was Tolnai doing that? His office lay in the opposite direction.

The Detective Sergeant brought the newspaper up and slipped downward in his seat, as though dozing while he waited for a carpool partner to finish breakfast. He watched the departing white sedan in his mirrors. When his target reached the corner, Usulak peeled into a driveway, backed up, and roared to the intersection. He caught sight of Tolnai a half-mile away, at a junction to the main road.

Otto turned into a brief gap in the flow and Usulak raced his little Fiat engine through gears, jamming on the brakes at the last second. The traffic flow was now seamless and forced him to risk an accident in his effort to move through the unrelenting stream. Brakes squealed when Usulak squeezed himself into a too-small gap. Where was that damned Volvo?

Detective Sergeant Usulak maneuvered along the main road in a vain effort to catch Tolnai, cutting across lanes, ignoring protesting horns. He glimpsed in his peripheral vision the tail of a white sedan vanishing down a side road. Usulak was trapped on the main thoroughfare for a kilometer before an opportunity to reverse direction occurred. He ignored the chance to turn around. It was way too late now.

The Detective Sergeant cursed under his breath. Tolnai was very good – and very clever. It was the first time in his career that Usulak failed in tailing a suspect. Usulak forced himself to relax. Now he had a few minutes to find a birthday present for his youngest daughter. Then he'd visit the rental car agency and ask about that delivery van Ryder wanted investigated.

* * *

After lunch, Detective Sergeant Usulak flashed his badge at a young girl behind a Hertz counter. She smiled politely but had no idea what he wanted. She'd been trained to rent vehicles, not to answer police questions. Usulak gave up and asked for the manager. He wandered with hands folded behind his back along the front windows of the office, examining travel posters of exotic locations worldwide where he could rent a car from Hertz. Usulak found his favorite in Tahiti, where a bikini-clad girl was climbing into a small Ford. He found it necessary to examine that poster several times before moving to the next one.

"May I help you," interrupted Usulak's reveries and he turned to confront a stocky man in his late fifties, wearing thick glasses.

"Yes, I'm with the police …"

"I know," came the impatient interruption.

"Well, since you're so smart, you also know that you rented a delivery van to Mr. Hans Mueller of Stuttgart approximately a month ago. Mueller neglected to register his extended stay. I'm looking for his address and a physical description of him. Was it you who rented that delivery van to Herr Mueller?"

"No. The van hasn't been in an accident, has it?"

"It may have been used in a crime," the Detective Sergeant exaggerated.

"I assure you we had no …"

Usulak cut him off. "Of course. I do, however, need to see the rental agreement."

The manager walked quickly behind the counter, pulling out a thick sheaf of rental forms held on a clipboard by large metal hoops. He shuffled forms until he found the right one, broke the clasp open and removed Mueller's transaction. "One moment, please. I can't give you the original." When he returned, the manager handed Usulak a copy. "Will that be all?"

"No." Usulak scanned the form to find what credit card was used. He spotted an American Express charge number. That would be easy to trace. Then he noticed the employee's name who filled out the form. "Is she here now?"

"No, she arrives in an hour. I can have her call you when she comes in."

Usulak glanced at his watch. "I'll wait." He folded the copy of the rental agreement in a neat square and slipped the paper in a coat pocket. Then he sat down opposite the bikini and conducted a more thorough police examination, wishing his wife had even once looked that sexy. Well, he had three children and a stable job. A man couldn't ask for everything. He did love his children.

* * *

"He'll see you now." The leggy brunette spoke to Ryder in a tone frosty enough to create ice in the room.

Alec followed the arrow of her slender finger into the Commissioner's office. There were men in expensive suits seated in chairs flanking the Commissioner's desk. He'd never met them before. The Commissioner's royal presence was also seated, hands folded, looking even more condescending than his secretary. No one bothered to offer Ryder a chair.

The Commissioner of City Services scowled. "I'm going to come right to the point."

Alec interrupted. "I haven't met these other two gentlemen."

"It would change nothing if you had, Mr. Ryder. They are the City's attorneys, here to witness the proceedings. You've gone mad, Ryder. Budapest is overrun with crimes and you're watching the Department of Property Titles and Vital Statistics as though it was the headquarters of a Mafia don. To add to this absurdity, you assigned your colleague, Mr. Usulak, to tail the Director, Otto Tolnai. In the meantime, we are no closer to the arsonist and brutal murders have been committed."

Ryder tried to speak. "I …"

"No. You aren't going to waste my time with a confession of your incompetence. If you want to defend squandering the City's resources, put it in writing and send your letter to the City Attorney's office."

"Is that all?" Alec snapped.

"No. Where have you taken that consultant who was working with Tolnai?"

"She's in protective custody. For her safety, I can't reveal her whereabouts."

"I fail to see how she fits into random arsons by a psychotic killer. I terminated her contract and revoked her travel visa. She has, however, been given a fair, in fact, handsome, settlement. The money is in that envelope. If you are as concerned about her safety as you pretend, take the money to her and escort her out of Hungary – today. If she's here tomorrow, I'll have her arrested."

"Fine." Alec scooped the envelope from the table and put it inside his breast pocket.

"You agree to follow the orders I've given?"

"Yes."

"Do you have any questions regarding their interpretation or my intent?"

"No, I think you've clarified a great deal for me today. Thank you."

The Commissioner leaned over further to emphasize his next point. His double chin squatted on the tight knot of his necktie. "I sense a certain amount of sarcasm, Mr. Ryder, in that last remark. Let me make it clear that you are on probation. Insubordination by you would be grounds for immediate dismissal as our Interpol liaison. Do you really want to return to Virginia? Think about it." A fat hand waved dismissal.

* * *

Clouds of shiny globe lights echoed across the mirrors, brass lamp stems and polished carvings of the New York Café. Alec Ryder slouched in a leather chair and sipped a double scotch, waiting for Usulak to show. Ryder sat alone at a large round table, anchoring a theater-box in one of the balconies. Several groups of tourists had come and gone, a parade of strangers whose gaiety didn't lift his ugly mood. A spill of light filtered through the cascade of French sheers, irritating him with its brightness. Through that picture window, he spotted the familiar shape of Usulak's car as it parked.

A group of noisy Japanese tourists moved past and occupied the adjoining box. They couldn't be seated until each had taken a flash picture of the ornate interior. Alec was nearly blind by the time Detective Sergeant Usulak sat down and ordered a coffee.

"I found the surveillance bugs in our office, just as you suspected," Usulak volunteered when the waiter left.

"How many?"

"Five that I could see."

"Busy little man, that Commissioner." Ryder sipped again from the tumbler of scotch and checked his surroundings for eavesdroppers. The Japanese had settled into a loud discussion in their native tongue, partially solving Alec's concerns.

"How about my apartment?"

"Several more there, too."

"And your home?"

"Clean so far. My wife is there almost all the time, neighbors come and go, the kids arrive, bring their friends. It's a zoo. They'll play hell to get a bug in there."

"Jeanette?" Alec asked.

Usulak paused while the waiter served his coffee. "She's in that spare bedroom. The kids don't like it. They can't go in there and watch TV any time they want, but tough luck."

"Is she working?"

"Appears to be going through the printout every which way. 'Course, I'm not a computer guru, so she could just be wasting ink for all I'd know." The Detective Sergeant picked up the cream and poured some into his cup. "I lost Otto this morning, Alec. He was ready for us."

"Think he was tipped?"

"Don't know. He certainly acted like he expected a tail, but he could have been doing this every morning. It's like you said. We should have been on him from the beginning. I'll get him tomorrow, though."

"No, you won't."

"Hey, look, just because …"

"No, Szige, you and I've been ordered by the Commissioner to drop our tail of him or else."

"How the hell did he know?"

"That's why I asked about the bugs. Did you sweep our cars, too?"

"Yeah, twice. Nothing."

"That leaves only some very unpleasant possibilities."

"Well, I sure as hell didn't tell him. Did you?" Usulak looked genuinely offended, like a puppy that got spanked for something he didn't know was wrong.

"There's you, me and Jeanette."

"She hasn't been out of my sight - or my wife's."

"Could she have used the phone without your wife knowing it?"

"Maybe . . . I'll check the phone company, get a dump of all the numbers that have been dialed from my house in the last 48 hours. I don't think Tolnai spotted me, but maybe. He acted more like this was a routine with him, a way of life."

"My guess, Szige, is that he has every car on his street memorized. For him, that would be child's play. He decided to assume that strange Fiat was us."

"I'll check the phone company anyway." Usulak finished his coffee and reached for his wallet.

"Before you go, I need to know what happened at Hertz." Alec drained his scotch and also prepared to leave.

The Detective Sergeant responded to the Hertz query by dropping a photo on the table. He tapped the black and white photograph with an index finger. "I showed them this. The girl gave me a positive ID on him as Herr Hans Mueller of Stuttgart."

Alec Ryder idly fingered the snapshot of Otto Tolnai and pushed it back in Usulak's direction. "Credit card?"

"Yeah, American Express. Belongs to Hans Mueller of Stuttgart. But, Alec, the card's been used all over the world in the last decade. You ever know Otto to travel?"

"Once. To that crazy publicity stunt Bobby Fischer staged in Yugoslavia. Tolnai is nuts on Fischer. Says he's the only guy that added anything to chess in this century."

"This card's been everywhere, Alec, not just to our always-killing-each-other neighbors."

"Wonderful, just wonderful. Well, stay away from him. No sense in both of us getting fired, at least, fired in the same day. Take the safe stuff for a while, Szige. Visit the phone company."

Usulak gave a mock bow and departed gracefully through the convoluted maze of chairs and tables. Alec changed his mind and ordered another double scotch. He needed to think and there was no better place for him to do it than here.

19

Robot

He turned down a narrow alley and checked the clearance of his mirrors as he eased a rented delivery van between buildings. He kept his eyes on a ribbon of dirty water seeping down the center of the alley. There was a snick as one mirror clipped a drainpipe. Bright sunlight jumped the roof of a stucco facade on his left and bounced off windows on his right, nearly blinding him. Squinting, he came to an open square jammed with small cars. A loading dock harbored vans with "Federal Express" stenciled on their white sides.

He maneuvered among cars, backing up to the loading dock. He slowed to a crawl at the end, hitting soft resistance from a dirty bumper of old tire sections caterpillaring across the cargo dock. His left hand reached in a shirt pocket and clipped a badge on the lapel of his blue coveralls.

He wove between pallets of plastic wrapped boxes to the front counter, smiling at everyone he met. They politely smiled back, as did the woman behind a countertop lined with stainless steel scales.

"You should be holding several packages for Mueller Industries. I'm here to pick them up."

"Oh, yes. They're in the back. Can you pull around to the loading dock?" She glanced at his badge, checking to make sure he was authentic.

He wasn't worried. His badge advertised Mueller Industries in bold letters, with a five year pin for good service. The plastic was yellowed with age, even though the badge was only a week old. "I'm already parked at the loading dock."

"Oh, good. I'm glad you know the way in here. It's pretty complicated. You must come often. I'm surprised we haven't met." She handed him a stack of forms to sign as receipt of delivery. There were eleven separate tracking forms and a customs form.

He signed forms while talking to her. "I usually pick up from the railroad. But the other guy was sick today. They needed this stuff in a hurry, so I called him at home and got directions. Good thing I didn't bring a big truck. It would never fit in that alley. What a tight squeeze!"

"Yes," she answered, taking the signed forms back from him. "I don't even like driving my car down that alley. I can't imagine taking a van through it."

A line of customers was forming behind him. He didn't have to turn around to know they were there. His instincts counted the footsteps and tracked each of them, categorizing people according to threat potential.

The Fed Ex clerk glanced at the line. "Would you mind taking these forms to the loading dock for me? Someone on the dock will help you load the packages."

"Sure. You're needed up here." He jerked a thumb over his shoulder at the line. He rounded her counter and strode down the hallway, twisting sideways as he passed a Fed Ex employee.

It took three helpers to load his van. While they did the job, he glanced at the forms. They indicated insurance values of ten thousand dollars per box. He smiled at that low number. Over twenty-five million dollars of electronics and machinery was being loaded into his Hertz rental van.

The box contents were created in the shadow of Mount Fuji by Fanuc Laboratories. Only the engineering had been done by man. Assembly was performed in a factory where robots made the next generation of robots, who would in turn build their successors. The men also worked like robots, living in barracks for a six-day week and commuting home by bullet-trains for a brief reminder they were husbands and fathers. A little sex, pat the kids on the head and return to a drone role in Dr. Fanuc's ant hill. By exploiting the Japanese work ethic, Fanuc buried his competition worldwide and gave Japan an insurmountable lead in robotics.

The robotics squeaking down a narrow alley had been en route to a trade show in Tokyo when Korean movers hijacked them. The Koreans shipped their cargo to the Democratic Peoples Republic of Korea, whose bankrupt regime needed money. North Korean officials shopped the robots worldwide via diplomatic pouches, along with illegal drugs and counterfeit American currency.

Once he verified what the North Koreans were offering, ownership tags changed on blocks of gold bullion in a Swiss bank vault. The robots began moving toward him. Now the finest technology of its kind anywhere in the world was here in Budapest, ready to assist him.

* * *

He parked his van inside the warehouse and got out. He filled his lungs with the fresh river air and stretched. He savored a last look at the Danube before pulling down a huge metal door. With a tug, the door slid in its rusted track until the awkward thing slammed against iron brackets. The air inside reeked of exhaust fumes and spills from every kind of cargo. He walked the length of a soccer field through a cavernous interior, his vision adjusting to bleak remnants of sun falling through grimy skylights. Dust stirred behind as he walked. He turned once to marvel at the spectacle of the dust idling inside square cones of light from the windows. He flipped on bank after bank of lights and the warehouse became an isolated world, the windows turning an opaque yellow-gray.

He drove a small crane to the back of the van and wrapped its hoist cable around each box. Dragging them from the truck, he arranged the crates in a circle, with him at the center. For the better part of an hour, he pried open wooden boxes and pulled bubble pack off machinery. When he was satisfied with the contents of each crate, he took out a large salesman's sample case, the kind used by airline pilots to hold manuals and charts. He spread diagrams on a table and began studying.

He reached to turn a page and realized he was still wearing the Mueller Industries badge. He pulled the false ID off, tossing it on a wiring diagram for the robot cell controller. He laughed at the badge – after all, he was Mueller Industries. He, the famed Dr. Hans Mueller, electronics genius who helped NATO build so much of their Command and Control facilities. Dr. Mueller held top security clearances, and used those clearance to bug NATO offices and conference rooms. It amazed him none of the bugs had been found yet. Even more amazing to him was that none of the tons of explosives had been found either.

They'd trusted him, courted him, given him sole-source awards where other firms were forced into grueling competitions. He rewarded this special treatment by building bombs into all the key NATO installations. For decades, he awaited the signal that the Third World War was beginning, that Soviet tanks were coming to crush the grain in West Germany's fields and shatter that brilliant economy with tactical nuclear weapons, nerve gases and napalm. While he waited, he made a fortune from both sides and stole the best in technology that each had to offer. He hoarded exotic technologies for a day like today, when he satisfied a lifelong obsession.

The Russians twice thwarted him from his obsession, first in the streets of Budapest when they occupied the city. The second time, they forced him to live in West Germany as their agent, a deep plant, a vital mole.

He'd had no choice. He'd awoken at the end of World War II in a Russian field hospital. His Soviet Army clothing was cut from him to treat his wounds. In the process of removing his uniform, they found the Gestapo pig's identification papers.

His interrogation began respectfully. A highly decorated officer who witnessed his heroism was present. In those days, being a hero of the motherland who fought and killed Nazis was enough to restrain an embryonic KGB, keep them from their worst behavior.

He hadn't known what to say about the Gestapo pig's ID documents. He tried lying, telling them he'd found the papers in the concentration camp. In two days, he was dragged back into the same room. The interrogation was preceded by withholding all pain killers for eight hours. This time, the KGB was alone and they knew exactly where to jab him with their batons, clamp their electrodes. He passed out from the pain several times.

The KGB man would ask a question and press on his wounds. It didn't take long before he'd told them the truth, all of it. He only managed to withhold the secrets of suite 115 of the Grand Hotel. Somehow, even their type of extreme pain couldn't force that treasure from him.

A month later, he'd recovered from their brutal treatment. He was again pushed in a wheelchair into the interrogation chamber with the same KGB agent. There was another man present, a stranger who didn't speak at first.

The agent said that they verified much of his story. The other man offered him a job. When he didn't accept, the agent explained his other option. He could serve Mother Russia in a labor camp, until he died. He might last a year. Most did.

So he became Hans Mueller, a deep plant in West Germany, a man whom everyone helped from a horrible sense of guilt. After all, the poor man was a Holocaust victim and deserved every chance after that atrocity.

He got a Ph.D. from the University of Göttingen in mathematics and began work as an engineer at a West German electronics firm. Dr. Hans Mueller was born. Only five years were necessary before Dr. Mueller started his own firm, specializing in secure military communications.

Then, the KGB contacted him. They made it clear he would cooperate or be killed. On the other hand, his cooperation would be rewarded. He was neither surprised nor frightened. This was the opportunity he wanted very badly.

He maneuvered cleverly, and a few years later took his first trip back to Budapest. It seemed his life goal was again within reach. Then tanks rolled through the streets. The Hungarian Revolution of 1956 blossomed into its full tragedy. In the chaos that followed, he sowed the seeds for today's accomplishments.

* * *

Dr. Hans Mueller stood back from the van and admired his precise installation of the robots. They would serve him unfailingly in tonight's performance. Mueller couldn't admire long. There was much work left before the van was ready.

The next hour was consumed in masking the trim and windows of the vehicle. He started the Hertz rental van's engine. The smell of its exhaust fumes irritated him, but he had no choice. He drove the van inside an improvised paint spray booth built of light wood and plastic sheeting. An exhaust vent pulled out toxic fumes through a sparkless fan. An intake vent supplied fresh air from a duct leading to the outside.

Wearing a disposable painting outfit, he started an air compressor and adjusted the spray nozzle on a sheet of plywood. In a few minutes, he'd changed the van from white to dark blue. The paint wasn't normal automobile paint, designed to last years. Instead, this was a special paint used in preparing cars for television advertisements, quick to apply and easy to remove with the right solvent. It didn't take long for the paint to dry sufficiently for him to tack on authentic Lufthansa Air Freight decals. Dr. Hans Mueller admired his work for only a few seconds before backing the van out and shutting off his equipment.

The next station was by far the simplest and yet the most dangerous. There were no adequate safety precautions, so he worked with a surgeon's care. In the van's cargo area, he spread out a small weather balloon and connected its inflation valve to a pressurized tank. With great care, he slowly filled the metallic silver balloon. At the end, it lay on the cargo floor like a beached whale.

Lethal chemicals inside the balloon were volatile enough without its companion. Yet to accomplish tonight's mission, he had no choice but to lay its fiery lover alongside. He smoothed another silver globe into the remaining space. The second balloon didn't quite fit. He was very careful where it touched the already inflated weather balloon.

He began filling the second balloon He laughed at himself when he realized he was standing farther back this time.. A yard wouldn't delay his death even a millisecond should the second balloon rupture. Sweat beaded on his forehead as the silver globe rose and billowed, filling cavities in the van's ribbed floor and sides.

He tore his fascinated eyes off the rising death and stared at the pressure gauge. It crept up one hairline mark at a time, moving toward a threshold where he was supposed to stop. He loved the fear now. It brought him to life. Fear touched him as only the eroticism of death possibly could. He deliberately let the pressure go one hairline mark above the threshold. He panted in excitement. A second mark was masked by the rising needle. He could hear his pulse in his ears. His hand trembled over the shutoff valve.

It seemed an eternity as the third mark slowly disappeared. He wanted a fourth. He wanted it to rupture, to consume him. But he would not let himself have that pleasure. Perhaps, after he'd consummated his obsession, he'd make his funeral pyre far more spectacular than Hitler's pitiful end. His crematorium would not be made of brush. He'd use hypergolic rocket fuel, stolen from a Russian submarine-launchable ballistic missile (SLBM).

His left hand twisted the valve shut. The weather balloon trembled and held.

20

Zoo

Alec Ryder sighed as he paid for his first pack of cigarettes in fifteen years. He pinched a set of matches emblazoned with the hotel's crest before exiting the gift shop. He stood exhausted and numb for a moment before orienting himself to the lobby. Alec shuffled wearily to the front desk and asked for the manager. There was no response from the clerk until Alec's Interpol badge was flashed.

An impeccably attired Austrian swaggered to Ryder, accompanied by the hotel's security man. The Interpol badge again changed their attitude. The manager cleared his throat. "Are you looking for someone?"

"No, I'm just dead tired. Do you have an empty room I could use for a few days?"

"The hotel is booked." The manager shrugged, as if there was nothing he could do.

"How'd you do on your last fire inspection?" Ryder scanned the lobby for mandatory extinguishers and their certification tags.

The Austrian coughed. "Even if I free up a room today, there might not be one available tomorrow."

"You heard about Satan's Touch? He killed a bunch of firefighters. I'm working on that case. Think maybe the Budapest Fire Department might be on my side?"

"We passed our last inspection." The Austrian looked haughty.

Alec gave him a cynical smile. "You'll flunk the next one. Can't operate without a certificate, can you? Have to close you down. Think your masters would give you a raise if I close you down?" Ryder leaned on the counter to watch as the manager used a front desk computer to bring up reservation information.

"Hmm. I've found one, all made up, but it's got no view. A non-smoking room, single bed. Next to the elevator, though."

Sweet bunch, Alec thought. "OK, for now. But you'll move me to a better room tomorrow. Sorry about the short notice."

"Any luggage?" The manager's eyebrow arched disdainfully.

"Not yet. I might bring some in tonight. How much for the room?" Alec pulled out his wallet.

"We require a credit card imprint, even when you pay in cash."

"No you don't." Ryder put a thousand dollars on the desk. "Either we skip the credit card or I'll have the fire department here in five minutes. Your sprinkler system better work fine. No dead alarms. We'll have to test them all, and do an evacuation drill."

"Cash is fine." The manager flagged a bellman and gave him a plastic card dotted with holes used as a key. He told the bellman to take the Inspector to Room 305.

They exited the elevator and turned right. Room 305 was indeed next to the elevator shaft. The bellman held the room door open. Alec entered and looked around. Smallest, noisiest room in the building, no doubt. The last one booked, the first one complained about.

"Will there be anything else, sir?"

"Yeah, bring me a bottle of good scotch, Johnny Walker or Chivas – and some ice. Oh, and a sandwich of some kind."

"Club sandwich be all right, sir?"

"Yeah, fine."

The bellman left and Ryder lay on the bed without removing his raincoat, suit coat, shoes, tie, anything. In seconds, he was asleep despite the elevator noise.

He awoke to knocking at his door. Alec started violently, rolling off the far side of the bed. He swept his automatic from its holster. The cobwebs vanished as the gentle knocking continued. He recalled ordering items from room service. "Who is it?"

"Bellman with your order, Mr. Ryder."

The voice was familiar. He holstered the gun and let the bellman inside, squeezing into the bathroom to avoid a large tray. The bellman was tipped and left gracefully, closing the door. Alec lifted the lids. There was a bowl of fruit, a chef's salad, a bottle of Chivas, ice, a club sandwich and a rose in a small vase.

He peeled the seal off the bottle of Chivas and poured it generously over a tumbler of ice. Ryder attacked the food, drank the scotch, lit up a smoke. He got up and went into the bathroom. In the mirror he saw a very haggard vagrant with 48 hours of stubble and bloody eyes. No wonder the manager nearly kicked him out.

Alec went back to the bed and laid down again. He stared at acoustical flocking on the ceiling, then fixated on the chrome sprinkler head centered above the bed. Would that maniac be able to burn down a modern hotel like this one? Where was Alec on the list of those to be killed – or was he on it at all?

The more he thought about the fires, the more confused and enraged he got. Finally, he dragged a collection of phone messages from his pocket and shuffled them until he had the right one. Guilt made it impossible not to respond to this one. He picked up the phone and dialed. It was, after all, why he needed the room, to make unbugged calls. His call was answered on the first ring.

"I need Michael Toth, the Fire Captain. Is he still there? Well, screw the visiting hours. This is a police matter." Alec picked up a small pencil and tapped it nervously against the hotel-supplied pad.

"Michael? Yeah, this is Alec Ryder, Interpol. Sorry to take so long to get back to you. I've been going after this maniac non-stop. What can I do for you?"

Alec listened and wrote two words on the pad – rocket fuel.

"OK, I'll keep you posted. Thanks, Michael. How're you healing up? That's good. OK, yeah. I'll be in touch."

Alec reassured the obsessed Fire Captain three more times that he'd find where the maniac stole his rocket fuel and then hung up. He looked at the two words on the notepad and got out the pack of Kools. Alec guiltily scanned the non-smoking room, then yanked out a cigarette, lit it and laid back on the bed. After a second smoke, he sat up and pulled out his address book. He licked a finger and pushed thin pages out of his way until he found the right number.

Interpol headquarters was no help and took an entire hour to tell him they were useless. But he could feel free to call them anytime – lucky Ryder. The last buddy he had at CIA was home watching Jay Leno. No, the U.S. wasn't missing any rocket fuel. But there was a KGB guy responsible for Hungary since the Cold War began. If Soviet rocket fuel was missing, this guy would have the details.

There was only an answering machine on the other end when he called, but Ryder expected that ploy. The answering machine was a blind mail box for the correspondent, a technique the KGB used since answering machines were first available after World War II.

He paced the room, regretting it had no view. A third cigarette disappeared. His raincoat, tie and shoes came off and went in a closet. He debated a fourth cigarette and tried the sandwich instead. The clock showed an hour passed since his KGB call. He had other people to contact, but he didn't want to tie up the line. He poured himself more scotch.

The phone rang and he jumped, splashing liquor on the tablecloth. Alec restrained himself and finished pouring, carrying a tinkling glass of ice and scotch with him to the telephone. He picked up and answered. "Ryder."

"Mr. Ryder, how are you? My name is Gregory Yevchentko."

"I'm fine, but over my head on a case."

"How can I help?"

Alec sipped from the tumbler. The Chivas felt wonderful when it burned down his throat. "Rocket fuel. Are you missing any?"

There was a long pause before KGB section head Gregory Yevchentko replied. "Many things leak out of Mother Russia that should not. There are desperate people in charge of precious items, powerful people, connected people."

Ryder understood the warning. He kept on anyway. "Is it the kind of rocket fuel that melts concrete into glass when burned – and how much is missing, Gregory?"

The response wasn't an answer but a question. "Do you have any suspects, Mr. Ryder?"

The man's arrogant tone and avoidance raised hairs on the back of Ryder's neck. He sat the tumbler of scotch down and thought to himself for a minute before replying. His stomach jittered. "Does the name 'Hans Mueller' mean anything to you?"

There was a long delay. Alec wondered if the line was dead before a familiar voice came back. "Yes, I've heard of this Mueller. I'll send someone to give you our data on him. Someday, I'll collect on this favor, Mr. Ryder. I'll expect full reciprocity."

"You'll get it. When can you arrange a rendezvous?"

"The meeting will be at 3:00 P.M. today, in the Zoo near the rhino cage."

Alec looked at his watch. "Sounds very spy-like. Why not just fax me the sheet?"

"I have more to communicate to you than a single sheet, Mr. Ryder. Humor me."

* * *

Alec Ryder stared at a hooded black eye and it stared back with an unblinking challenge. The rhino lowered its enormous horn and backed up, his armor pressing against a low fence of round logs stuck in the pen. Alec decided it was best to cede dominance to the monster, so Ryder blinked and looked away. The huge beast announced its disdain by sauntering toward its private cave. Before disappearing, the rhino stopped and looked at Alec in scorn, then plodded defiantly through a Roman arch in the art nouveau façade.

Alec yawned and looked at his watch. It was exactly three o'clock.

Within five minutes, a man approached Alec, gave him a manila envelope and waddled off casually. Alec sat down and read in silence. A churning began in his stomach. What the hell was going on that Yevchentko and Ryder had to act so secretly? He had no idea.

Still, Alec decided to be cautious. To make sure the rendezvous wasn't observed, he left his car at the zoo and walked to the Arts Hall. He took wrong turns leading to dead-ends, hid himself in shadows and waited. There was no sign of a tail. Still, he went inside the Arts Hall, found its restroom and crawled out a window. He jogged downhill to the street, flagged a cab and returned to his hotel room, where he could make the necessary arrangements in relative safety.

* * *

An hour later, another taxicab dropped Alec back at the zoo. He got in his car and drove to the office. The Commissioner's deadline for getting Jeanette out of the country expired at eight o'clock that night, when the last plane left Hungary. Alec called American Airlines from his desk phone and booked reservations that took her back to Santa Monica, California. When he hung up, he grinned at the walls of his office. With all the eavesdropping bugs in those walls, there was no need for a written status report tonight. The Commissioner knew Alec was complying with the bastard's orders.

21

Software

He picked up the telephone and dialed a number in Stuttgart, Germany, listened to a voice-mail and erased the message. "Dr. Mueller" ran a hand across stubble on his chin and replaced the telephone receiver in its cradle. He reached in a drawer and pulled out an electric razor, trimming away the infant beard of an all night session programming Fanuc's robots. After that phone message, it was necessary to alter their programs with new instructions. He sat at a computer console connected to the robot controller and spewed out a string of new commands for the robots inside his freshly-painted delivery van. He was teaching them how to drive the van holding rocket fuel.

Two hours later, the delivery van with rocket fuel turned into an air freight entrance of Ferihegy I, the twin of Budapest's other airport,

Ferihegy II. Mueller sat two hundred yards away, inside a van he'd driven behind the robots, shadowing them when they navigated Budapest traffic. He watched a TV monitor, concerned as the delivery van slowed to a crawl to ease across a deep storm gutter. Inside the robot van, weather balloons bursting with volatile rocket fuel jiggled. Their explosive load washed back and forth inside the weather balloons. Servo mechanisms feeding data to the robots dictated braking. The van abruptly halted.

He could see from his television that a large truck was behind the delivery van. The truck driver wasn't expecting the robot van to halt suddenly. The truck swerved and missed the van by inches. The truck driver roared past the van with a blast of horn, ignorant of how close he'd come to a violent death.

Inside the robot's van, sensors detected vapor from one of two weather balloons. There was a pinpoint leak in a seam, Mueller decided. He wiped sweat from his forehead and watched the van move around the corner of a building. The vehicle rolled toward a low fence dividing the parking lot from the aircraft area.

The robots again halted when they ran across a hole in the pavement. The leak detectors indicated more spilled fuel, but only one of the two types needed for intense combustion. As long as there was no spark, the mission would go ahead as Mueller planned.

A red light flashed on his command console. A large tractor-trailer rig blocked a gap in the fence he'd programmed the robots to find. They were supposed to park in front of that gap. At the right moment, he'd toggle them to drive through the gap in the fence.

He switched from monitoring the rocket fuel to scanning with a wide angle periscope, a piece of advanced fiber optics appearing to be only a cellular telephone antenna atop his delivery van. He spotted a uniformed policeman walking near the truck obstructing the robot's path.

The policeman was now alongside the robot van, banging on the tinted driver's side window, demanding the occupants open up. The policeman put his hand on the door knob of the motionless van and pulled. In response, the door flung open violently, knocking the cop to the ground. When the policeman rolled to his feet and sought to pull out his gun, sophisticated pattern recognition logic found the man's eyes. A laser capable of welding steel pulsed into the soft flesh of the cop's retinas.

The gun clattered to the asphalt as the policeman's hands flew up to cover his painful wound. The laser pulsed again and again in a chainsaw of millisecond bursts, razoring across the elevated wrists and exposed neck. Like a defaced marble statue, the man's body stood for a moment with headless torso and handless arms erect, then crumpled on the severed face.

The van door shut.

The automatons glided forward and parked, only feet from their first victim. Patiently, they waited.

22

Deceptions

Alec Ryder left his car in Ferihegy I's long term parking lot and walked to the bus shelter. He helped a retired Englishwoman load her luggage on a rack behind the driver before weaving his way to the back. He yearned for another cigarette, more food, a good night's sleep. The bus snorted diesel fuel that seeped inside and nauseated him. Scotch and nicotine had done serious damage to his already tender stomach. The driver curved around an obstacle course of unloading cars and Alec thought he might have to vomit. He was relieved to see the bus waved to a stop by a uniformed policeman. The cop stood in front of a patrol car with its Christmas tree of blue lights spinning, casting a disorienting glow down the roofline of his bus.

Ryder got up and showed his badge to the driver, who opened the bus door. More patrol cars cordoned off the area. Alec walked toward the terminal, pausing only for the automatic door to open. Policemen lined the area, pushing onlookers to one side. Queued passengers were annoyed when cops parted to let Ryder pass. To make their life easier, he showed his badge to the crowd and kept going toward an escalator.

He bounced up escalator steps until he got to the next level and headed for a security checkpoint. Alec cut in front of a slow group of tourists and slid through detectors. Alarms shrieked when his gun went through the magnetic field. Heads turned. Guards ran. He pulled out his badge and waited coolly for them to settle down. A uniformed policeman verified his identity and Alec started along the concourse, flipping a glance at gate assignments. It wasn't hard to find Usulak and Jeanette. Another cordon of police guarded a sullen group of airline passengers waiting for their flight.

His eyes caught hers. Alec's stomach churned into a tight little knot when she smiled. Ryder forced himself to say, "Hello."

"I thought I wasn't going to get a chance to say goodbye to you. But Szige kept telling me you were coming."

Alec ignored her friendliness and cut to his bottom line. "Did you crack the data?"

"No." She puckered her face in disappointment.

"Did you bring the data with you?" Ryder looked away from her and scanned the room.

"Yes. I was told to bring the printout. It's here." She pointed to a cardboard box, taped shut and tied with string.

A gate attendant interrupted. "Do you want her to board first, Inspector, or last?"

Alec reacted automatically. "First."

Jeanette shuffled a bit. "Well, I guess this is it. I'll miss you, Alec."

"In that case, I'll walk you onboard." Ryder picked up the cardboard box by its string.

When they got to the gate attendant, Alec gave the woman Jeanette's ticket and reached for his badge. The gate attendant waved her hand and passed them through a turnstile. The boarding ramp sloped down and bent at an angle. The rubber mat under his feet undulated when they walked. The tunnel reeked of jet fuel carried on bitter cold air through a window. A steward with a pleasant smile extended a hand to help Jeanette onboard.

Alec asked the steward, "Is she booked in the computer for being on this flight?"

"Why, yes. Isn't she boarding?"

Alec ignored him. He asked Jeanette, "Have you ever been to Moscow?"

She looked shocked. "No . . . I haven't . . . why do you ask?"

"Because we're going there tonight."

"I'd love to … but my luggage is already on this airplane. I don't know how to get it transferred."

Alec cut her off. He queried one of the men standing near the aircraft door. "Is Ms. Murphy's luggage on this flight?"

"Why, no sir." A policeman dressed as an airline ground crewman played along with Ryder: "There was a mistake, I'm afraid, sir. The lady's luggage was placed instead on the Aeroflot flight to Moscow. My apologies, ma'am."

"It'll only be a short stay in Moscow and then you can continue to Los Angeles," Alec explained.

Jeanette was angry. "Why didn't you tell me?"

"Couldn't. Sorry." Ryder jerked a lever and icy wind blasted his face. A spotlight illuminated a metal stairway to the tarmac. "Aeroflot is holding their departure for us."

Across the tarmac sat Aeroflot flight 405 to Moscow. A set of portable stairs rested against an open door in the side of the airplane. The jet was fueled and ready for immediate departure. A bank of bright lights flooded the path between the planes and the area swarmed with heavily armed policemen.

23

Collisions

A robot slid the side door open on the delivery van and rolled out. It fell hard to the pavement and tumbled on its side. A mechanical claw reached out, extended against the asphalt and pushed the automaton erect again. A motor whirred and the drive belt ran furiously. The two-foot high welder oriented itself with a rapid 360-degree turn.

The ten million dollars worth of prototype lab equipment drove its treads at different speeds, turning like a miniature army tank. The onboard computer calculated a path to the center of the closest fence section. The robot stopped a yard short of a chain link fence, measured by a laser range finder.

The welding laser pumped itself to maximum power, far more than it used to dissect the policeman. A beautiful blue-green beam of light, thin as a scalpel's edge, struck the fencing and razored off the entire section from the rest of the fence. The chain link flopped in a smoldering curl, pipe stanchions ringing against the pavement.

A cousin robot's arm shut the van's door and started the engine. The robot drove over the downed fence. The welding robot tried to follow but fouled a rubber track on a ragged piece of chain link. It stalled and went into reverse, still caught. The welding robot seesawed back and forth, dragging the offending piece of chain link deeply into its gears. The entire drive mechanism jammed. The welding robot shut down to conserve battery power.

An alarm buzzed inside Dr. Mueller's control van. He selected the welding robot's camera and his monitor went blank with snow, indicating no reception of a signal. What the hell happened?

Mueller picked up a headset and listened to the ground controller. The instructions were spoken in English, the international flight language. The American Airlines 747 was cleared for departure, though the jet hadn't yet moved from the gate. There was no other flight with higher priority than the American 747.

Mueller slid open the door of his control van just a crack. Street traffic roared past only yards away. Across the boulevard, the freight terminal looked normal. He got out and waited for a break in the heavy traffic flow. Once across the street, he tried to stay in shadows, but it was impossible. Warehouse floodlights and street lamps for the employees' parking lot left few shadows. On the back side, though, where the gap had been cut in the fence, it was much darker.

He heard gravel crunch behind him and a car motor. He slipped into a niche in the concrete wall of a warehouse. A police car moved toward him. He pressed harder against the wall and felt its damp cold pierce his coveralls. The police car slid past, two worried faces shown him by the green light of dashboard instruments. The car lurched when it bumped over something and stopped abruptly. It backed up and lurched again. Both doors opened and the cops got out, shining flashlights on the decapitated corpse of their comrade in arms. He heard their soft gasping.

One of the cops had doubled over to vomit when Mueller opened up with a silenced Uzi. There was a cascade of soft "whumps" and then quiet. A quick inspection verified both of them were dead. He placed the Uzi in its shoulder holster and felt the warmth of its hot barrel nestled against his ribs.

A glint of moonlight off aluminum revealed the location of his immobilized robot. The galvanized wire of a chain link fence was too firmly entrenched in a sprocket gear for Mueller to free it with bare hands. He went to the police car and removed the keys from its ignition, wincing as he saw the time – 8:01 P.M. He listened to the distant whine of jet engines starting. But no aircraft was moving into position for takeoff. Fast as he could, Mueller opened the trunk and stripped the carpet from the spare tire well. He spun off a wing nut holding the lug wrench. Moving to the robot, he used the lug wrench as a crow bar, tearing fence wire loose.

He pressed reset on the device. The robot came to life and identified Mueller as a threat. The welding laser whirred and he jabbed his finger at the emergency off button, missing. The laser glowed and Mueller jabbed again. The laser shot only one quick pulse before ebbing away its energy.

Mueller checked his arm for a wound and found none. A burning smell caused him to turn around. He saw the police car's door smoldering with a wicked gash cut all the way through the door's panel and into the driver's seat.

He carefully set a delay timer on the robot and re-armed the device. Glancing at his watch, Mueller cringed. From behind the police car came the sound of huge jet engines moving toward him. The American Airlines 747's bright runway lights swept past him and continued along the runway. He bolted for the command van.

In the 747, pilot and copilot went through their preflight checklist and didn't see a Lufthansa Air Freight van move into their path. They braked to a halt at the beginning of the runway and applied power to massive Rolls Royce engines, knowing they would need all of the runway to raise their lumbering giant off the ground.

As the Boeing 747 strained against its brakes, Mueller knew he was too late to change the outcome. The van would collide with the wrong plane. He was certain from information given him in the last phone call that Jeanette Murphy and Alec Ryder would be on an Aeroflot flight to Moscow, scheduled to leave after this American Airlines departure.

Inside their van, robots continued their program with a logic he'd forgotten even existed. They scanned for the plane's identification transponder and found it. In response, the driver robot started the van's engine and engaged the automatic transmission. The robot van crept off the runway, seeking to avoid a collision with this plane instead of its intended target.

The 747 pilot released his brakes and the blimp-sized plane accelerated. Halfway down the runway, the copilot glimpsed a van and screamed. The pilot saw a Lufthansa Air Freight decal rushing toward him and tried to deflect the 747's enormous inertia. The plane's right wingtip missed the van by less than a foot.

Behind them, the Aeroflot jet waited for the 747's turbulence to subside before following that massive jet into the sky. To minimize delays for ensuing flights, ground controllers vectored the Moscow-bound jet to an alternate runway. The Aeroflot flight wouldn't have to wait long for the air flow to calm down.

While they sat, the Russian pilot let his eyes idle over the cockpit. He detected an error in the switch settings and corrected it by turning on the Aeroflot's transponder, transmitting international ID codes for the flight.

Inside their van, the robots heard the plane's transmission and understood what they were to do. Obediently, they committed suicide. Their van moved so its dark rear faced the jet. The van's transmission was put in neutral. The plane would now drag the van's inferno along the runway, maximizing damage. The two weather balloons were ruptured. An ugly, seething mess became an inferno, consuming everything inside the metallic shell of the van. At the end of the runway, the welding robot sat and waited. Its mission lay ahead – mop up survivors.

Fascination with the impending doom prevented Mueller from returning to his command van. The raw sexual power of death to come pulled him to a low fence along the runway. He paid no attention to three bodies lying at his feet. His whole being pulsed with anticipation of the climactic moment ahead. The Aeroflot flight began to move, rolling forward, gaining speed.

24

Betrayal

First class in the Aeroflot flight was two rows of battered leather seats separated by a shower curtain from a dense pack of people, animals and cargo. The stewardess tried to make up for lack of atmosphere with lots of wide smiles. Her grins cracked heavy makeup on her stolid, aging face. She poured lots of cheap, sweet champagne. Alec gagged on his first glass and the urge for a cigarette overpowered him. He couldn't light up. The "No Smoking" sign was on. He felt himself pressed in the seat as the jet lurched forward. It seemed to him the pilot was really gunning the throttles. He forced a smile at the stewardess sitting in a fold-down jump seat opposite him. She cracked the makeup again in an automatic reflex but stared past him down the aisle.

The plane bounced across the concrete sections and his champagne glass kept time by splashing bubbly syrup on his hand. He stole a look at Jeanette. Her face was taut and hard. She was turning the pages of a multilingual in-flight magazine, examining each page briefly before rejecting it for the next. To him, she looked annoyed and tense.

The instinct that kept him alive as a CIA operative told Alec disaster was coming even before he felt anything. Engine pitch changed to a frantic whine and the champagne flew onto his sleeve when the aircraft's nose jerked upward. The engines' power pressed him hard into the seat but only for a short moment before the seat belt cut deep and his head flew forward.

Alec felt his eye socket jump with pain from a collision with the rising knee of the stewardess. There was a flood of sound and bitterly cold air attacking him from behind. The chill was immediately replaced by worse heat than he'd ever felt. Drops of melted plastic embedded themselves in the back of his head and neck.

Then silence and cold. Sick fear swirled in his guts. He started to look toward Jeanette and was driven into his seat. The horizon twisted and tilted. The noise of the jet's fuselage rending against the runway shrieked in his eardrums. The cabin flinched, twitching violently while his feet jumped around. His seat bent at an unnatural angle against the rest of the enclosure.

The pilot appeared, his face dripping blood from hundreds of glass cuts. One shard jutted from his cheek. His eyes were lifeless and dazed. He walked past Alec and into the void that once held the rest of his plane. The back half was now a crematorium, left a football field behind. Alec heard the dull thump and moaning of the pilot as he fell from the sharp, jutting edge at the back of the first-class section.

Ryder stared uncomprehendingly at the stewardess, whose face twitched as she unbuckled her seatbelt and stood. She staggered to the edge of the precipice where the pilot fell and leaned against Alec's seatback. His chair pivoted in response and he nearly tumbled backward onto the pilot, stopping only by grabbing Jeanette's armrest.

The stewardess teetered on the brink and he shot an arm out to catch her. She fell on him and clumsily righted herself, slumping into her little jump seat.

Ryder managed to look at Jeanette. She was terrified but intact. He struggled upright and realized the seat was attached to him, pulling him down with its weight. He unclasped the seatbelt and the assembly tumbled on top of the dead pilot. Alec went inside the cockpit and found the copilot and navigator. Ryder shucked chunks of glass windscreen off the copilot's upper torso.

"Are you badly hurt?" Ryder muttered.

"No, I don't think so." The copilot was amazed to be alive.

"Can you help me with the navigator?" Alec asked.

"Ah, sure." The copilot twisted out of his seat and nearly fainted from the pain of broken ribs. But he got up and leaned over the limp form of the navigator.

Alec felt the man's neck and gingerly lifted his head. His eyes blinked to life.

"What the hell happened?" the navigator demanded.

The copilot pointed toward fiery remains behind them. "We hit a truck parked in the runway. Some idiot from Lufthansa Freight parked there. The damn thing tore off the back of our plane. It must have been carrying some hellish concoction, because it blew us to pieces, incinerating the passenger compartment."

"Come on, let's get out of here. Help's on the way," Alec suggested. He pulled on the man's elbow and lifted the navigator to his feet.

The copilot suddenly became aware that his pilot was missing. "Dmitri! Where's Dmitri?!"

"You can't help him," Alec responded. "He's dead. Fell off the back of this section and was impaled. Come on, let's get the hell out of here before a fire starts."

Ryder dragged them with his words and his hands. They staggered toward the exit door behind the cockpit. Jeanette had it open and was deploying a slide with the stewardess. The men insisted the women go first. The women declined firmly. They would not be the first to try the slide.

Ryder told the navigator to go. When he wouldn't, Alec pushed him and he tumbled head first down the soft, slick plastic, arriving at the bottom in a heap.

When the copilot refused, Alec ordered Jeanette to go and she grabbed her briefcase and jumped gracefully, feet out, landing on the slide. At the bottom, she startled Alec by rolling to her feet and disappearing. Instinctively, he followed, far less gracefully and rolled on his side. He lurched to his feet, brushing dirt off his slacks and sports coat.

He looked for Jeanette and stopped, riveted by the molten passenger compartment in the distance. "Rocket fuel. How did he know which plane we took …?"

The thought was cut off by a scream behind him. Ryder turned to see the copilot kneeling at the end of the ramp, his hands to his face. An invisible sword cut into him and the man's chest severed from his stomach. The copilot fell apart in sections. The stewardess bowled into him from behind as she completed her slide.

Alec watched in horror as a blue scalpel slit her face, then dissected her also. He whirled to see the welding robot sliding toward the plane. He grabbed for his gun and found it missing. The laser turned in his direction.

Alec tumbled to the ground and heard hissing as the terrifying weapon cut off a chunk of the cockpit. He saw his gun where it had fallen when he'd tumbled off the end of the slide. Ryder sprang to a crouch and threw himself at the 9-mm automatic.

The red lights of an approaching fire engine slid across the broken cockpit windscreen and glinted vividly, confusing the robot. It cut viciously into the airframe and ignited magnesium fires where it touched.

The distraction gave Alec time. He fired and was ashamed at his erratic aim. Three shots went high and wide. He tried to breathe calmly and failed. His hand jerked the trigger and another burst went low.

The laser came around to him and Alec rolled, seeking cover. He tried to hide behind a chunk of the fuselage, but the laser tore through it and seared flesh on his leg. Ryder howled in pain and the automatic fell from his grasp.

On his hands and knees, Alec waited to die and prayed for it to be quick. The laser pulsed intensely and tore away his cover, moving toward him.

Then it died. The robot battery, drained by its fight with the chain link fence, expired. It would sit and wait for some charge to return, then fight as much as it could.

But Alec gave the robot no second chance. He picked up the gun and hobbled over to the vicious automaton, exhausting his clip at point blank range into the machinery.

Pain from his leg wound came in nauseating waves and threatened to force him to pass out. A rescue worker put an arm around him and helped him to walk away.

"What in God's name caused all this?" the astonished man wondered, looking at the wreck and the bisected corpses.

Alec muttered, "We were betrayed."

"Betrayed? What do you mean?"

"The KGB. Only they knew in time to set us up." A wheelchair was unfolded and Alec refused it.

"The KGB? They're gone from Hungary. Here, sit down. You're delirious," the rescue worker demanded.

"No. They're here. They want something. Very badly. They wanted me to put myself, Jeanette and the data . . . Oh, God, the data!" Ryder limped back to the slide and tried to climb a slick chute. He tore furiously at the plastic and collapsed from exhaustion.

"All right, all right!" he heard shouted at him. "What is it you want?" Alec looked at firefighters in the doorway above him. A ladder was propped against the torn section of plane.

"A cardboard box. In an overhead compartment. It's very important," Ryder shouted with all the energy he could summon. The firefighters disappeared, looking puzzled.

Alec felt a soft touch on his arm. He turned and saw Jeanette, her face soiled with dirt.

Ryder screamed at her. "Where did you go, damn it!"

She retreated in shock. "To that other piece of the plane, to see if I could do any good. It was way too late. Hopeless. They were doomed. There was nothing I could do. What happened to your leg? It looks horrible, but surgical, like it was cauterized."

"Is this that box you wanted?" The shout came from above Alec. He turned from Jeanette, feeling ambivalence about her story. Her concern for him seemed false. He screamed over wailing sirens. "Yes, that's the box."

The cardboard box slipped to his feet along the escape chute. The box was still tied with string. Jeanette bent to pick it up and he stopped her. He grabbed the box himself. He pushed her away. She looked angry and puzzled.

Damn, she's good, he thought. Very fast on her feet. Where did she really go? What was she looking for when she disappeared? Then again, maybe she's for real and I can't believe it.

A clipboard appeared in his path, with a pencil and a woman attached. "What's your name?" demanded the clipboard woman. "We need the names of all the survivors."

"Mr. and Mrs. James Smith."

"Smith?" she wondered, looking skeptical.

"Yes. From Louisville, Kentucky. Don't worry. We'll get a cab to the Hyatt and call our children to let them know we're safe. Thank you." He brushed the clipboard woman aside.

"Smith?" Jeanette asked, as he limped toward the freight area. "Why the deception?"

"For the moment, the people who tried to kill us tonight may not know we're alive. That gives us an edge and we need all the edge we can get. These people are good and they won't stop. What are they after, Jeanette, that's worth killing a plane load of people?"

"How would I know?" She acted stunned.

"Because you've looked at this data. Because the answer is in here somehow."

"Alec, you've had quite a shock tonight, from this accident. None of what you say makes any sense." Her tone was perfect, but she couldn't quite look at him.

"How long have you known, Jeanette, that the data you were compiling was for a search? How long have you suspected?" His hand bit into her arm and she winced, jerked her arm away and rubbed it.

"Not long," she whispered at the ground.

"How long, damn it!"

She looked at him with defiance. "I didn't date you because I wanted your protection. If that's what you think, go your own damn way. I can take care of myself." She turned and walked toward the air cargo area.

A movement caught his eye. "Jeanette!" he screamed and tore the gun from its holster.

He saw the silenced Uzi pivot from her to a more immediate threat, himself. Alec squeezed the trigger, but his gun dry-fired on an empty clip. A stream of bullets wove toward him, tearing out dirt and grass. "Get down," he shouted. He threw away the box and rolled behind a clump of dry brush. His left hand furiously sought the extra clip and couldn't find it. The bullets must have fallen out somewhere, he thought.

Alec heard "whumping" again and her muffled scream. More dirt flew around him and he rolled, pained by a hard lump in his right pocket. The stupid clip, that's where it is, he thought to himself. He jammed the clip home and fired blindly, hoping to hit a man in dark coveralls with a Lufthansa logo above his breast pocket. Alec rolled again, shooting and scooting, avoiding return fire.

He waited. Nothing. He crawled forward and waited some more. Sirens wailed. He flashed his head up and then down. In the distance, he thought he saw a man in Lufthansa coveralls running away. He dared expose himself again. Yes, the man was running through street traffic toward a van.

Alec moved to Jeanette and found her trembling, holding her rib cage. "How bad," he asked.

"Grazed. Shocked the hell out of me. I'm sorry, Alec. I didn't think it was for real before. A man killing all those people was too crazy to be real. Do you know what I mean?"

"Yeah, sort of. Come on, let's get out of here. We've got to hide so we can think."

They got up, grabbed the cardboard box and staggered off. Alec watched the van disappear into traffic and felt a strange presence from its driver. Where in the hell had he felt that man before? It was recently, damn it. He should be able to remember the guy. Ryder was certain he'd met the killer in the last few days. Alec had stood close enough to touch him.

25

Flight

Retreating galled him. He could have run Alec Ryder out of ammunition and shot Jeanette Murphy. Instead, police converging from every direction forced "Dr. Mueller" to retreat. He left his targets as unfinished business and boarded an unmarked private Learjet waiting for him at Ferihegy II airport. It'd taken considerable political muscle to use the field reserved for the Hungarian national airline *Malév*. But there was no choice. Budapest's other airport, Ferihegy I, would be closed for a long time due to the collision between the Aeroflot flight and his robot-controlled delivery van.

He tore heavy makeup from his face and flung it away in the privacy of his Learjet. He yanked off the rubbery nose and slapped it down. Damn!

Tens of millions wasted and irreplaceable robots destroyed. Why had a welding robot simply quit when it was set to vivisect Ryder?

But then, why did an Aeroflot pilot become a jet jockey and gun down the runway? If he'd done a normal takeoff, the cockpit would've made contact with the van. The first-class cabin would've been a crematorium. No one could have survived when the inferno shot through the plane.

He pulled out a new mask and prepared his face. When he was done, he compared the results to a passport photo – identical. Now he was Ray Stewart, Captain U.S. Navy, retired. Ray Stewart worked as a recruiter of top talent in the aerospace industry.

His Lufthansa coveralls were put in a Top Secret "burn bag" and then inside a diplomatic pouch. The locked briefcase was handed to a courier in the back of the plane. "Captain Ray Stewart" dressed himself in a $5,000 blue suit with silver pinstripes and a bold red silk tie. Cordovan wingtips completed the conservative power look.

A short flight and the Learjet received permission for taxiing into the Concorde area at Orly Airport, outside Paris. He went from his private plane to the Concorde with less than a minute to spare. French Customs waived any inspection of his luggage, passport or briefcase. Captain Stewart helped the *Surete* and French Intelligence with jobs over the years and this small favor in return was not a problem.

26

Run

Alec saw light pushing against the dirty curtain of a cheap hotel room. The night was over and he wasn't ready. Alec needed time to think and yet couldn't seem to think. He just saw the horror of the crash replayed in an endless loop, the certainty of death until the welding robot failed, the numb fear of being shot. The laser swath burned into his leg didn't help. The wound wasn't in danger of becoming infected, but the deep cut throbbed when he sat and nearly killed him when he tried to walk.

He watched the sunlight become more insistent with each minute. Ryder felt the hunted animal's fear of certain death when it's cornered. The fear paralyzed him. Only raging hunger drove him to awaken Jeanette and leave the illusion of safety provided by four walls.

The hotel had no elevator so he let Jeanette carry the cardboard box of data. Ryder agonized down each step, gripping the banister with both hands. There was a chair in the dingy lobby and he tried sitting in it. The throbbing pain was worse than when he moved. Alec got up again. The smell of rancid cooking oil hit him when he exited to the street. He followed his nose to a six table restaurant. There was no room to stretch his leg when they sat and waited for whatever the cook/owner/waiter/busboy would make of their order.

Jeanette took a well-read newspaper off the counter, returning to their table and folding the daily back to its front page. She glanced at it for a second before placing the front page in front of him. Her eyes were dull and glazed. Jeanette spoke flatly. "We're in trouble."

He responded sarcastically. "I don't need a newspaper to tell me that."

She tapped her finger on a new column. "More trouble."

Alec tried to focus bleary eyes on a companion article to the airport tragedy. A picture of him accompanied a minor headline – "Budapest Interpol Inspector Implicated in Crash." The Commissioner of City Services was interviewed and flatly stated that Alec Ryder had disappeared from the area after surviving the crash and was wanted for questioning in regard to his aiding a fugitive from justice in her attempt to escape Hungary. Jeanette Murphy's passport photo was at the bottom of the first page.

The owner didn't pay any special attention when he brought them a basket of stale bread and instant coffee. Undissolved crystals still floated in the lukewarm water. Then Alec realized that they looked like street bums, not like the photos. Ryder turned the paper over anyway.

He tore at the bread and drank some of the "coffee" just to soften the dry loaf. Through his clogged mouth, he asked a question. "What's in this data that's worth killing us for?"

"Killing us, Alec? I assume it's your KGB, again. You told me they don't need an excuse for killing us." She tore the bread into small chunks and dipped them in her coffee.

"They aren't, unfortunately, *my* KGB. Look, you said you didn't crack this data. I think you're lying."

"Fuck you, Ryder." She grabbed the bread, put it in her briefcase and started to get up, then looked at the street and sat down again, defeated. She didn't meet his stare, just gazed at the empty grayness outside.

"Why don't you leave?" Alec felt genuinely puzzled.

"Because I've nowhere to go," came her laconic reply.

"Then you better tell me what you know." He slapped the taped lid of the cardboard box to emphasize his point.

"There's nothing in that box but old newspapers."

"What did you do with the damn data?" He seethed.

She whispered an answer. "I sent it to a friend."

He could barely hear her. He leaned closer. "Where is your friend?"

"He works at an Air Force think tank. Nothing but Ph.D. geniuses. He's the best at databases." She turned and looked at him now. There was nothing in her eyes but fear. "If he can't crack the puzzle, Alec, no one can. I sure as hell can't. I've no idea what they're looking for, other than us."

Fury built inside him but Alec controlled it long enough to ask another question. "Who sent the package for you?"

Jeanette didn't answer.

"It was Usulak, wasn't it? That stupid, horny fool, always gawking at everything in skirts."

"No. I sent it. I gave the package to Federal Express. They came to the house and picked it up."

"Bullshit!" exploded from him. Now the owner was watching them intently. Ryder folded the paper under his arm and staggered to his feet. He grabbed her with one arm and the box with the other. Then he realized there was no need to carry that stupid box anymore and dropped it. "Come on, we're getting out of here."

She let him drag her into the street. "Where are we going?"

"Somewhere I can call Usulak and you can call this *genius*," he snorted.

Ryder tried to focus on finding a payphone but just kept seeing her running a hand over Usulak's crotch and telling him how policemen really turned her on. He'd been an idiot to leave her with that weak shit.

He found a phone booth on the other side of the street and pulled her inside. Instinct made him turn around and Alec saw the restaurant owner's wife pointing at them. Ryder forgot the phone and ducked into a used clothing store, limping through racks to an alley behind. Alec hobbled to a corner and flagged a taxi.

"Where to?" the driver asked.

Ryder's mind went blank.

"Lady, do you know where you want to go?"

"Yes, but you can't take me there," came her dry reply.

The driver started to say something but lost the words. Before the cabby formulated another question, Alec spoke. "Take us to the main fire station in Budapest."

27

Cauterize

Ray Stewart slept a little on the Concorde and felt refreshed when the supersonic transport landed in New York. He walked to an executive lounge and sipped a Perrier until his flight to Los Angeles was called.

At LAX, a limousine driver fetched his suitcase and drove him up La Cienega, through Beverly Hills to Sunset Boulevard, finally arriving at the Bel-Air Hotel. He wandered the gardens, enjoying swans gliding in their moat, until his appointment showed.

They went to the terrace for dinner, exploiting the balmy Southern California night, a marked contrast to the bitter damp of Budapest, only hours away for him. Ray Stewart was charming and sensitive, inserting the answer to each objection and portraying the advantages of a few well-paying years abroad to his flattered subject. Glossy brochures for Ray

Stewart Executive Recruiters and a photo album showed other Americans in Saudi Arabia. Photos of attractive women lounging around a pool were effective when combined with all the right technical challenges. The man was ready to sign.

The stroked ego and full bladder excused himself and left for the men's room. With perfect – and paid for timing – the target's entrée arrived the moment he vanished into the restroom. Once the waiter turned his back, Ray Stewart planted small time-release capsules in his victim's entrée. The object of Ray Stewart's non-stop attention returned and ate one of the best meal of his entire life. He didn't notice even one of the soft gelatin capsules.

Stewart walked the man back to the canopied hotel entrance and had a limousine driver take the overwhelmed technician to his small, rent-controlled apartment in Santa Monica. Then, Ray Stewart changed both his clothes and his appearance and waited. In an hour, he let the doorman tuck him into a taxicab and rode to the Century City Marriott, where he sipped a non-alcoholic beer, then caught another taxi.

When Ray stepped out and paid the modest fare, he was only a block away from a small, rent-controlled apartment in Santa Monica. The apartment was up a flight of concrete stairs floating on a pair of dingy steel beams. He reached the top and walked with light footsteps. Thin decorative lines etched in the walkway once matched a turquoise metal railing's shape. Now the lines were filled with dirt and the thin leaves from a nearby acacia tree dusted the walk. Only a single porch light was lit in the run-down building. Unfortunately, that glowing bulb sat outside his target's door. Ray halted to unscrew the glass cover. Hundreds of fried insects fell out when he removed the cover and loosened the bulb.

Ray Stewart waited and listened. There was a television set pulsing light through a curtained window at the end of the landing. Somewhere a phone rang in a first floor apartment. Ray knocked on the cheap door below a tarnished brass "3." He watched the peep hole for a change that meant someone had come to the door. There was no response. The adjacent window was open and only a screen kept Ray outside. The window screen came off easily and he stepped into a mildewed apartment. A dim light filtered along the hallway.

In the center of the green shag carpet was a grotesque replica of the man who dined with Ray at the Bel-Air Hotel. The victim's face was tortured, his hands rigid, clawing the air. One shoe had popped off and the foot was arched in spasm. The man's eyes were shut, but his tongue had been swallowed and his face was purple with suffocation.

Ray Stewart made certain to be careful when he moved around the corpse, avoiding contact with the dead man. Ray didn't want to take an antidote to the deadly nerve agent contained in the gelatin capsules. The antidote drug would slow his reactions and dull his mind.

The closest bedroom served as the victim's study. Stewart ran a low-intensity flashlight over the study, avoiding windows. Clutter lay heaped on clutter in layers, like an archeological dig. Ray sighed and went over the top layer of computer printouts and scribbled notes, careful not to disturb anything. Discouraged, he left and tried the bedroom and the bathroom. Ray found an attic crawl space hatch in a closet and opened the access door. He swept that hidden space with his light and found nothing. Ray played back messages on an answering machine and made certain they were saved. Again nothing. He returned to the corpse and opened the man's coat with reluctance. A careful check of his pockets also turned up nothing.

Disgusted, Stewart tried to find satisfaction in the man's clever mode of death. The drugs wouldn't be looked for in an autopsy. They were intended for battlefield use only and would be impossible to detect by the time this body was discovered. The gelatin caps had already disappeared in the victim's stomach. His symptoms could be mistaken for an epilepsy attack and the technician had a long history of that disease, a frequent companion of genius. The man had been a recognized genius in his field.

Still, this setback was going to cost Ray Stewart another day away from his lifelong goal, an intolerable delay when he was so close. Yet Ray had no choice but to go inside where the man worked, an Air Force think tank.

28

Hide

Alec accepted a sandwich from Fire Captain Michael Toth, back at work after the hospital stay. Ryder ate and talked, giving Toth a summary of events leading to their arrival at the fire house. Alec finished talking and asked Michael if he had any questions. Ryder took a bite of his ham sandwich while the Fire Captain examined the new facts.

"Well, there's really only one thing you left out." Toth gave Ryder a wan smile. "What do you need?"

"A safe place to hide – with an untapped phone. Some money, not a lot. Ammunition for my gun."

The Fire Captain reached in his desk drawer and took out a door key and an envelope. Michael pushed them across the desk to Alec. "My father-in-law died in the warehouse arson. The City Commissioner slammed my father-in-law as an incompetent. Nothing could be farther from the truth. So I believe you and not that self-serving politician."

"Thanks." Alec mumbled through a mouth stuffed with food. He'd been starving.

Michael tapped the thick envelope. "This is cash from his last paychecks, including a lot of unused vacation and sick leave. He left it to my wife and me in his will. The money should keep you going for a while. What kind of ammunition do you need?"

"NATO 9-mm. Some extra clips would be nice."

"I'll work on it, Alec. In the meantime, you'll find a hunting shotgun in his closet. Ammo is on top of the bathroom cupboard. Just birdshot, I'm afraid. No good for stopping a maniac like that arsonist." Michael reached in his drawer again and shoved car keys across the desk to Alec. "My father-in-law's car is still parked in the apartment garage. Battery's good. I checked, started the car yesterday. Fired right up. How do I contact you?"

"Don't. Let me call you. You're likely to be watched."

Toth thought for a moment. "How do you know I'm not being watched right now? They might have seen you come here."

"Maybe, but that was a chance I had to take."

"How will you get out without being followed, assuming they were watching?"

"Is there a back way out?" Alec wondered.

"I've got a better idea. Wait here." The fireman glanced out the door of his office at a truck. Toth left them alone.

Jeanette spoke for the first time since they'd left the cab. "Alec, I'm sorry."

His face turned to stone. "How much, Jeanette?"

"What do you mean?" She blushed.

"No, not how much did Usulak pay you for screwing him. I know what that cost, a little detour on the way to the airport so you could fedex the data package to your friend. I want to know how much this shit they're after is worth. A million dollars, U.S.? Ten? A hundred?" He glared at her.

"Possibly a hundred million. Assuming you're right about the KGB involvement, the total value is a lot more." She looked normal for the first time since they'd left the hotel room that morning. Her pretense dropped and her energy returned.

Ryder had expected some bullshit evasion. He was stunned by her candor. He couldn't help but ask, "How valuable is this treasure?"

"I think the KGB is trying to steal Budapest. They might be playing table stakes for all of Hungary."

"What would the KGB do with Hungary?" Alec was skeptical.

"Live. Prosper. Russia's crumbling, at the moment. It may come back, but that's a long shot." Jeanette gave him a calm but cynical look.

"OK, I buy that. Hungary has Western European ties. Living here, it's easy to move contraband goods between Russia and the Common Market. How close is the KGB to reaching its goal?"

"I'm not sure, Alec. Whatever this killing machine is really doing, it's not psychotic blundering. He wants something that's absolutely key to their conquest." She looked keen and alert to him now.

"Do you want to stop them or profit from them?"

"I don't think they can be stopped, Alec, not after what I saw last night. They're going to find a way to rule Hungary, even if this path doesn't work. It's like drug lords being the real government of Colombia. Enough money and they can be legitimate, not a Mafia. The only thing that would stop them is war. They won't let it come to that. They're too smart."

He studied her in amazement. "So you want to find whatever they're after, first – your strategy is beat them to the goal and sell this hidden treasure to them."

"Yes." Her eyes brightened.

"What happens then?"

"We'll spend the money, live like a king and queen." Jeanette radiated

"What makes you think they'll let us live to spend it? You mentioned the Mafia. The KGB has a better reach than even the Mafia."

"No they don't, Alec. Their empire is washing away daily. A lot of their power vanished with the turnover of East Germany. A huge portion of their intelligence network was exposed, broken. The cracks went everywhere. Plus, Alec, they only want Hungary. We can convince them to leave us alone. We'll live like royalty."

He wondered if the gleaming in her eyes was from greed or madness? Maybe greed like that caused madness. He sensed someone in the office doorway. Ryder turned to see a firefighter carrying turn-out gear for them to wear – helmets, coats, boots and pants.

A few minutes later, the Budapest Fire Department responded to a false alarm in the neighborhood where Michael Toth's father-in-law had lived. The firetruck parked in the street and firefighters checked surrounding buildings. After the search, the truck departed, carrying the same number of firefighters as when it left the station house. Two of them, though, had come off the cab's floorboards to fill vacant slots left by Alec and Jeanette.

* * *

The apartment was tiny, like Alec's, but modern by Paris standards, meaning the building was only thirty years old. When Jeanette excused herself to use the bathroom, Ryder made certain there was no back exit where she could evaporate on him. He found a rusting fire escape ladder crossing the bedroom window, but the frame was painted shut. She'd have to shatter the glass and that should give him plenty of warning. Anyone breaking in would make enough noise to awaken the dead. Before they got to the bedroom window, the metal fire escape would have to be extended to the ground. Even a ladder placed against the wobbly structure would cause its metal frame to creak and groan.

He found the shotgun in a closet, as Michael indicated. Alec waited until Jeanette was out of the bathroom, went inside and pocketed the box of shells. Michael was right again and the loads were only bird shot. But an adversary wouldn't know Ryder couldn't kill them. At close range, the bird shot would remove a face from someone's head. Alec decided against loading the shotgun in the apartment. He didn't want it used on his face.

Ryder sat at the kitchen table and realized how far beyond exhausted he was. When would the abuse end? Not for a long time was the honest answer. In contrast, he couldn't go much longer without sleep.

Alec picked up the telephone and dialed Usulak's office number. He tracked the seconds dial on his watch. Ryder didn't want this call traced.

The familiar voice answered. "Detectives, Usulak speaking."

Ryder didn't bother to introduce himself. "You're an asshole, Szige."

"Alec? Where are you?"

"Who did you send Jeanette's package to, Szige? You owe me one, buddy. I almost bought it last night because of you."

"Alec . . . I didn't think there was any harm . . ."

"In screwing her while the wife was out of the house, Szige – or in mailing a little package for her?" Alec saw thirty seconds had passed, but he waited for the answer.

"Alec, no man is safe with her, I swear it." There was a nervous cough at the other end of the phone. "Listen, Alec, we ought to meet and talk about it. You can't throw away our friendship like …"

"I'll meet you in hell, Szige. These bastards won't keep you around long. Your wife won't keep you either after I tell her. Is she home now, Szige? Or should I call her at her school? Think she'd believe me, Szige?"

"OK, Alec, I got your point. What do you want?" The question sounded more like a hiss than a whisper.

"A clean call. One payphone to another. Some answers, no bullshit. In fifteen minutes exactly. You know where. Don't get tailed. I'm not going to live very long, but it'll be long enough to kill your kids, Szige. You, I'll leave alive. You can fall asleep each night remembering what happened. I'm not bluffing." Ryder hung up. Less than two minutes. Not traceable.

He found Jeanette lying on the bed asleep. He woke her and she jumped up, startled. "You have to make a phone call. I can't do it. You've got to call that genius of yours and find out if he knows anything. You've got to do it now. Do you have his home phone number?"

"Sure." Jeanette looked in her briefcase for the address book. She found the number and started to dial, then stopped. "Alec, he'd be at work now, not at home."

"So dial him at this think tank. Keep the call short, so it can't be traced."

"Traced?"

"Yeah, my brilliant computer guru. You sent him a package, remember? Usulak knew. Usulak has a wife and kids. He's not hard to threaten. He's also not being chased all over Budapest. I just checked. That means he sold out. So they know about your friend. If the guy's in one piece, they may have some way of tracing this call. Be terse and hang up when I tell you."

"Oh, God, Alec. I'm so sorry." She deflated into a kitchen chair. "I've been so stupid."

"And so greedy, Jeanette. Stupid greedy. Plus ruthless. Play any angle you can to make it, huh?"

"Alec …"

"Just dial, Jeanette. Maybe we can walk away from this thing in one piece. I don't want to hear your crap."

She looked at him with her mouth slightly open, unable to find anymore words. Her fingers hit the touchtone pad and she waited. "Fred Jennings, please." She waited some more. "No message. I'll call back." She hung up. "They said he wasn't in yet. They wanted me to leave a number where he could reach me."

"Good girl. Now you're getting smart. Call back in five minutes and we'll see what happens."

They sat in the kitchen and stared at the cabinets and waited for the eternal five minutes to pass.

Alec got restless. Ryder decided to try retrieving messages from his office recorder. Maybe the other side had been a little careless and left his messages intact. He was delighted to find he had two voicemails. The first was from the girl at the phone company, leaving her name and number. The second call was from Gregory Yevchentko, giving a long string of characters Ryder was supposed to think was an encoded message. Alec hung up. It was a trap. They wanted him on that line long enough to locate him by tracing the call.

A few more minutes and they'd try the think tank again. A lot would be learned in a few minutes.

29

Think Tank

FBI Special Agent George Halliday surveyed a metal desk and filing cabinet. A computer terminal blinked at him, demanding a password. "Is this the only office Fred Jennings had?"

"Well, I don't quite know how to answer your question, Mr. Halliday. Perhaps if you came back tomorrow, we could arrange a transfer of your clearances," the head of security hedged.

"I'll be in Rome tomorrow, unfortunately, Mr. Browning. We have very strong reason to believe that Fred Jennings compromised several Top Secret projects. We think he's about to leak more sensitive data to the other side." Halliday leaned closer. "If it's true, Mr. Browning, we have to change the President's itinerary for the next month. That will raise diplomatic hell and the President won't do it without solid evidence. On the other hand, Mr. Browning, imagine what happens if Air Force One is knocked out of the sky by a missile with the President onboard."

Browning paled. In thirty years playing the security game, he'd never come even close to such an electric moment. He'd known his work was very serious and important. But now, finally, he personally could make a difference. "Come on," he said.

They went past an open bay of 1950's-style gray metal desks and into a corridor ending at a door whose lock was a keypad. Browning shielded the combination with one hand while he keyed it in with the other. "Wait here while I sanitize the area."

In a moment, the door opened again. Halliday walked along a narrow corridor pulsing with a rotating police light. Blue flashes hit a dozen curious stares, people standing in office doorways to get a look at this important visitor. Halliday smiled a thin, controlled smile, looking official and important. Browning led Halliday to a small office with Moseler safes and the same 1950's gray metal desk, battered by decades of tenants.

A metal table in the same dead gray and edged with the same gray rubber sat wedged between the door and the desk. Stacks of dusty papers flooded the table. An old-fashioned chalkboard was properly erased to conform with security procedures. The desk chair had an Air Force property tag visible on a front leg.

Halliday was about to leave when he looked under the desk, almost as an afterthought. Electricity pulsed through him. He'd found the data box, Federal Express label prominent on its top. He urged Browning backward, pushing the desk chair away and dragging out the box. "This is it. Exactly what we needed. No wonder Jennings hid this back here. Mr. Jennings never thought I'd get this far. Thanks to you, Mr. Browning, the President is safe."

The security man blushed.

Halliday ran his finger across the return address. "There's his controller. She uses 'Jeanette Murphy' on all her correspondence to him. Has a residence here as cover and a full set of tax records, everything." Halliday started out with the package, but the security man stopped him.

"This is awkward, I know, but we have very strict procedures here, Mr. Halliday. I can't just let you walk out of this area with a package."

"Can I sign for it?"

"Of course. I didn't mean you couldn't take it with you. I just have to open it and make certain nothing classified is inside. Then, I'll get you to sign a receipt and you'll be on your way."

Halliday reluctantly set the parcel down on the table.

Browning flipped open the unsealed package and rifled through pages. "Well, I don't see any headers on this computer printout saying the data is classified. It doesn't look like anything a terrorist would care about, though. Are you sure this is the right thing?"

"Definitely."

"Well, it'll just be a minute while I round up the form. One of the secretaries has it, I'm sure. Wait here." Browning went across the hall and a middle-aged woman opened her desk and drew out a yellow pad of forms.

Halliday couldn't hear their conversation completely, but he did hear the word "FBI" and smiled wryly.

The telephone rang. He hesitated, then picked up. He decided not to say anything, let the other person speak first. There was a long pause.

"Fred?"

"Is this Jeanette Murphy?" He was astonished to hear the Impostor's voice.

"Who the hell is this? Where's Fred?"

He smoothly improvised. "Jeanette, this is Special Agent Halliday of the Federal Bureau of Investigation. Where are you?"

Another pause. "Where's Fred?"

"Fred Jennings is dead, Jeanette. Where are you? Are you with Ryder? Get away from him Jeanette. The KGB's trying to kill Ryder. You'll get hurt too, if you stay with him. We can bring you in. Where are you?"

Another long pause.

"OK, look, just get away from him, Jeanette. Ryder has to sleep. Get away and go to the American Embassy. Understand me?"

He waited but there was only a click and the line went dead. He put the phone down and swiveled in the desk chair to see Browning staring at him in disbelief. "Come in, Browning, and shut the door. I can see I need to brief you. What I said can't go any farther. We can't afford leaks."

A few minutes later, most of which were spent waiting for credibility, Halliday opened the door. He thanked Browning for his cooperation and began walking out of the security area unescorted. No one challenged him. With luck, he thought, they won't find Browning's corpse until I clear the building.

He could feel the stares on the back of his head when he cleared the second door of a man trap buffering people between sets of cipher locks. He exited the outer door and moved in a quick walk to the stairs. Security guards were in the lobby. They were carrying guns.

He tried to bluff his way through. He began his descent, moving at a sedate, confident pace. Their phone rang. A guard picked up, stared at Halliday in astonishment, then pulled his gun. The other automatically pivoted and drew.

Halliday stopped, looking into the muzzles of two .44 magnums.

30

Movement

Jeanette hung up the phone exactly on Alec's cue.

"It wasn't Fred, was it?"

"No. It wasn't Fred." Jeanette realized Alec was staring at her and looked away.

"Who was it?" he requested gently.

"I don't know."

"What did they say?" he prodded.

"Nothing, other than Fred wasn't there. That's all."

He watched her very carefully. She looked honestly tired and scared. If she was lying, she was really good at it. He got up from the table. "I have to go out. You get some sleep. You're safe here for tonight. Don't be a fool and leave. You've got food here, a bed."

"I'm not going anywhere, Alec." She talked with heavy bitterness. "I've got nowhere to run."

"OK. I'll be back some time tonight. It just depends on what happens in a couple of phone calls. I can't make them from here." He moved to the front door and looked at her again. She was staying put, it seemed to him. He opened the door a crack, peeked out.

"Alec," she called out.

"Yes." He slipped the door closed.

"Nothing." She looked at a vanishing point on a distant horizon, way beyond the walls of the apartment.

Yeah, he decided, that word summed it up. Nothing. He started to leave and remembered the shotgun. He didn't want to walk into the apartment and have its barrel pointed at him. Besides, a weapon might prove handy. He went along the hallway and picked up the gun. He was surprised to catch a trace of disappointment in her eyes, just a brief flash. He really ought to handcuff her to the bed. But then, he thought better of it and left.

She stayed in his gut as he started the car Michael Toth said would be there, stayed in his gut as he drove to the phone booth miles away. Finally, he refocused and called the "safe" phone where Szige was supposed to wait. There was no answer after eighteen rings and he hung up. Maybe Usulak was delayed trying to lose a tail.

Ryder dragged out the sheet of paper where he'd written the number of the phone company girl and tried her. She picked up on the first ring.

"This is Ryder. You left a message for me."

"Oh, yes, Inspector . . ." she stalled distantly.

He checked his watch. Could they trap him in less than three minutes because she was directly at the central switch? He'd give her only two and a half, then cut it off. "Look, I'm in a helluva hurry. You got something for me or what?"

"Well, maybe. We had a funny call from an old woman who said a fake telephone lineman came around. He talked to her and left without repairing her phone. I handled the initial call from her. We got cut off just as I was transferring her to a supervisor. Yet she claimed she'd talked to a supervisor and been told this lineman was OK. We sent someone out and they found her wires had been tapped. The outgoing circuit was cut at the junction box in the basement. I remembered you finding where this Satan's Touch creep did a phone tap. Maybe he did both taps."

"Yeah," Ryder cut in. Two minutes and a half exactly. Did he dare risk it?

"I got her number here and address. You want it?"

"Sure." He wrote the information down and hung up without saying goodbye or thanks. Three minutes, five seconds. Damn. He'd blown his location – if they were listening. Quickly, he tried Usulak again. Still no answer.

Ryder got in the car and sped away at random, twisting down streets until even he was lost. Finally, Alec hit a major boulevard he recognized. He was certain they hadn't tailed him. Then he remembered the old lady's address. It wasn't far away. He decided to go there. He wasn't ready to face Jeanette again.

* * *

"Some tea, Inspector? The girls in my apartment house say I make a wicked cup of tea," she chimed at him.

"Sure. Black tea, strong, please –some lemon in it, if you have some." Ryder peered around her small living room as the elderly woman sloughed away, moving toward a kitchen filled with unwashed dishes. His concern over contracting a disease from her unsanitary china was lost in his astonishment that she possessed no television. There was no stack of newspapers waiting to be thrown out. How in the hell could two people have missed his image, the telephone girl and this elderly spinster?

Then it hit him. He'd been too tired to see the trap. He had to get the hell out of there. He'd foolishly walked into an ambush. Ryder went to the curtains and drew them back. The street was empty. But these guys weren't amateurs. They wouldn't stand around so he could spot them. He had to get some sleep before he made a real blunder – assuming this wasn't already his best and final blunder.

Alec's hand was on the doorknob when she squeaked at him from the kitchen. "You're not leaving already, are you?"

"Ah, emergency call came through."

"I didn't hear the phone," she pouted.

"Radio," he improvised.

"Don't you want to know what this man looked like?"

"Well, he was probably wearing heavy makeup. You know, a disguise." He had the door cracked and was carefully peeking down the hallway. No one. No sounds.

"I don't care," she whined. "I'd know him anywhere."

"How?" he asked mechanically. Ryder studied what little he could see of the street through the glass of her apartment house's outer door.

"His eyes," she insisted. "They were the most intense eyes I've ever seen. Like coals, no, like a dog I hated as a child. That dog always terrified me when I walked to school. The animal just stood and glowered at me. I knew that one day it would eat me up and it nearly did. If it hadn't been . . ."

He gaped at her. "What did you say?"

"I said that dog tried to kill me." She was pouting again, but seated in her favorite chair with yellowing doilies on its arms.

"No. Before the dog attacked, you said something about its eyes."

"Yes. They were terrible, vicious eyes. Blank and cruel, yet calculating at the same time."

"What kind of dog?" But he already knew the answer and was halfway down the hall when her voice reached him.

"It was a Doberman Pinscher," she yelled after him.

"A Doberman," he acknowledged, spinning around and waving thanks to her. A broad smile creased his face. "Thanks, you've been a big help, a very big help."

31

Shot

Halliday decided he wanted to be shot in the back. One armed guard he could've taken out, but two with drawn guns was hopeless. A shot in the back would hurt less, take less time to heal and he'd have a better chance of living.

The two guards stared at him. One talked in a voice made high-pitched with excitement. "Put your hands behind your head."

Halliday scorned the man with his look. "Get your guns out of my face. I have a plane to catch."

"You're not going anywhere."

He glowered arrogantly as he cut the man off. "I'm Special Agent Halliday of the FBI. Now get the hell out of my way." He pushed forward and they stepped back, hesitant to shoot. One of them stood in front of him, blocking the doors. He sensed a crowd forming on the stairs behind him. Halliday must leave before someone identified him as Browning's killer. "Get out of my way," he demanded. Halliday stepped right at the guard in front of the doors.

The guard backed into the exit doors, pushing them open.

It was time. Halliday hit with enough violence to snap the man's wrist when it was trapped against the door frame. Tendons in the broken wrist contracted the trigger finger, firing the guard's .44 magnum revolver. The bullet smashed harmlessly into the guard's console, shattering a TV monitor and burying its energy in the cinder block wall behind. Then the hand opened convulsively from shock and pain, dropping the gun.

Halliday clenched himself against the injured guard and twisted, using the man as a shield. Together, they crashed against pavement and he heard a shot, felt a bullet scream through a hamstring. The guard he was wrestling with begged his companion not to shoot again. They rolled and Halliday clawed at his opponent's eyes, effectively blinding the guard and forcing the man to defend his precious vision with both hands. Halliday found his precious stiletto, taken from the Gestapo pig.

His peripheral vision saw a nightstick and Halliday's instinct reacted, forcing another roll. The stunning blow hit home on the wrong head, turning Halliday's wrestling opponent into a limp weight. Another blow hit his left arm and needles of pain shot to fingers holding the knife. He heard but couldn't feel the knife fall loose. Halliday flipped mace from the inert guard's utility belt and sprayed upward, buying time while his right hand sought the knife.

A terrific kick hit him in the stomach, driving all wind from his lungs. Halliday trapped the foot with his unresponsive left arm.

Halliday's right hand grabbed the stiletto and its blade shot out. He drove the knife into the trapped leg and twisted. The club flogged his back twice before he yanked the stiletto out and rose enough to bury the knife in his enemy's groin. He used the knife handle as a stanchion to pull himself up. Halliday loved seeing terror in his opponent's eyes. That emotional reaction bought enough time for Halliday to position a leg behind the opponent's knee and push, felling the man and freeing Halliday's knife.

He threw all his weight behind the thrust when the stiletto cut into the guard's neck.

A frenzied hand savagely yanked Halliday's own head backward, tugged by the hair. The guard's other hand pulled out his revolver and brought the gun up.

Halliday let go of the knife, letting the handle bob around, stuck in its target's neck. They fought over control of the gun. Another shot rang out, then another. A burning line traced across Halliday's stomach, but the bullet didn't enter his flesh.

Halliday was tiring and the guard was younger, more fit. Should the fight go on much longer, Halliday would lose. He had to gamble. Halliday drove all his weight into the gun and twisted. The weapon fired again.

The form under him jerked and momentarily lost strength. That opening was all he needed.

The knife came out and this time its blade hit the guard's jugular vein. Blood drenched Halliday's face. In seconds it was over and Halliday snapped out the knife, dragging himself to his feet.

Everyone ran away when the shots began. He was alone with two dead guards. Halliday limped to the box he'd killed to possess and picked it up, clutching the box with his briefcase. Around the corner, he paused at a metal dumpster and forced the lid open. He tossed the box in the dumpster and pulled out a thermite grenade. Halliday extracted the pin and placed the thermite grenade on the Federal Express package.

Sirens wailed nearby, but he waited until the magnesium sparked to life and licked everything into its fiery mouth. In seconds, the Federal Express package was ashes and the dumpster was well on its way to being an inferno.

His rental car was an agonizing block away. When Halliday got in, a white police car with blue stripes shot past. He started the Ford and backed out of his slot, careful to look casual.

Halliday glanced at himself in the rearview mirror when he turned on Ocean Avenue. He looked the way he felt – a bloody, battered wreck. Damn, he thought. This is going to waste more precious time. Damn, damn, damn. He hadn't expected this mess.

32

Rabbi

Alec awoke to the warmth of a new dawn thawing his frozen face. He looked around in a daze and tried to separate the street outside his windshield from a nightmare of a Doberman Pinscher, tearing out Alec's throat. Where was he? Ryder was upset to realize he sat parked near the old lady's apartment. He'd gotten in his borrowed car and hit the wall, fallen into the kind of sleep combat troops experience in war after several days of continuous operations. Sometimes, the troops even fall asleep in the middle of a firefight with the enemy.

Frost blurred Alec's car windows. His condensed breath had frozen on the steering wheel. His fingers and toes were numb. Ryder opened the car door and got out, nearly falling when his wounded leg gave way. He slapped his hands against his arms and stumbled for a block to warm up. Then he returned and started the car.

Alec had driven to the father-in-law's apartment when the car heater got toasty. He parked for a while and turned up the fan, enjoying the roasting heat, before getting out and climbing the stairs.

Ryder knocked gently at first, then insistently. He gave up and tried the key. "Jeanette?"

No answer.

There was a draft of cold air coming from the bedroom. He went in mindlessly, still half asleep. The window glass was broken out, a premeditated, sanitary job. Nothing panicky about it. Alec stuck his head out the opening and saw broken glass on the fire escape and peppering the ground below. The fire escape was extended to the ground. He snorted in disgust.

Jeanette couldn't get out the door because it had a double deadbolt lock and he'd latched it shut. So she escaped via the bedroom window. Well, fuck her. He was too starved to care.

Alec went into the kitchen and saw the cupboards were open. Most of the food was gone. Alec tore open a box of crackers and greedily swallowed them.

Where had Jeanette gone, Ryder mused as he sat down at the table? Then he remembered Usulak stood him up. Well, he thought, I know with whom she went, even if I don't know where. He poured a glass of water and drank to the bottom without stopping.

Alec was sitting on the toilet when he realized she might have turned him in, given the apartment address to the KGB. Good way to eliminate him as a competitor, looking for treasure. Or maybe the bitch cut some other deal with the devils. Her reasons didn't matter. The only important thing was leaving right away, before the apartment house was sealed off by KGB thugs.

Alec got up and pulled on his pants, leaving the bathroom without flushing the toilet. He looked outside the broken window and saw no one. How long ago did she leave? There was no way of telling. Ryder decided to also take the fire escape. He watched the street for some time before getting in the car and roaring away.

* * *

He didn't like the risk of being recognized but the gas tank was empty. He pulled in a gas station and pumped himself a full tank, then used a payphone. He popped a few coins in the phone and dialed Fire Captain Toth.

"Hello, Michael," Ryder announced when the phone was answered.

"Yes, Alec. Are you making progress?"

"I know who Satan's Touch is, Michael. I need your help in finding him."

There was a pause. "Shouldn't we be careful. My phone line might be tapped."

"Good point. I'm getting careless in my exhaustion. Listen, meet me at the same place we first met. I'll wait a block away. Be careful about being followed, but I'll watch you anyway before approaching you."

"OK, Alec."

They both hung up.

Alec drove to the burned out warehouse and parked two blocks away, in case the line had been tapped. He walked to where he could see the charred building remains.

Toth arrived and parked. The Fire Captain got out, one arm in a sling. Behind him, an innocuous-looking Peugeot slid in a parking space.

Alec began walking. He rounded the block and approached the Peugeot from behind, hiding in a doorway and watching. Both men in the car had short haircuts and thick necks. KGB thugs, he thought to himself. Not the cream, but still very deadly. One of the Peugeot occupants chatted on the car radio phone. Ryder waited until the talker finished the call.

Alec thought over his options and swallowed hard. There didn't seem to be any other way. He rationalized they'd kill him with a lot less thought and no regret. He pulled the shotgun from under his raincoat and walked to the passenger window. Ryder leveled the gun as the man turned in surprise to see him. The window exploded and half of it became part of the man's face.

The driver cleared an automatic from a shoulder holster and Alec fired again, hitting that guy in the side of the head. Ryder leaned in and removed both their weapons. He smiled. They also carried 9-mm automatics, standard NATO issue for officers. The KGB weren't fools. They didn't use any crappy Warsaw Bloc equipment when so much NATO gear floated around the black market. Alec fished in their pockets and found extra clips, ID papers and money. He took their car keys and threw them down a storm drain. Finished, he walked to the startled Toth.

"So you shot them." Toth said it flatly, as a fact, not an issue.

"Yes. You were followed. Sorry. I couldn't think of another way. Let's get out of here."

"Right." Toth jumped in his car. They drove aimlessly for a while. Toth finally pulled to the curb. "Who is it, Alec? Who is Satan's Touch and when can I kill him?"

"He's an Hassidic rabbi."

"What! A Jew? He couldn't be a rabbi. I mean, Alec, this makes no sense. I can't just . . . just kill a rabbi without knowing. It's not like those two that followed me. I understand you can't let them get you, but damn, Alec, a man of God …"

"Satan's Touch was posing as a rabbi when I first met him. He made several mistakes. For one thing, he let an old woman live who'd seen him when he entered her apartment. He was looking for whatever in the hell is worth all this killing."

The Fire Captain stared at Alec.

Ryder grew impatient. "He's not of God, Michael. He's of the devil, of Satan."

"But how do you know . . .?"

"I saw him in the very beginning, at the Department of Property Titles and Vital Statistics. Satan's Touch stared at me. I'll never forget those eyes. He could wear a thousand disguises and I'd know. It's his fiendish presence. I felt him at the airport when he ambushed me. He damn near got me then. I don't know what caused him to quit. He could've forced me to waste my shots and slaughtered Jeanette and me when we tried to run away."

"Alec, excuse me, but you've just killed two men on a hunch. Damn, Alec, I didn't think it would be like this. I thought you'd know for sure . . ."

"We'll find him, Michael. Then we'll know for certain. He'll be carrying something that ties him to the crimes. Or we'll break the bastard, make him talk."

"But where is he, Alec?"

"In a hotel somewhere with a group of nine other legitimate Hassidic rabbis. They're on a tour sponsored by the Holocaust Foundation in New York. What a bastard . . ." Alec's voice trailed off. He was enraged at himself for not knowing from the beginning. But how could he? He tried to forgive himself as he inventoried the carnage.

Toth interrupted the depressing list. "Alec, there are a lot of hotels in Budapest. You can't go to the desk and ask about these rabbis. I mean, you'll get caught. I'll have to help you. Where do I start?"

"There are only a few places they'd stay, the better hotels. Probably not the most expensive, but a really good one." Then Ryder knew the answer. The solution was obvious. It explained how the son-of-a-bitch knew a pair of policemen were in suite 115. "Drive to Margaret Island," he ordered. "He's at the Grand."

* * *

"Can I help you, sir?" The front desk clerk talked politely.

"Ah, yes. I'm looking for an uncle of mine," Michael Toth lied. "He's a rabbi, traveling with a group of them. It's very embarrassing. He called me and invited me to have dinner with him tonight at his hotel and I lost the slip of paper. Do you have a group of ten Hassidic, that is, very orthodox, old fashioned-looking rabbis staying here, by any chance?"

"Well, yes. What's your Uncle's name? I'll ring his room," the clerk offered.

"Oh, that won't be necessary," Toth retreated. "I'll just wait in the dining room for him. Uh, thank you."

Alec overheard their exchange from behind a magazine. Ryder held the pages in front of his face to avoid being recognized. He heard Toth sit next to him on a plush lobby bench. Alec whispered. "Now, we have the problem of finding which room when we don't know his name. Don't suppose he was obliging enough to register as Hans Mueller, do you?" Ryder broke a wry chuckle, surprising himself. His nerves were going. Too long on the edge, too little sleep, just too much of everything, especially Jeanette. He really hated her now. He wanted to put the shotgun between . . .

"Alec, look! We're in luck," Toth whispered.

Ryder lowered the magazine enough to see a gaggle of Hassidic rabbis shuffling inside an elevator. He rose quickly and followed, shoving the closing doors backwards, allowing himself and Toth to enter. The damn elevator crept from floor to floor. It made his skin crawl to think a madman could be behind him. But his instinct told him otherwise. There was only peace and solitude in those rabbis, not the sick passion he'd felt at the airport.

The doors cranked back and he let the rabbis ease around him, like Alec was going to another floor. His hand stopped the elevator doors from closing and he pulled Michael with him. They sauntered along behind and kept going as the rabbis went one by one into a chain of rooms along the floor. Ryder walked past the last one and pulled Michael away from their doors. Alec heard his pulse pound with excitement.

"He probably has that room they skipped, 211," Ryder whispered to Toth.

"How do we get in?" the Fire Captain asked.

Alec took out one of the KGB guns he'd confiscated. "You'll need this. Make sure this safety's off and don't shoot me, OK? You wait here."

Ryder went to the door and knocked. There was no reply. He talked sharply. "Open up, please, this is hotel security. We need to check your room for an electrical short. It's urgent." He rapped his knuckles on the wood and waited.

A rabbi exited from the room next door. "He's not in tonight."

Alec jumped at the voice behind him and then recovered. "Oh, I didn't know. When will he return?"

"No idea," the bearded face replied. "He's not like the rest of us. He needs more time to himself."

"I see. Well, uh, thank you, rabbi." Ryder wanted to ask a million questions, but then he wouldn't seem like a hotel security man.

"Why don't you just go in," the rabbi offered. "I'm sure he won't mind you checking for an electrical short."

Alec could feel Michael Toth standing nearby. "Did you bring a master key?" Toth asked.

"No, Michael. I thought the rabbi was in his room when I saw all the others enter without him. No need for you to go with me. I'll get one from the desk and be right back. Good night, rabbi." Alec waved and moved toward the elevators.

He heard a "good night" and the click of a door shutting. Ryder breathed a sigh of relief and punched "down" on the elevator panel.

* * *

The rabbis didn't go to dinner until hours later. Alec and Michael waited in the dining room, eating slowly, their eyes tracking shadows in flickers of candlelight. Waiters hovered near their table like circling birds, yet they dragged out their stay until the rabbis filed inside the restaurant. One of them bent stiffly, tipping his broad-brimmed black hat at the pair. Alec acknowledged the greeting and stood up, quickly paying the waiter.

Ryder's shirt was damp with sweat when he stood outside room 211. They hit the door together, causing a loud rending. The doorjamb gave way, almost parting from the wall. Another blow and the door slapped open.

Alec looked up and down the hallway, checking for anyone curious about the disturbance. "Michael, cover me while I search the room."

"Sure. I hope this is the right suite. We'll get caught for sure if we try battering down another door."

Alec ignored Toth's pessimism and threw the mirrored closet door back. "It's the right room," Ryder hissed. When Toth stuck his head in, Alec pointed to the black robe, button shoes and hat in the closet. He returned Toth's wide grin.

* * *

For nearly half an hour, Alec opened every drawer in the room and looked under every piece of furniture. There was no sign of anything inappropriate to a rabbi. Ryder was beginning to doubt his own sanity when he heard Michael approaching. There was a knock on the closed but damaged door. Alec opened it.

"Housekeeping is on the floor. I think they're turning down beds and putting mints on the pillows. Thank God they started with the other end. Did you find anything?"

"No. Come in. We'll get out in a second." Ryder knelt and examined a pair of old-fashioned button shoes. He put them down and rifled pockets in a robe. Alec picked up the hat and ran his fingers inside the lining, feeling the silk for a ninth time. Nothing, like the other eight attempts. Ryder stood in disgust and stared at the robe.

"Housekeeping's getting close, Alec. We've got to leave. They'll see the broken door."

"OK, OK." Ryder spoke without conviction. Something pulled him to the robe.

Toth hissed urgently. "Alec!"

Ryder ignored the warning and took the robe off its hanger. He began patting it down.

"Alec!" Toth demanded. "Come on!"

Ryder shrugged off the fireman's grip and patted down the robe. There was a heavy lump in the back of the waistband. Alec turned the robe inside-out and discovered a hidden pocket. He tore the Velcro tab loose and pulled out a small book.

There was a tentative knock at the door and Alec pocketed the book. Ryder hung up the robe and shut the closet.

Alec moved around the frightened Toth and pulled open the door. A surprised maid looked first at Alec and then at the shattered door jamb.

"We were just leaving" Ryder talked suavely and stepped around her. They went to the stairs, disregarding the elevator.

Toth asked quietly, "Did you find something?"

"Everything," Alec replied. "We found everything, my friend."

33

Animal

He drove away from the Air Force think tank, heading south on Pico Boulevard toward Overland Avenue. "Special Agent Halliday" was getting more and more desperate. He needed medical attention for the leg wound from a .44 magnum bullet. A tourniquet stopped the bleeding, but he had to loosen the tourniquet every few minutes and waste more precious blood. He passed two hospitals, but didn't dare use them. Emergency rooms were the first place cops would look for him. By now, every hospital close to the Air Force think tank was alerted and swarming with police.

Overland Avenue was useless, he quickly decided. He turned on Venice Boulevard and immediately saw what he wanted. He pulled into their parking lot, moving as far back as possible. It would be a long wait until they closed, but he had no choice. He reached behind the passenger seat and groaned with pain, twisting to get his emergency briefcase. It contained his "crash kit." He flipped open the attaché and administered a vitamin B shot to himself. His energy returned and he injected a gram positive antibiotic, followed by a gram negative one. For the blood loss and pain, he swallowed iron supplements and a massive dose of ibuprofen. That was all he could do for his wound.

Special Agent Halliday felt cold despite Southern California sun baking him through the windshield. He wanted to sleep. Amphetamines were the next thing he took. The amphetamines soaked into his overloaded system and he felt restless, then wanted to get out and run around like a crazed maniac. With iron will, he remained in the car, turning on the radio and scanning for a news station. He hoped to find a mention of his murders at the Air Force think tank.

He listened to weather, a traffic report, the stock market, international and national news, a special report on the trial of a local sports celebrity. The "All News, All the Time" pattern repeated for several hours before he could make a crucial phone call. He turned off the car radio and took out a crude version of today's cell phones, weighing about five pounds, with a long antenna jutting from the heavy device. He dialed a number glowering at him from the side of the building in front of him.

"Venice Animal Hospital," a receptionist answered.

"This is an emergency." He talked in a panicked voice. "Someone just shot my dog. You've got to help me. She's dying."

"We're closing for the night. But let me ask the doctor if someone can stay. Otherwise we can recommend …"

"Tell him I'll pay anything. Anything," he urged.

"What kind of dog is it?" came the skeptical reply.

He thought quickly. "Lassie, a collie. You know, like in the movies." Everyone liked them. How could they turn his away?

"I'm certain we can help. I wanted to make sure your dog isn't three-quarters wolf or something. Please hold."

He held the cellular phone close to his ear and looked at the receptionist through the window. The twenty-something with long, dangling earrings put down the phone and straggled away out of his sight.

Soon she came back and picked up the phone. "How soon can you be here?"

"Well, fifteen minutes to half an hour. Depends on traffic. He can wait, can't he, the doctor, I mean? She needs help, bad."

"Oh sure. Come around the back, though. The front door will be locked. Has your collie lost a lot of blood?"

"No, I got to her right away. Thanks, I mean it."

"Oh sure, yeah. Drive carefully, now. Don't panic. The doctor is real good. People come to him from all over."

"I'll bet," he smirked as he hung up.

As much darkness as Los Angeles ever sees settled comfortably around him in the next half hour. The twenty-something receptionist walked to her car next to his and drove away, ignorant of his presence. There were still lights in the building windows when he forced himself out of his rental car.

Dogs in the kennels started baying and wailing. Ignoring the barking, he put the Uzi under his coat and struggled to the vet's back door. He didn't have to knock.

A cute girl in a white smock opened the door, anticipating his presence from the kennel noise. "You have the collie?"

He put the Uzi in her face. "Get inside."

"OK," she begged, backing up and raising her hands.

"Anybody here besides you and the doc?" he demanded.

"No . . ." She realized why he asked that question and her face showed fear. "Look, the money is up front. You can have it all." She stammered to a halt.

"Take me to the doc. NOW!"

In response, she walked sideways down the hall, one eye looking in front of her and one eye staring at his gun.

* * *

An hour later, he hobbled to his rental car with all bullet fragments removed and the wound cleaned. A fresh supply of antibiotics and any other medicine he might need bulged in his pockets. Behind him, the doctor and his assistant lay on the floor face down with bullets from the Uzi in their brains. The cash register was empty and several drugs that might be of interest to addicts were cleaned off the shelves and flushed down the toilet. He hoped the killings would look like a junkie's rampage.

Now it was a matter of going to ground. He needed to hide long enough for his wounds to heal. He was in the right place for anonymity, a large urban area with enough violence every day that his killings didn't rate a mention on the local news station.

He drove to Overland Avenue and rented a furnished studio apartment on the ground floor, called Abbey Rents and got a hospital bed delivered with an IV stand. There were bottles of saline solution from the veterinary hospital in the back of his car. He gave an extra tip to the kid who wheeled in the bed and had him bring in the saline solution.

He turned on the TV, switched to a local station and tried to last through the news. The amphetamines wore off and he was swallowed by the void they left behind – no dreams, no pain, just exhaustion.

34

Diary

Alec Ryder quit turning pages in Hans Mueller's diary. He sat in a comfortable chair in the Christian Science Reading Room and looked into the anxious eyes of Michael Toth.

"Did you find out why he killed my men?" Toth was eager to know.

Alec handed over the book. "Would you like to read it yourself?"

"Sure." An hour later, the Fire Captain sagged in his chair and looked out a window at one of Budapest's main streets. "I don't suppose it matters any more, but I'd still like to know why he did it."

"So would I, Michael. I know Hans Mueller had an obsession, a fixation on revenge. We still don't know what he's after or where it's located. I wish I had the data Jeanette stole." Ryder joined the young Fire Captain in staring out the window at the street.

Toth interrupted their silence. "Where do you suppose Jeanette is, Alec?"

"I think she's with Usulak, hunting the treasure. Whatever the damn stuff is. Wait. I've been an idiot. We've got the solution. It's only one step away and I've been wasting valuable time." Alec jumped out of his seat and stuffed the diary in his coat. "Come on." Ryder opened the reading room's door and didn't wait for his companion.

Toth caught Alec by the arm. "Where're we going?"

"To see that stubborn fool Otto Tolnai."

"But I thought Otto might be Hans Mueller. What if he's the killer?"

"Otto can't be the killer." Alec sat in the driver's seat of Toth's father-in-law's car. "He's the fall guy and Otto is so stupidly smart he doesn't see it coming." Alec pulled into traffic. "Trust your guts, not your heart. It was your heart that said to send your men up the ladder when your guts said it was a trap. Now my guts say the killer isn't Otto. He can't be. He'd have to be in too many places at once. No, our satanic rabbi isn't Otto Tolnai. But Otto probably knows enough, with the help of this diary, to put the pieces together."

"I thought Otto wouldn't cooperate, Alec. Why will he help now?" Toth wondered.

"Because Otto is Jewish, Michael. He lost a lot of his family tree to the Gestapo. When he finds out this bastard helped the Gestapo, Tolnai won't care how much they paid him – I hope."

They crossed the Danube and twisted along cobblestone alleys until they stopped within sight of the Archives. Alec parked and scanned rooftops, looking for observers.

"Is there a back way in?" Michael asked. "The Archives must be under surveillance. We're sitting ducks if we try to walk inside."

Alec started the car and turned into an alley. They got out and Ryder walked around, peering into every grating in the pavement.

"What are we searching for Alec?" Toth felt puzzled.

"Alice's hole, where she fell into Wonderland, so we can join her. There!" Alec walked to a low wall and looked into the garden a story below. He knew from the plants that this was it, the atrium bordering Otto's office. Alec announced, "We need a ladder and we're inside."

* * *

Ryder went down the ladder fast as he dared, gun drawn. When he got to the bottom, he surveyed the office. He couldn't tell for certain, but Otto appeared to be at the computer, slumped in a nap.

Alec heard Toth follow him down the ladder. The Fire Captain appeared alongside, peering inside the glass.

Ryder placed a finger on his lips to silence Toth and tried the garden door. It was unlocked and they tiptoed inside. He went to Tolnai and placed a hand on the Director's shoulder.

Alec saw a trickle of blood coming from the base of the skull. He picked up the head and turned it. Glazed eyes of the late Otto Tolnai stared back. Ryder dropped the head in disgust and it fell hard on the keyboard, leaving a string of typomatic characters chaining across the screen. Some irrelevant sense of propriety caused Ryder to pick up Otto's head and lay it alongside the keyboard.

"He's been shot?" Toth asked.

"I don't think so." Alec bent down to the floor and picked up a wooden handle with his handkerchief. "Ice pick. Driven in the base of the skull and twisted around until the handle snapped off. The killer made scrambled eggs out of the top of the spinal cord. That area houses primitive brain functions controlling your lungs and heart. Death comes soon, but not instantly."

"My God, Alec. What a way to kill. It's so damned cold-blooded. Mueller again?"

"Yeah, it looks that way." There was another possibility, but it revolted Alec too much to consider Jeanette seriously. "Do you know anything about computers, Michael?"

"A little. Why?"

"Can you search this machine?" Ryder asked.

"Maybe. Let me see." They moved the limp form of Otto aside. The Fire Captain sat at the console. He read what was already on the screen, tried one command and gave up. "They've formatted the hard disks, Alec. Wiped out everything."

"Isn't there any way to get back the data?" Ryder was furious at himself for not getting there first.

"An expert could do it, Alec, but not me. Maybe there's some kind of backup. Diskettes?"

They tore the room apart before Alec remembered them. "At dinner, Otto said they dumped the hard disk to CD something or the other."

"Yeah, CD-ROMS, compact discs. Where would they be, Alec?"

"In the security room with the printer. I've seen them there. Come on." Ryder cracked the office door and made certain the hallway was empty. He led Toth to a cipher lock and keyed in "1956."

There was an incinerator inside, still warm, and the compact discs were gone from the shelves. Ryder wrapped his coat around a hand and opened the incinerator. The smell of melted plastic flowed out. He got a metal ruler and poked the ash. He found a corner of one disc and dragged out the fragment. "Too late."

Toth looked at the incinerator in disgust. Then his face lit up. "Where did they get the data, Alec? I mean, from what documents? Maybe we can get a hint from the books."

Ryder was almost out the door when he remembered how most of the documents lining the Department's shelves were gone. Once a document was scanned, it was burned in that same incinerator. "I'll look, Michael, but I think it's useless. Come on. We've only got a few minutes. Then we better get the hell out of here and find a place to think."

Ryder held the cocked gun in front of him, sliding along the hallway toward the public area. At each office, he pushed the door open to make certain no one was hiding inside the office. He turned the last corner and stopped. Toth bumped into him.

"What is it?" Toth whispered.

"Nothing." Alec put away the gun. They moved into the stacks and Ryder sighed. It would take forever to look through the remaining documents in the Archives. "No wonder they used a computer to organize things."

"It's hopeless, isn't it," echoed Toth.

"Yeah, looks that way. Let's get out of here." Ryder turned around and headed for the Director's office.

"What are we going to do, Alec?" Toth wondered.

"Think and run. Run and think. You should get your wife and kids out of Hungary. I'm infectious and you touched me. They'll know it soon, if they don't already. They can get to you through your kids. Let's get your family safe. Then we'll worry about that lunatic and what he's after."

"OK, Alec."

They climbed the ladder and laid it down next to an electrician's truck, returning what they'd "borrowed." Ryder started their car and drove toward the Fire Captain's home.

35

Red Square

Gregory Yevchentko opened the liquor cabinet in his Zil limousine and poured himself a stiff shot of Jack Daniels, a non-Russian taste he'd acquired in Cuba. Landing that sought-after assignment was the crowning achievement of his career, he thought to himself as he gulped the whiskey and poured himself another one.

Yevchentko was drunk when he staggered from the back seat and ignored the scowl of his new driver. Gregory waddled into the offices of his masters on the Kremlin side of Red Square. He walked head down, bulky frame shoveled forward like a rhinoceros he admired in the Budapest Zoo. Gregory's only concession to the masters of his destiny was popping a breath mint before shedding his fur hat and coat in the cloak room.

Gregory squatted in a chair, running nervous fingers over brass tacks holding red leather on a solid wood frame. The room filled with middle-rank bureaucrats and became overheated. Yevchentko didn't exchange chit chat with others as he had in the old days. They ignored him, treated him as a dinosaur who'd soon fade away. Well, he thought, this dinosaur has some teeth left and that's why I'm still here when all the other dinosaurs are gone to die in poverty or live off what little they'd stashed in foreign accounts. Most just had heart attacks.

He rose with others as their boss entered the room, followed by bodyguards. Gregory listened without any display of emotion when another reorganization was announced, the fifth this quarter that eroded his personal importance. Since the third reorg, they didn't bother to consult him. At least, they still informed him. Soon even that grace would stop. Then, he knew, the end was less than a year away, probably within a month unless he could pull another rabbit out of the hat – or the Americans did something even the new bunch of idiots couldn't tolerate.

He looked at the bureaucrats filing out. One day, it would be his last time to see these smug faces. He'd leave, but on his own terms, not as a poor man but as a rich man of influence. The Kremlin kept him as a convenience, a placeholder. He was their liaison with Hungary, a lost piece of their empire that didn't matter to these idiots. They felt Hungary was neither threatening nor essential to a loose confederation that replaced the centrally mis-managed Soviet Union. Let them think Hungary doesn't matter, he told himself.

He retrieved his hat and coat. The limousine wasn't waiting for him as it should have been. He stood in the cold for nearly forty minutes before the disrespectful idiot who replaced his loyal chauffeur bothered to return to his duty station. Gregory ignored the slight – this time. There'd be a final trip soon, to the airport. Then Gregory would probably leave the asshole a little present behind the seat, one that'd blow his brains through the windshield and halfway across Red Square.

There was just one troubling problem, he mused as he poured another Jack Daniels – Herr Mueller. Mueller was no longer controllable. He was doing too many things on his own. Worse, he hadn't reached closure on the first and most frail step in their grand plan for turning Hungary into Gregory's private country. It was fortunate that Gregory Yevchentko hadn't been fooled into believing Mueller and had taken precautions.

He sadly placed the nearly empty whiskey bottle in its rack. Gregory lamented that he'd no longer be able to get Jack Daniels until his emigration to Hungary. Russian vodka was such a coarse way to get drunk.

They arrived at his office and he trundled inside. An aide was waiting for him with a message. Gregory let the man leave before opening his safe and pulling out a pad of sheets with nothing but columns of numbers on them. He used the next sheet from that pad to decode the message, which created gibberish. Then, he got a similar pad from his briefcase and did the exercise again. This time, the message was clear. It was from his operative in Hungary and it caused him to smile.

Yevchentko picked up the phone and called operations. "Where is he?" Gregory asked. "How can you have lost Mueller? He leaves a trail of dead bodies behind, wherever he goes now. Yes, I know about the think tank episode. Well, find out who else was killed nearby. Their bodies will lead you to Mueller. Then terminate him. He's become a liability. Yes,

I'm not mistaken. Kill Herr Mueller. That's right. Good-bye. Yes, let me know when it's done."

Could they do it, he wondered? Well, it didn't really matter if the first team succeeded. Eventually, they'd get him. It was only a matter of days, not weeks. Of course, Alec Ryder was still running around and they hadn't gotten him yet. But then, that was another of Mueller's mistakes. Gregory believed some men were lucky and some were not. Mueller had been very lucky. Not anymore, because Gregory didn't need Hans Mueller anymore.

* * *

Hans Mueller, aka Special Agent Halliday, aka Ray Stewart, flipped open yellow pages and found another restaurant that delivered. He never used the same one twice. He didn't want them noticing anything. A delivery boy might connect him with the deaths at a nearby veterinary hospital or killings at an Air Force think tank. But that was a manageable risk, less than hobbling around to get food in a supermarket. The worst risk of all was the damn rental car, now well overdue. But there was nothing he could do about that problem. The vehicle sat in an assigned parking space for this apartment, waiting for Mueller's leg to heal.

What he needed to speed the healing was a transfusion, but it was far too risky. So he ate pizza, submarine sandwiches, ribs, fried chicken, Chinese food and watched the same stupid television programs. There was a knock at the door. It was too soon for his food to be delivered. These kids always took thirty minutes, sometimes an hour after he'd called. His instincts told him not to answer the knock. Muller waited in silence and took the safety off his Uzi submachine gun.

Another knock, louder and more insistent, yet still no voice announcing a food delivery. Short hairs bristled on the back of his neck. Mueller squeezed out of his bed and felt chilled. His hand shook, making his aim unreliable.

Was it a wrong address? Then they'd go away. He didn't dare venture to the window. He slipped backwards instead, away from the hospital bed in the living room. American police, he thought, would announce themselves. He found supplies he'd brought from the car and struggled to open a taped box. His television blared while he fought at tearing the tape. But the TV didn't matter. A lot of people left the television on when they went out, as a deterrent to burglars.

Frustrated, Mueller tore at the box and knocked it off a little table. The package caught the phone cord and dragged off the phone also. Both of them landed on the carpet with a soft crash. The living room window dissolved in a spray of bullets, sending him to the floor and covering him with glass. Grenades parted the shredded curtains and fell hissing on the floor, waiting to explode.

He pulled a mattress off the bed and doubled it between himself and the grenades. They exploded a second later and one chunk of shrapnel broke a rib, but he was mainly unhurt. He crawled from under the mattress. Its thick padding shielded him, but the assassins outside wouldn't know he'd lived.

Mueller heard scraping at the front door and resisted the urge to blow away the man on the other side. He'd have backup and Mueller needed to get both of them. He'd wait and finish the pair when they rushed through the door. It came down to timing. Would his reactions be faster than theirs?

The scraping quit and Mueller raced to open the box, not caring what sound it made. Ironically, this part went quietly. He pulled the pin on his own grenade and cradled the explosive device, fingers clamped on a safety handle. He moved in a crouch down the hallway and into a bathroom. He was grateful there was no sound of explosives being laid on the back door. Mueller laughed. Few men in any organization knew how to kill a man like him. The scraping stopped and he rolled his grenade toward the front door, then ducked in the bathroom, closing its door against the impending concussion.

With a crushing sound, the front door came off its hinges and flew halfway across the living room. Two men rushed behind the tumbling door, firing assault rifles blindly. Mueller's grenade exploded, cutting the first one in half. The second killer was still moaning when Mueller finished him. He turned the man over and was sickened to recognize the face. Mueller identified the other body as well. There was no mistaking what happened. Yevchentko had turned on Mueller.

A crowd was forming, gawking at the shattered apartment. Mueller had no time for bitterness. The KGB would tip Los Angeles police as a backup in case their own men failed. They could always have him killed in jail. That would be easy in such a violent land as America.

He stepped over their bodies and hobbled away. Mueller would have to get a new car - that must've been how they found him.

36

The *Mohel*

Ryder turned on the main road from the miles-long gravel lane they'd been bouncing along for an hour. Michael Toth's family were left with relatives on a farm at the other end of that dirt road. Tomorrow the family would be driven across the border to Austria. Alec scolded his companion. "You should've gone to Vienna with them, Michael."

"You need help. You're wounded from that fight with the robot. Laser burns are serious." The Fire Captain sulked in response to being criticized.

"You should talk." Alec grunted, using his cut leg to press the accelerator and merge with traffic.

"I'll be fine," Toth insisted. "You just find Mueller." Michael Toth crossed his arms and looked out the passenger window.

"All you want is to kill him? What about afterwards? What about living? How will your family live when you're killed in return? The KGB might also decide to take out your wife and children. Quit now. You can still get out. I don't think they know about you yet."

"The maid saw me at the Grand Hotel, when you got that madman's diary. Have you forgotten? Some detective you are."

Toth was right, Alec knew. He and his family will be dead because of me. Ryder sagged deeper into his seat.

A long mile passed before Toth interrupted the ex-CIA agent's misery with a comment. "There must be *something* in that diary we can use to find this bastard. I mean, it's got his whole story."

"Otto was my only link. And he's dead. Maybe Jeanette knows. In fact, I'm pretty certain she does know. It's hopeless."

"One crazy long shot first. Then it's hopeless," Toth insisted.

Ryder steered into a faster lane and sped up to get around the diesel exhaust of a tourist bus. Sun glinted off its back window and sharp pain shot through his exhausted eyes. Alec looked at the ribbon of asphalt spinning under him and then at puffs of clouds chasing in a herd across the blue sky. He envied their freedom. "What's this crazy long shot?"

"OK. I'm Jewish."

Alec re-focused on the speedometer and realized he was going way too fast for his bone-tired reflexes. He lifted his foot off the gas and the car jerked. "You're Jewish?"

"Yeah, I'm Jewish."

"Well, Michael, that's fine but how's that going to help us?"

"My grandfather is still alive, Alec."

"I'm glad, Michael." Ryder was sarcastic.

Toth ignored the insult. "My grandfather told me he used to be a *mohel* before the war."

"What's a *mohel*?"

"Circumciser of Jewish boys. Now they have doctors do it."

"OK, so he made little Jewish boys more Jewish. You think maybe he knew someone or heard something during the war?"

"Yes. I think he hung out with our man Mueller."

Alec gave Michael a skeptical look. "Yeah, sure. And my Dad hung out with Adolf Hitler."

"One thing you don't know." A neat smile traced Michael's lips. "My grandfather had one of his feet blown off near the end of the war."

"Where is he? How long to get there?" Ryder came wide awake.

* * *

The nurse pushed open the door to Abraham Toth's little room. "You can't stay long, even if you're family. He's had a stroke. Mr. Toth doesn't have much strength."

Michael Toth tried to assure her. "We'll only be a moment, nurse." Toth approached an age-spotted face with oxygen tubes winding up both nostrils. Michael put his mouth close to the man's parchment-like skin. "Grandfather, this is Michael. You were a *mohel*?"

A flicker of life returned to the blank eyes. Abraham's mouth twisted in silent struggle.

Alec ran his eyes down bedcovers to where one leg ended in a foot, but the other leg quit at the ankle. A scratchy, faint "Yes" brought Ryder to Abraham Toth's side, leaning over the sunken face.

"You once circumcised a *goi*, a non-Jew, to make him look Jewish to the Gestapo. Didn't you, Abraham?"

Life force ebbed and waned several times in the old man's eyes. Finally, he spat out an answer. "He was evil!"

"Yes. He's back, Abraham." Toth moved away and surveyed the fear rising in his grandfather's yellow eyes.

"Then kill him," came the feeble reply. "We can't stay here. I told them. But they wouldn't listen." What little energy Abraham possessed went into alertness, but his mind soon faded, like a Christmas toy with dying batteries.

Toth persisted, ignoring the closing eyes of the old man. "What did the *goi* want?" Michael waited for an answer, but there was none.

Ryder stood next to Michael and reached out a hand, then hesitated. Finally, he jostled a skeletal shoulder.

Michael placed fingers on the old man's neck and searched for a pulse. "We'll kill him if we keep going. He may already be dying. I'm sorry, Alec."

"You did the right thing. Your grandfather hadn't any time. You don't kill a man by asking him a few questions."

"You think Abraham knows?"

"Knows what and where? Possibly, unless the treasure's lost forever in the chaos after World War II." Ryder stared at the old man. "Did he ever mention . . . Did he ever say anything . . . ?"

"Yeah, he gave me hints about a treasure. I thought at the time, as did everyone else, that he'd gone a little crazy from the torture. We all thought he wanted to make himself seem more important."

The nurse glanced at Abraham, then scolded them. "Your time is up. Come back next week – if he lives." Her body language said they were guilty, if he died, of killing him by showing up.

They left in unbroken silence, not talking until they sat in the car again. Alec stared at the retirement home, an old mansion in poor condition, like its occupants. "Did Abraham have any close relatives?"

"None of them are alive today. My mother died of cancer."

"And the rest?" Alec persisted.

"The Camps. It shortened their lives. Except for Abraham. He was too tough to die."

"Isn't there somewhere we can look?"

"Yes . . . There's somewhere we can look. The treasure probably isn't there. Still, we need a place for the night. This spot isn't one they're likely to know about."

Ryder started the car and released the handbrake.

"Where are we going, Michael?"

"Home. I'm going home."

* * *

Bitterness seeped like acid across his guts when Michael Toth looked at a run-down house at the edge of Lake Balaton. Even the "For Sale" sign was battered into meek submission by wind and sun, tilting its edge on the ground for support. Michael kicked down the sign and pushed on the fence gate. A hinge broke loose from rusted screws and he had to drag the gate over weeds claiming the front walk. His mother's pride tea roses were only scraggly counterpoints along the crusted porch.

Yet the house seemed bigger than he'd remembered. How had Abraham afforded a large home, Michael wondered? He'd never asked that question as a child, taking it all for granted – a splendid location, plentiful rooms, well-kept gardens and beautiful furnishings. Michael lasted until he was fourteen and then he ran away. None of those material things mattered to him. His mother was gone. Michael's father was an unknown, dead from the Camps. People told Michael his mother wasn't right. Well, she loved him and that was more than Abraham ever did.

Toth heard Alec's footsteps and turned around. He found respect and surprise in the Inspector's countenance. "You didn't think I came from a rich family, did you, Alec?"

"Well, no. You didn't act wealthy."

"I'm not."

"But you will be, assuming you inherit this property after your grandfather dies."

Michael shook his head. "Abraham wouldn't leave his estate to me, even if he could. Property titles in communist Hungary were scrambled like a deck of cards. There's no way . . ." Michael halted. A new awareness crept into his mind. He suddenly knew why Otto Tolnai was so important to Satan's Touch. He couldn't grasp all the logic. Parts of their plan floated out of reach, hiding in the corners of his mind. Michael saw Alec shiver in the lake's biting wind. The same harsh gusts pushed a solitary, brave sailboat across a gray expanse of lake water. "Let's go inside," Michael suggested.

He pulled open a familiar, now decrepit, screen door and was surprised to find the front door ajar. Had realtors handling the property visited and left the abandoned house unlocked? More likely some kids explored the old wreck during a boring summer break.

Toth was startled when Alec Ryder pulled out his gun and gestured for Michael to arm himself also. Inside, a beam of sunlight bored through a hole in a broken window, shining on ages of dust layered on the parlor. The spotlight illuminated its creator, a rock thrown by a truant child. The stone occupied center stage, laying between chairs draped with dusty sheets. Burnt fireplace logs gave off a charred odor, as though the fire were kindled recently, by a vagrant spending the night. Michael stopped and listened, but heard only wind and their breathing.

He backed out of the parlor, telling his mind to quit bringing him memories of his last quarrel with Abraham, an ugly scene after his mother's funeral. It was the last act in an ugly relationship, staged before the fireplace he'd just visited. Michael needed his attention on the present, on the dining room he was about to enter and a kitchen that lay beyond.

There were footprints on the dining room floor, outlines of steps in the caked dust. It was a fresh trail, without new dirt to mute the patterns. One set of tennis shoes led from the kitchen door toward Michael. The other footsteps went up remnants of stair carpeting and came down again.

Michael listened for anyone moving upstairs. He remembered how as a child he could tell exactly where everyone stood, when he waited in the entry hall to sneak into his room from a forbidden nighttime excursion.

There was no sound now to give anyone away, no snoring and restless tossing. Toth skirted the dining table with Ryder. A chair lay in the corner with a broken leg. Cobwebs filled the candelabra with smoky lace.

Michael pushed open a door separating the kitchen from the dining room. Part of him expected to see uniformed servants preparing a meal, the floor glistening in a new coat of wax. Instead, the floor held a man's body, his head in a pool of blood turned black in a sponge of dirt coating the linoleum.

37

Waiting

Agent Halliday, aka Hans Mueller, parked his rental car in front of an office building near a Santa Monica Freeway off ramp. He got out. An injection of morphine made walking possible. He was increasing his recovery time by walking, but he had to get rid of that damned car. It'd almost been his downfall. Keep the same vehicle and they'd nail him for sure.

Within a few blocks, he saw what he needed – a small used car dealership. He showed a phony California ID. The owner made no effort to validate the driver's license. He simply pocketed a wad of cash in exchange for a low mileage BMW sedan with many previous drivers. The salesman made his living selling flashy cars to drug dealers. The area was a sort of Stop 'n Go for cocaine sold to the Beverly Hills set on their way home. The rich found it convenient, just hop off the freeway and get your high. When the boys selling dope got busted, their cars were confiscated and sold at auction. The owner snapped up cars at a fraction of the going price and re-sold the vehicles. His business was simple, fast and clean.

Halliday-Mueller got out of there in ten minutes and went to his rental car, retrieving everything he needed from its trunk. He left the Hertz vehicle unlocked, keys in the ignition. Soon the car would be in Tijuana, stripped, its parts recycled to Southern California body shops.

The next step was tricky. Mueller needed a place where no one would look for him. He'd been too professional and logical with that other apartment. The KGB could analyze his every move and hunt him down, if he kept thinking like a chess player. His next move would have to be the unpredictable, random shot of an amateur, something a pro would never do. He sat drumming the BMW steering wheel with his fingers, thinking.

Abruptly, Mueller flipped open his briefcase on the passenger seat. He'd figured out the best possible place to hide. He looked in his notes and found the address. It was in a fashionable neighborhood of Santa Monica, near the ocean. He started the German car and drove away.

* * *

The BMW was comfortable and went unnoticed parked north of Montana Avenue and west of 26th Street. There were, after all, nothing but BMWs, Range Rovers and Volvos here. This was yuppie heaven. He, however, was in hell and forced to use his last shot of morphine.

Soon the shot freed him to walk again and Mueller approached the house he'd targeted. He limped to the backyard, examining window jambs. The alarm system appeared comprehensive, with a switch set to trigger when any window was opened.

He tested his theory by jiggling one of the double-hung sashes. Wailing erupted at a deafening level inside the house, and an electronic counterpart under the roofline sang its discordant repertoire. He walked calmly past the security company's warning sign in the lawn and sat in his car. For half an hour the alarm kept on going. Finally it shut off.

He waited another ten minutes and was about to get out of his BMW when the private patrol car showed up. A rent-a-cop got out of a large domestic sedan and walked the home's perimeter, testing its doors. The security guy got back inside his car. The dome light went on, a clipboard came out and five minutes passed while the paperwork was filled out. Then he left.

Mueller triggered the alarm again and the private security service dutifully, if slowly, showed up again. This time the rent-a-cop flashed by the home but didn't get out. The third time was a repeat performance, but the fourth time, the rent-a-cop didn't show. Not once did a neighbor go outside to check what was happening.

Hans got out slowly. By now, the morphine was making him woozy. His scheme was going to work or he'd be caught, too slow to run away, too doped up to react quickly and kill the security guard. He went into the backyard and simply smashed a window. All hell broke loose as it had before. This time, he carefully pulled himself inside the house.

Even earplugs didn't make the sound level tolerable and in the living room there was an intense strobe light flashing. The alarm's control unit must be in a closet. Mueller tore all closet doors open, but didn't find the control. He tried the kitchen. The damn thing was in a cupboard over the refrigerator and hard to reach. He took a stepstool from the laundry porch and used it to stand on while he disconnected the alarm from its sirens and strobes. The house fell quiet.

He went to the back door and found it double-deadbolted. His brain was still fogged from morphine and it took forever for him to pick the door lock. Then he went outside and opened the garage doors. He was in luck. It was empty enough for him to park his BMW. Perfect.

After he put the car away and carried his things inside, he checked the refrigerator. It had been emptied for an extended trip, but left plugged in. The freezer held ice cubes and a few Lean Cuisine frozen dinners. He read their instructions, popped one in the microwave and waited for breakfast.

It would take a week for him to heal enough to travel out of the country, but he had all the conveniences available. It had been very thoughtful of her to stock up on frozen meals before going to Hungary. What would Jeanette think, he wondered, if she knew he was in her house?

38

Crisis

Alec Ryder knelt over Szige Usulak's body and touched the back of his skull with a fingertip, parting the hair. "Shot once, small caliber, close range." Ryder spoke without a trace of pity for the dead fool. "Help me," he asked the Fire Captain. Together, they managed to turn over the rigid corpse, stiff as a mannequin. Alec checked for Szige Usulak's weapon and found it still holstered. There was nothing in Szige's pockets beyond a wallet and the usual crumpled papers, including a market list. His wife used to force Usulak to do the grocery shopping on the way home each day.

Alec and Michael left Usulak's body in the kitchen and followed the pattern of tennis shoe marks upstairs. Footprints went in and out of every bedroom on the second floor. The door to Abraham's suite was ajar and Alec pushed it open with a certainty that Usulak's killer was long gone. Faded drapes framed a window nearly opaque with grime, but still letting in enough light to show the mess. The bed's canopy was piled in one corner. A dresser, nightstands and bureau were intact, though drawers were rifled and contents pulled out. Fresh sawdust filled Ryder's nostrils and made his nose run with irritation. A chainsaw and gasoline can sat in the center of the room, surrounded by wooden pieces of the bed no larger than a man's forearm.

Alec bent down and picked up a thick, heavy piece of oak. He turned it over in his hands with a bemused smile, looked through the hollow core of the piece in the light from the window, then tossed it on the floor. A harsh smack echoed when the oak piece landed in the barren hallway behind him.

He caught a glimpse of himself and Toth in an old mirror above the Grandfather's bureau. Ryder's own eyes and lips were tight in a smug, ironic smile. Toth looked bewildered and shocked. Michael's gun arm hung down limply at his side.

Alec turned and faced Toth. "Put that away," he told the Fireman, pointing at the gun. "You won't need it. Usulak's killer is gone and won't be back." Toth slowly complied and put the gun into a side pocket of the coat he wore on one arm and draped over the other, still in a sling. "Come on, Michael. We've got a phone call to make if we want a chance to live."

* * *

They drove monotonously for thirty miles along the flat, open southern shore of Lake Balaton. Reaching the resort town of Siófok, Alec parked before a five-story modern hotel, a blank and soulless reflection of how he felt. As a decoy, Ryder checked them into a room he had no intention of occupying. They left and drove to another town, where they ate in silence, his fear poisoning the food and his companion's mood. When the phone call could be postponed no longer, Alec went to a booth and called Gregory Yevchentko. Alec didn't expect the KGB section head would answer the phone. "Gregory?" Alec asked, failing to mask his astonishment at making direct contact.

"Who is this?" Yevchentko asked suspiciously.

"The late Alec Ryder. We should talk, Gregory, before you try to kill me again. You might succeed and that would be a tragic mistake for you."

"Don't be absurd …"

Alec cut him off. "Cut the crap, Gregory. You tried killing me at the airport. Our relationship needs some mending, as they say. Unless you prefer I talk to CIA, who will in turn talk to … "

"Alec, it's ridiculous to think the Russian government authorizes me to assassinate foreign nationals. Be reasonable, Alec."

"Gregory, I think you were sitting in your office expecting a call and got one. But I'm not the person you were waiting to hear from, am I right? Well, no need to confirm it. You can explain when we talk in person."

There was a prolonged silence. Alec smiled at Michael Toth. The longer Gregory was silent, the more confident Alec became that he finally understood the game of cat and mouse they were playing. Alec the mouse was becoming the cat. It was Gregory's turn to run, but not from the cat. This time, to live, the mouse must run right into the cat's mouth.

Finally, a low hum of static on the line was broken by a guarded voice. "What do you propose?"

"You leave now. You come alone. You don't, I burn what you really want and flush the toys into Lake Balaton where no one will ever find them. But first I make copies of the …"

Yevchentko cut in. "There is no need to be explicit."

Now Alec knew for certain that Yevchentko was a fallen star. Gregory had lost his former stature with the KGB and even his most private line was tapped. The Kremlin was just waiting until they no longer needed the old man or until they were certain he was toothless.

"Where are you?" came to Alec over the phone.

"Where I won't be ever again. But I'll leave directions here for you and I'll watch very carefully that you come alone, Gregory. Together, we can have a good future. But apart, Gregory . . . apart we each die. I'll sell you what you want. I have it. You have six hours to get here."

"Six! You're mad! I can't possibly get to Lake Balaton in six hours!"

"Gregory, you're a powerful man. Arrange it."

"I need at least twelve hours. You said that apart we each die. Six hours is killing yourself."

"But I have the satisfaction of taking you with me, Gregory."

"Ten, Alec."

"Eight." Ryder hung up. He turned and looked into Toth's anger.

"So the bastard who started it all is coming to grovel before you. After all my men . . . Well, at least we're safe." Michael sighed.

"Safe for two hours. Then we might die any time. Or live to be drugged and tortured. Or . . ."

"Or what?" the Fire Captain demanded.

"Or Gregory Yevchentko is a renegade, working alone for his own benefit. In that case, he'll show up here. I'll write down directions and leave them at the desk for Yevchentko. Then we'll drive to your grandfather's home. I'll wait there for whatever happens. I promise you they won't take me alive. They'll never know where you've gone."

"And where am I to go?"

"Austria. Join your family. Get the hell out of Europe. Live as long as you can."

"Alec, he killed my father-in-law. He killed my men. He's wrecked my life. I can't simply leave."

"Yes, you can and you will."

"But you have the upper hand!" Toth nearly screamed.

"No, I've only bluffed. If Yevchentko takes the bait, I'll bluff some more. I'll keep bluffing until someone calls my bluff. Then the game is over and I'm dead. There's no reason to take you down. Forget being so damned noble. Think of your children and live."

* * *

Alec Ryder watched the Fire Captain drive away. Cold seeped into his body and matched the emptiness in his soul. Ryder limped to the edge of Lake Balaton and watched the sun prepare to set over reedy marshes and low hills. He bent down and picked up a stone. Alec sent the pebble spinning across the calm water and was a little boy again.

He stood and fought against the cold to watch the lake for as long as he could. In the end, the cold won. Alec went into the house. In the parlor, he tore dusty sheets off the furniture and re-lit logs in the fireplace. He settled into a chair for the long wait.

* * *

Electronic beeping from his watch told him to wake up. Alec swept away a fitful sleep that had overtaken him. There were still embers enough in the fireplace to stir into a renewed blaze, but no more logs.

Reluctantly, Alec went into the kitchen, aided by a small pocket flashlight. Stepping around Usulak, he located a kerosene lantern in the broom closet and lit it, holding the light before him. He found a small pile of logs not far from the porch, but ignored them.

He felt the pull of the barn, as he had since entering Abraham Toth's property. Alec tugged at the barn's sliding door and went inside. The lantern cast jagged streaks of light on dirty floorboards, rafters and leaky walls. There was a bale of mildewed hay rotting near the far wall and he walked over to the straw block. A sense of the forbidden tingled in him as he took rusting tongs off their huge, square-headed nail and dragged the hay a few yards away from its origin.

Alec's feet scraped away dirt on the floor. He knelt and lifted up a ring, using it to open a trap door. The smell of damp earth rushed to meet him. Alec flipped the door on its back and peered down a ladder. It appeared to be solid, so he tested a foothold, then a second.

He descended into a large pit with wooden shoring to keep its sides from collapsing. Shelves lined one wall, holding pickled food in glass jars. He moved jars aside and found a hidden latch. Setting the lantern down on the dirt floor, Ryder shouldered into the wooden shelves. They swung back and his lantern flooded a square room. The sleeping quarters were complete with table, chairs and bunk beds. He assumed a door at the far end of the room led to an escape tunnel reaching the lake.

Alec hung his lantern on the main ceiling beam's hook and went over to a little writing desk. Ryder opened the center drawer and pulled out a thin ledger. He smiled and put the book on the desk to study. He carefully turned aged and rotting paper, etched with fountain pen entries.

Half an hour later, he finished reading. For the first time, Ryder felt he understood the bizarre web spun around him. Alec rose and went to the shelves. Using instructions from the ledger, he found a hiding place and removed a metal strongbox. Carrying the strongbox, ledger and lantern, he climbed out of the cellar. Alec replaced the trap door and hay bale before returning to the house.

When the fire blazed again, Alec sat and stared at the cover of the strongbox. Its rusted lock was useless and fell apart when he pried with the fireplace poker.

* * *

Headlights swung across the parlor windows. Their beams were muted to a diffuse glow by wind-blown sand, caked by winter fog to a crust even driving rain couldn't erase. The car's tires crunched on gravel and rolled to a stop. Alec hit a button on his watch and saw the time was 4:32 A.M. Yevchentko was only two minutes late. Ryder thought all night long about where to hide, how to see if Gregory was alone, when to flee. In the end, he decided to sit in the parlor and wait.

Alec was too damned tired to keep running and hiding the rest of his life. He lit a cigarette and turned up the lantern. It silhouetted him in the parlor very boldly. An easy shot, a clean kill – if that was the game. They had him now. Sadness crept over Alec. He thought of his wife. Was there a heaven where she waited for him? Certainly not his destiny, though. Not after killing her murderer, not to mention a pair of KGB thugs.

The car door was shut quietly. Only one door. Only one set of footsteps. Didn't mean the house wasn't surrounded by a dozen heavily armed men, though. Didn't mean Gregory Yevchentko wore those shoes scraping across the porch.

Alec picked up his automatic and pointed it, but not at the door to the parlor. He'd promised young Michael Toth a head start and was determined to keep his promise. Ryder had no illusions he could hold out against drugs and probes the KGB had refined on thousands of victims. He cocked the hammer and held it with his thumb, pressing the trigger. If they shot him, even with a tranquilizer dart, his thumb would release the hammer. The gun would blow a hole in his heart. He'd barely live to see his killer's face.

The front screen door creaked, then the main door. The screen door slapped shut, then the front door was eased closed. Alec started to believe the visitor was Gregory. Dangerous, he told himself. Knock it off. They have you zeroed in. It's over.

Slow footsteps in the hallway. A flashlight leading the way. How long could his thumb hold on and not make a mistake? What a time to die because your hands are sweating and the hammer slips . . .

"Alec?"

Ryder let up on the trigger, pointed the gun at the doorway and eased the hammer down. "In here," he said softly.

"I'm alone, Alec. As you requested. Alone."

A man who'd ordered the death of hundreds of men, women and children, was now a lonely, frightened bureaucrat.

"Turn off the flashlight. There's plenty of light in here." Alec saw the beam disappear. Hesitant footsteps shuffled to the door. A rhinoceros appeared, clad in a heavy coat with a fur collar, gloves, fur hat and fine leather boots. His wardrobe shouted – "Moscow *apparatchik*, circa 1975." No doubt that outfit was the dress of choice for May Day parades in Red Square, when they rolled tanks and missiles by the thousands past Kremlin elite.

Gregory's eyes stayed fixed on Alec's gun. Ryder had forgotten about the weapon. He flicked on the safety and holstered the automatic. "Sit down, Gregory, by the fire. You've had a long, hard trip. I'd offer you a drink, but there's nothing alcoholic to drink in this old house."

Yevchentko moved stiffly to a dusty chair and sat, remaining upright. His eyes never left Alec. They exchanged stares for several seconds before Gregory spoke. "You have it?"

"I have several conditions first, Gregory."

"Yes, of course. Reasonable conditions can be met. How much?"

"I want your asshole Commissioner of City Services removed. He doesn't have to be killed. Nothing old fashioned like that. I have a man I want in his place, someone competent."

"Who?"

Not maybe, not yes, just who, Alec thought. Well, here goes. "Otto Tolnai, Gregory. He's one of your buddies. But I don't care. Otto's smart enough to actually run the God damn city, not screw it up."

"Fine."

A little piece of Alec died and he felt sick. Gregory didn't order Otto's killing. Yevchentko looked like a fat, scared little shit, not a consummate bluffer.

That left only Jeanette – and he'd wanted to make love to her so badly his whole body ached to touch her sex. He'd been stupid enough to run to her rescue in his apartment house. Damn her. She came to Abraham Toth's house with Usulak and killed Szige in the kitchen. If Ryder lived, he'd add to the score against himself in the afterlife. Jeanette callously used that poor horny Usulak, let him saw up the bed, then sent him to the kitchen for a glass of water. She'd run her hand over his crotch, put the barrel to his head and squeezed the trigger.

"Is that all you want?" Yevchentko sarcastically interrupted Alec's reverie.

"No. I get a quarter of the jewels, not a quarter share of what you get for them. I'll fence them myself."

"Yes, I'm sure you know a lot of good fences, Alec. But that kind of thing is risky to the operation as a whole. I must require that I hold your share in escrow for a while."

"Then I'll hold a quarter of the . . . what shall I call them, Gregory? The papers. I'll hold a quarter of the papers in escrow."

"You have them?"

No poker face, no attempt to hide their true value, thought Alec. "Yes." At least on this score, Ryder wasn't bluffing.

"Where are they? I must see proof that you have them." Gregory leaned forward, unconsciously rubbing his hands together, unaware of the stealthy feet behind him.

Alec heard the soft footsteps and assumed they were Gregory's backup team. The noise could've been wind, but it wasn't wind creaking a loose floorboard in the hallway.

"Killing me won't keep the truth from falling into hands that will destroy you. I've set up a deadman's switch, Gregory. Someone has to get my messages each month to prevent delivery of my sworn affidavit and copies of the papers."

"Very thorough, Alec, but unnecessary. You'll be a centerpiece in the new Hungary. Forget Otto. You can be City Commissioner. The job'll make you rich. Richer, by far, than your share of the jewelry. You have them, too, Alec?"

"No."

The Russian frowned. Alec traced the man's thoughts in his face as Yevchentko's expression turned from puzzlement to outrage.

"Easy, Gregory. I do have the papers. As you said, they're worth far more than the jewelry, at least to a man like yourself, with the connections and the influence and the plan to exploit them. A lesser man, Gregory, wouldn't have seen the bold outline, the great strategy like you did."

"Thank you, I think," was the wary reply.

"No, Gregory, it's not mere flattery. It's the truth, just as I tell you truly that if you don't instruct your man in the hallway to toss out his weapon . . ."

Yevchentko's frightened twist toward the doorway caught Alec by complete surprise. Alec barely stopped himself from firing into the thick upper body of the Russian. It was the look on the man's face that prevented the act. Ryder took a moment to recover his thoughts and guess who had entered the house. "Throw down the gun, Michael. Then come out – slowly."

"Where's Mueller?" was the unresponsive reply.

"Dead," Gregory interjected. "I had him killed. He was too … unpredictable."

"I'll bet," Alec said flatly. "Now throw down the gun, Toth. If you want revenge, there'll be plenty of opportunity in the future." Alec waited. There was no sound, no movement. Ryder added, "Michael, I don't want to shoot you, but I will." Alec leveled his gun at the wall where he'd heard the floorboard squcak. "I'll count to three, Michael. Then the games end. One . . ."

The automatic hit the floor in a dull thud and skidded close to Yevchentko. Alec rose and carefully picked up the gun, dropping it in the pocket of his overcoat. "Now come out."

Michael appeared in the doorway, rage glowing in his eyes, blending with mistrust of Alec. Toth didn't speak.

"Sit down over there, Michael, where I can watch both of you."

Toth sullenly obeyed and turned his furious countenance toward Yevchentko. "Why should I believe anything you say, Russian? Where's Mueller? He killed in this house. The body is still in the kitchen …"

"It wasn't Mueller who killed Usulak, Michael." Alec talked while watching Yevchentko carefully. "It was Jeanette." The shock of that statement registered in the Russian's face. Alec took out a cigarette and lit it. He puffed in a little and let the smoke out slowly. "Gregory, I'd like to know something. Is she a mercenary or a recruit?"

"She has the jewels?" Yevchentko asked in response.

"I'm pretty sure she does. What's left of them. Now it's your turn to give information. Independent mercenary or one of yours?" Ryder glanced at Toth, then fixed on Gregory.

"A very good mercenary, too good I see now. What do you mean when you say 'what's left of the jewels?' "

"I mean this, Gregory." Alec pulled a thin ledger from beside his chair and flipped open pages.

"What the hell has that book got to do with us?" Yevchentko sputtered.

Ryder glanced sideways and caught a bit of respect coming into Toth's glaring eyes. Then Alec replied to Yevchentko. "Another woman stole most of the jewels first, before Jeanette got the rest. This is her account ledger, what this other woman got for them."

"Got! All the jewels gone? How much did Jeanette take? I, that is, we, could get them back, but these others . . ." Yevchentko put a hand to his face.

"Well, that's hard to say. I don't know how much was there to begin with, you see. But I can estimate from the size of the hollowed-out portions of that bed upstairs, the canopied bed that must have originally been in suite 115 of the Grand Hotel. Subtract the cost of maintaining this home and the cost of a trust fund that now maintains Michael's grandfather in a private Jewish retirement home."

Yevchentko was too grief-stricken to say anything. But Toth spoke. "What jewels?"

Ryder smiled. "The crown jewels of the Habsburgs, accumulated luxury of the wealthiest of the wealthy. They had centuries to buy or plunder the best Europe offered. You owe your grandfather an apology, Michael. He used the gems to save Jews from the Holocaust. But how did your grandfather get them in the first place?"

Toth replied. "A con, a swindle. The Habsburgs lost power around World War I. They thought there was a chance to rule after World War II, or so Abraham must've told them. He called them all together in a gala ball at Margaret Island and got them to dress up with all the splendor, then leave it behind in a desperate, foolish attempt to rule again, at least in Hungary. Abraham told them they could pool their assets and finance a revolution to put a Habsburg in charge, some such nonsense at any rate."

Ryder interjected, "Sort of the same idea that occurred to Gregory. Was it Mueller who first proposed taking over the country, Gregory, or was he more modest in his ambitions, just getting the loot enough for him?"

Yevchentko muttered an inaudible reply and sank his face deeper into his hands. Then he bolted his face upward. "You still have the papers. Where are they?"

"Yes, the documents." Alec addressed Michael, deliberately ignoring Yevchentko. "Your grandfather was a very thorough con man, Michael. He not only got the Habsburgs' liquid assets, but many of their properties as well. Now you begin to see where Otto Tolnai fits into this crazy puzzle, eh?" Alec dragged the strongbox from under his chair and pushed it toward Gregory.

The Russian fell to his knees and seized the box, dragging it open and spilling a great heap of yellowing papers on the floor. "They're here, they're here . . ." he murmured in ecstasy.

"Yes, all here, Gregory. The title deeds for great estates made out to the bearer, the codes and identification numbers and powers of attorney for Swiss bank accounts that probably still exist and have drawn interest for fifty years, including, from what I could tell, several vaults filled with gold bullion."

Alec turned his eyes on the Russian, who lifted the hoard with him into the chair. Yevchentko was examining each document, as Alec had done earlier. "Worthless to Michael's grandfather in a Communist era where all property is owned by the State," Alec explained. "But invaluable in a country returning to private ownership. Even if you can't possibly claim everything, the deeds give you power to cloud everyone else's title. You can force them to trade for what they want. It's like a Monopoly game, trading Boardwalk for Park Place. A quarter of what those aristocratic dupes pooled to restore the monarchy would make you King of Hungary. Imagine having the Department of Property Titles in your pocket, ready and willing to lose documents the other side needs – and willing to authenticate your own forgeries. You might keep half, even most of what those deeds indicate. Beautiful estates, like this relatively small one on Lake Balaton."

Alec continued, "Michael, your mother used the jewels your grandfather stole. She ran a sort of underground railroad, as it was called during the American Civil War. She traded jewels for the relocation of Jewish families to safety. They were hidden in the barn, in an underground room, until the arrangements could be made for Gypsies to smuggle them into Switzerland. A diamond-studded tiara in a platinum setting with incomparable rubies for accent equated to three generations of Jews, fifteen total, escaping the death camps. Your mother planned the whole thing. Imagine, Gregory, sleeping in that bed every night, surrounded by a fortune that would put King Midas to shame. But now the jewels are gone." Alec leaned toward the Russian and smiled.

"But Jeanette? She only has a few jewels, you said." Yevchentko stammered.

"She killed Otto Tolnai. Shocked Gregory? You thought you were being smart to use her as a check and balance on Mueller. In the end, it backfired. She corrupted Otto, got him to use the computer for tracing what happened to all the furniture in suite 115 of the Grand Hotel. After the War, the hotel was expropriated by the People's Republic of

Hungary. Most of the furniture went into the warehouse that burned. More furniture went to the arsoned apartment house. The State furnished that building with some of the warehouse contents before the bureaucrats forgot they even had the furniture. Mueller got a little carried away there. Made more of a fuss than he was supposed to, killing Michael's men. But he got away with it. Then Mueller worked to track down furniture parceled out in single sets. It's not too bad a job when you can disguise yourself as a telephone repairman. Plus, he only had to look for a canopied bed, so he didn't have to run around burning down everyone's apartment he entered. Have I missed something, Gregory?"

"All that careful work wasted. But I'll find another to replace him, Alec. Together …"

"Together we'll rule, is that it, Gregory?" Alec sneered. "I doubt it. Jeanette came to the same conclusion I did. You aren't needed anymore. Besides, I don't like you, Gregory. You tried to kill me. You killed a whole bunch of innocent people through this Hans Mueller."

Alec let the Russian go for his weapon, let his gun clear its holster. Only then did Ryder empty the thirteen rounds of a full clip into the Russian's jerking body. He didn't release the trigger until it dry-fired several times. Slowly he thawed and realized Michael Toth was shaking him hard by the shoulders.

Alec looked at Toth. Ryder saw a wide-eyed, opened mouth stare.

"Alec," the Fire Captain began.

"Mueller? Is that what you want to know?" Ryder muttered.

"I just wanted to help you, bring you out of it. But yeah, Mueller. He'll be back, won't he?"

"I doubt Yevchentko got him. That bastard Mueller's just too damn good. I'm sure Gregory tried. Soon as the loot was found, Mueller would've gone after Gregory."

"Can we kill Mueller too?" Toth asked.

"Maybe. And maybe he'll get us." Alec bent down and pried blood-soaked papers from the Russian's hands. He offered them to Toth.

"No, Alec. They make me sick."

"Then you won't have any objection to making certain Mueller can't have them either?"

"No . . . What are you going to do?"

Alec moved to the fireplace and tossed a mildewed stack of legal documents into dying embers. For a while, nothing happened. Then the fire caught hold and the stack flared into a brief glory that ended in curled ashes.

Ryder pulled his eyes off the fireplace and reached in his pocket. "There were three documents I saved before Yevchentko arrived. Here, take them. Go to Switzerland with your family and find out if they're any good. Take the money and disappear. Live happily ever after."

Alec dropped the documents in the Fireman's reluctant hand.

"What of you, Alec?" Toth asked.

"I'll stay here and try to kill Mueller." Ryder stated a simple fact.

"Don't you want any of the money? You need something to live on also."

"If I keep some, Mueller might get it."

"I'll set some of this up in your name, Alec, if you live. I see your point. Mueller is a killing machine." There was only silence for a brief while and then Michael Toth asked, "Where will you find him?"

"I don't have to find him. He'll find me. He'll come looking for what we've just burned." Alec pointed to the fireplace ashes.

"And Jeanette? Will you kill her, too?" asked Michael.

Alec was surprised at his pain when he thought of her. Had there been something there despite her professionalism, or had that all been in his own mind from the beginning?

"Will you go after Jeanette?" Toth insisted on knowing.

Alec turned away and gazed at the moonlight struggling through a window. "I doubt that will be necessary," he said. "Mueller, I believe, is taking care of that for me."

39

The Impostor

The cab door slamming caught him by surprise. Mueller rushed out of bed quickly as the broken rib and unresponsive leg would allow. He heard voices in the front yard, but couldn't make them out clearly. He'd left mini-blinds over the living room windows angled the way he'd found them, tilted to let sun inside. Unfortunately, there was no way to see outside, without disturbing the blinds. He heard leather-soled shoes clicking up the walk and rustling in a purse. Mueller stood before the mini-blinds, frustrated, wondering what was the best course of action.

Hans Mueller realized he'd left his Uzi in the bedroom. He took a step in that direction and heard a key turn in the door lock. There was no time to get his gun. He ripped the stiletto off his leg, ignoring the minor pain of some lost skin. Mueller focused on the opening door.

The woman who came inside was short and of Hispanic descent. One of his hands clamped her windpipe, the other stuck the knife against the side of her neck. Mueller dragged her with him, slamming the door shut. They rolled to the floor and pain from his wounded leg made him nearly pass out. But his instincts won and he found himself atop the cleaning woman with his knife point pressing hard beneath her chin.

She was trembling violently, but there was no resistance. He loosened his grip on her neck and kept the knife jammed hard enough to draw a trickle of blood. She began jabbering in Spanish. He knew enough Mexican to tell her to be quiet. She was too panicked to obey and he slapped her viciously until she only whimpered.

He pulled himself up, confident she was too intimidated to attempt escape. Mueller bound her in a chair at the dining room table. It didn't take long to extract that she was preparing the house for the Impostor's return from Europe. His next question was when and that was volunteered without the slightest hesitation. Mueller satisfied himself this woman knew nothing else of value to him. He led her into a closet, slit her throat and shut the closet door.

He had less than twenty-four hours to prepare for the Impostor, but despite the handicap of his wounds, he'd be ready.

* * *

This time when a cab pulled in front of the house, the mini-blinds were turned so he could watch. Jeanette had the cabby tote her luggage to the front porch. She tipped him and let him drive away before finding the key and opening the door to her home.

The instant she stepped inside, he saw them. They were still magnificent earrings, their diamonds and emeralds shimmering in the swath of a streetlight beaming through the open door. That Jeanette had the audacity to wear those jewels enraged him. They were not hers, this Impostor. They belonged to him and to the real princess, but really now to him alone.

He stepped behind her and jabbed a stun gun in her back. She dropped in a heap to the floor and tried to recover. But Mueller was on her, stunning her again and again, reveling in seeing her body twitch and jump to his command. He realized it would take her longer to return to consciousness, longer to tell him what he needed to know. But he had all night and she was finally his.

He'd been trained by the best for this night. The Gestapo pig had shown Mueller the way torture was done. Now he'd enjoy himself to the fullest, dangling hope before her and then taking it away, letting her think there was a chance to leave intact. Then he'd take away pieces of her until she knew there was only the final exit. It would give Mueller his greatest orgasm when she begged him to kill her.

40

End Game

Hans Mueller lay in a clump of low reeds that barely let him see the house. He watched Abraham Toth's mansion through binoculars, as he had for the previous days. At night, he approached the house closely, sniffing for danger. The weather was warmer now and a nearby estate was occupied, complicating his surveillance. There'd also been a small motor boat cruising at night, then turning off its lights and coasting for long periods. That night boat worried him more than anything. It was possible someone liked night trawling. But why did they turn off their running lights? To conserve a weak battery, perhaps. He'd tried to run down the explanation but hadn't found anyone who knew about a night fisherman on the nearby piers. There was also a local fisherman who hung around all day long, but he appeared legitimate.

Hans Mueller knew time wasn't on his side. A vandal would find Usulak's body in the kitchen, where she had so deliciously told him it would be after he worked her fingernails for a while. She thought herself a tough pro, but in the end he had everything he wanted. He even dragged out her torture a second day before putting a red satin cord around her throat. He delighted in watching life drain from her compliant body.

Those earrings he'd taken from the late Jeanette Murphy were with him in a small bag of gear by his side. He dragged the bag with him when he crawled from the reeds. Mueller brushed off sand from his clothes. The night fisherman was nowhere to be seen. The daytime one left when sunset approached. In the nearby estate, they were at the supper table. He was going in, going for the strongbox Jeanette didn't find.

Mueller walked a mile and didn't see any signs of trouble. It didn't matter. There was enough firepower in his gear bag to break a police ambush.

The barn was quiet as usual, but he went to it first. Nothing had been disturbed on the barn's exterior. He felt pulled to go inside, but disciplined himself to survey the main house first.

The back door was open. Usulak's body was in the kitchen, decaying rapidly with the help of a swarm of flies. Rats had found it and taken pieces of the hands and face. The stench was horrible as he moved around the corpse, looking at the floor to see the telltale marks of other visitors. The dust of ages seemed disturbed only by his flashlight and the late Impostor's tennis shoes, plus Usulak's footprints. Was there something else, though? It seemed there was a bit too much dust sometimes. Or was he just edgy as he neared the goal of a lifetime?

Mueller went into the parlor. A dusty stack of logs was in the fireplace. Only his footprints were on the floor. The chairs were covered with sheets that obviously hadn't been disturbed in many years. Why was Gregory coming to his mind now? He must focus on the goal, on the situation. Unless it was his intuition warning him that Gregory Yevchentko was nearby, ready to pounce. But how would that overweight has-been know of the existence of this house? Jeanette hadn't told Gregory. That fact Mueller confirmed in her terror and her muted screams as he'd sliced open the fingers of her right hand.

Her tennis shoes had gone up the stairs and he followed them, curious to see what she'd done to the bed he'd killed so many to find. Her chainsaw job was crude, stupid. She might've destroyed so much with that chainsaw. It was better the real treasure hadn't been inside the bed.

He turned to go and thought he saw something moving outside toward the barn. Carefully, he slipped across debris to the side of a window and waited. Cold was eating into his flesh by the time the object moved again. A cat, prowling like he was. He relaxed.

What happened to Alec Ryder since that abortive night at the airport? Ryder was now an outlaw, on the run, hunted. But no one had found him, not the local police nor the KGB. Jeanette hadn't known either. Probably left the country. Ryder was lucky but not very smart, not determined. He'd fallen for the Impostor. A stupid weakness.

It was time to check out the barn. The house was clean. If there were no clues in the barn, he'd tear the house apart plank by plank if necessary. He was careful in crossing the open space, moving quickly to cover, then waiting for a telltale response of someone who didn't have patience. It took Mueller nearly half an hour to go from the back porch to the barn door.

He slid the door open, forcing it against a resistance formed of decay. Mueller inspected the interior with the flashlight held at arm's length, so any shots would go wide of the mark. He still limped, but there was really no pain when he walked across the floor, careful to keep the light off any windows. Where his flashlight leaked through the walls, though, couldn't be helped.

A bale of rotted hay drew him. Why would someone have cleaned out every other possession and left this? Whoever was the caretaker years ago wasn't a careless person. So why make this mistake? He pushed the hay bale and it stuck against something in the floor. Mueller went to the other end and saw a rusted metal ring jutting from the boards. In seconds, the hay was pulled back and the trapdoor flung open.

He tingled with excitement. This was what he had expected. That bitch had been too stupid to realize that a man smart enough to steal those jewels would have dispersed the hoard, not risk it all in one location. What if the house caught fire? The papers might have gone also.

The ladder led him into a pit lined on one side with a shelf of old glass jars. He explored them, found a hidden latch. The shelves swung open. He trembled with excitement.

His flashlight found it on the table. The metal strongbox was sitting there, beckoning to him. Hans Mueller moved to it in a single bound and tore the lid open.

There was only a note inside, in German. Just two words were written on it and a signature. "You lose – A. Ryder."

Mueller leapt for the shelving as it slammed shut. Quickly he fell to the floor and grabbed for the bag, ripping out his Uzi. He traced an "S" with one clip and heard the shattering of glass jars on the other side as bullets ripped through the old wood.

His flashlight raced around the room until it found the other exit. He was moving to that other wooden door when he smelled a terrifying odor.

* * *

Alec bit his lip in anguish as he smothered the pain of bullets that tore into his left arm, shattering a bone. He waited until the fusillade stopped, hoped the pause meant a change in clip and fought his way up the old rickety steps as fast as he could.

Outside the barn, moonlight showed him a torrent of blood pouring from his arm. Ryder did not falter in his race to the small fishing boat pulled on the shore near the tunnel exit. Alec knew Mueller was clawing at that old door hoping to escape through the tunnel. There was precious little time.

Alec cursed his lighter as he clicked it repeatedly, trying to ignite the gasoline soaked torch he'd grabbed from the bottom of the boat. A fifty gallon drum of gasoline had already been dragged to the tunnel and was gurgling its contents down the stone-paved path toward Mueller.

Finally, the torch ignited and Alec threw the fiery rag into the tunnel, flinging himself on the ground. He bounced with the earth when it shook from the explosion. Flames leapt above him and descended on his head and clothing. Alec rolled to beat out the fire, threw sand on his burning hair.

He tore his shirt off with his good arm and made a tourniquet to staunch the flow of blood. The burns and the blood loss made him nearly faint as he moved back to Mueller's only other exit.

When he entered the barn, a human torch rose to meet him from its depths, the Uzi cutting a swath across barn walls. Alec fell to his knees and then on his face as the Uzi ripped above him. Ryder struggled to get off a shot, but it went wide. Another shot was closer to Mueller but missed. Alec's vision was blurring when he tried again, holding down the trigger and letting the gun kick around in the pitiful hope one round would find its mark.

The torch staggered on towards Ryder. Alec could see Mueller's face and Doberman eyes staring at him, the burning arm pointing an Uzi downward.

Then Mueller's burning flesh spun around and fell. Ryder watched it crawl toward him.

Alec stumbled to his feet. His gun dry-fired. He threw it at Mueller's head but hit the man's chest instead. Mueller was still alive, trying to reach Alec.

Ryder picked up the small gasoline can he'd brought to the barn the night before and hidden there. He clamped the can between his knees and twisted off the cap.

Alec walked calmly over to Mueller and poured a gallon of gasoline on the dying man's head, smiling when the fuel caught fire.

He watched until Mueller no longer writhed in agony, no longer screamed silently with lungs too burned to hold air. Then Alec dropped the empty can on the charred carcass.

Outside, Ryder sat down and began to feel his wounds. He didn't have much to live for. The KGB would consider it a matter of honor to hunt him down and execute him. Most likely, his wounds would take longer to heal than they'd take to find him.

Too bad he was out of ammunition. Even one bullet and he'd end it now. Why endure all the pain of healing from the burns and a damned shattered arm, only to die?

But he didn't have any bullets. So he went to the boat and pushed it into the lake. He draped his wounded body over the boat's gunwales and slowly hauled himself aboard. There was a Gypsy camp nearby. He'd ask them for help.

With a little luck, he'd make Switzerland. Maybe Toth left some of the money in Zurich. There could be a fortune in those accounts. It was possible he could pry the money loose with fifty-year old documents. Wasn't it? There'd be a future for him after all. He'd move to a place in the world where even the KGB couldn't find him. Maybe.

This novel is dedicated to my late father-in-law,
who survived the Nazi Death Camps
and was an inspiration to all of us.
It's also dedicated to those who protested Nazi policies
and paid for it with their lives – and to those who risked death
to shelter friends and strangers, leading them to safety.
May the courage and sacrifice of all of them,
and the troops who liberated Holocaust survivors,
always be remembered.

www.ingramcontent.com/pod-product-compliance
Lightning Source LLC
LaVergne TN
LVHW020533100826
845148LV00010B/1445

* 9 7 8 0 9 8 1 7 7 0 2 9 1 *